TOTAL RECALL

"Untie me, you assholes!" Quaid roared. "They'll be here any minute! They'll kill you all!"

Huh? "What's he talking about?" McClane snapped.

"Stop this operation *now!*" Quaid yelled.

How could the guy be talking so clearly?

"Mr. Quaid, please calm down," McClane said, trying to be soothing. Maybe they could change the mix, get him sedated all the way down, then explore the problem. A memory cap?

"I'm not Quaid!"

Multiple personality?

McClane nervously walked closer to examine Quaid's eyes.

"You're having a reaction to the implant," he said, though he was by no means sure of that.

Quaid strained again at his bonds. Suddenly the strap holding his right arm snapped. That arm shot up and grabbed McClane by the throat.

"Untie me."

Dr. Lull hastily readied a syringe gun and frantically jabbed it into Quaid's thigh. She fired dose after dose of narkidrine, until the man finally released his grip and passed out.

"Listen to me!" Dr. Lull said urgently. "He's been going on and on about Mars." Now it was evident that she was genuinely frightened. "He's really *been* there!"

TOTAL RECALL

Piers Anthony

Inspired by the works of
Philip K. Dick
and
Ronald Shusett, Dan O'Bannon, Steven Pressfield

A Legend Book
Published by Arrow Books Limited
20 Vauxhall Bridge Road, London SW1V 2SA

An imprint of Random Century Group

London Melbourne Sydney Auckland
Johannesburg and agencies throughout
the world

First published in 1989 William Morrow and
Company, Inc.
Legend edition 1990

Printed and bound in Great Britain by
Courier International Ltd, Tiptree, Essex

ISBN 0 09 974200 4

1

Mars

Two moons hung in the dark red sky. One was full, the other crescent. One seemed to be four times the diameter of the other, and neither was exactly round. In fact, both might better have been described as egglike: a chicken egg and a robin egg. Perhaps even potatolike, large and small.

The big one was Phobos, named after the personification of fear: the type that possessed armies and caused their defeat. The small one was Deimos, the personification of terror. This was appropriate, for these were the companions of the ancient Roman god of war and agriculture, Mars.

The landscape of Mars was ugly. As far as the horizon, which was closer than it would have been on Earth, there were barren rock formations, overhanging ledges, and dust. There might have been a war here, fracturing the terrain, but there was obviously no agriculture. This was no-man's-land in the truest sense.

Douglas Quaid stood on the jaggedly sloping surface. He wore a lightweight space suit with breathing apparatus, for the atmospheric pressure here was only a hundred and fiftieth that of Earth at ground level, and the temperature was about a hundred degrees below zero, Fahrenheit. There would have been arctic snow, if the scant air had had enough water vapor to form it. Any failure of his suit, any little tear on the edge of one of the rocks, would finish him just about as quickly as it would in deep space. About the only thing Mars had going for it that the vacuum of space didn't was gravity: slightly better than a third of Earth's. At least it provided some notion of what was up and what was down, and made it possible to walk.

Quaid hardly needed low gravity to help him walk. He

was a massive man, so muscular that even the space suit could not hide his physique. He seemed to exude raw power. His chiseled features within the helmet were set, reflecting his indomitable will. It was obvious that he was here by no accident. He had a mission, and not even the hell that was this planet would balk him for long.

He scanned the horizon. As he turned, the jumbled terrain changed, until it reared up into the most phenomenal mountain known in the Solar System: Olympus Mons, ten miles above the point where he stood. In its totality, it was closer to fifteen miles, more than triple the height of Earth's largest, Mauna Loa of Hawaii, most of whose mass was hidden beneath the Pacific Ocean. Like that one, this was volcanic, but on a scale unknown on Earth. The base of its cone was some 350 miles in diameter, with radially spreading lava flows now frozen in place. A mighty scarp over two miles high ringed its base, defining it strangely but clearly. Olympus Mons was a wonder to make even a man like Quaid pause in admiration.

There was a sound behind him, audible more as vibration in the rock than as any wave in the trace atmosphere. Someone was approaching: a woman. Quaid turned as if expecting her, unsurprised, and gazed at her with appreciation. She was worth it: she was as well formed for her sex as he was for his, voluptuous within her space suit. Behind her visor her hair showed brown, and her eyes were great and dark. She gazed back at him, and her posture suggested her interest: if she was not in love with him, she was getting there.

But this was hardly the place for romance! The suits would have made anything significant impossible, even if they had it in mind. This was business.

She turned and walked toward a pyramid-shaped mountain he hadn't looked at before. Hardly on the scale of Olympus Mons, it remained big enough to be impressive. It seemed almost artificial in its symmetry. How had such a curious feature come to be on Mars? Well, it was no bigger a mystery than the human faces sculpted in other rocks, or the many little alien artifacts scattered about, evidence that man had not been the first here.

Quaid followed, regretting that only her helmet was translucent. Even so, it was a pleasure to watch her walk. She led him to a tortured opening in the side of the mountain, evidently a fault that had sprung during one of the eruptions. It was a cave whose walls were sheer. Just enough light filtered in through crevices to enable them to find secure footing as the passage wound into the mountain.

They came to a ledge deep inside. They were in a roughly circular chamber of considerable size. No, it was a depression, a hole; the sky of Mars showed above. Its floor was a pit so deep that it seemed to have no bottom. Quaid's eyes, adapting to the deep shade at this level, made out only the curving rim and the cylindrical rise of the rock above. Was this a natural cavity or a chamber hewn by man? It had aspects of both, and neither. He felt an awe of it that related only partly to its size and mystery. Somehow he knew that the significance of the place transcended anything any ordinary man or woman might compass, and that what the two of them did here was more important than anyone on Earth could guess.

The woman walked to the right. She reached down and drew out a slender cable. It seemed to be anchored to a large rock or projection from the wall. She backed away, hauling on the cable, and it extended. She turned, and Quaid saw that the end she held was connected to an apparatus somewhat like a fishing reel mounted on a solid belt.

She brought this belt to him and stretched out its ends. She bent to reach around his waist, wrapping the belt until it snapped together behind him. Now the reel was in front, and he was tied to the rock.

Quaid tested it himself, stepping back and watching the cable pay out. It was coiled within the reel, flattening there but becoming round as it reached toward the rock anchor. There was actually a considerable length of it, but it weighed only a few pounds.

He put his two gloved hands on the cable and pulled them apart. The cable held. He increased the pull, his muscles showing. Still it held. He gestured to the woman, and she approached. He formed a loop in the cable and signaled

3

that she should sit in it. Awkwardly, she did, holding on to the top to maintain her balance. Quaid lifted his arm and drew her readily into the air. Of course, she weighed only forty-five pounds in the Mars gravity, but it was obvious that he could have lifted her full weight almost as easily. She smiled.

He let her down, smiling also. The cable would do.

They grasped their clumsy suited hands, bidding each other farewell. They embraced, touching visors, unable to kiss. If there was one thing he really hated about a space suit . . . !

Quaid let her go and stepped to the edge of the rim. He put his hands on it, then swung his legs over and down in a maneuver that would have been difficult in Earth gravity. He gripped the cable, facing toward the wall, and lowered himself into the dark chasm, hand under hand.

A lesser man would have rappelled, passing the cable under his left thigh and over his right shoulder, using a double line that he allowed to lengthen slowly for the descent. Quaid didn't bother; he simply handed himself down almost as if on a ladder. His feet jumped down the wall a yard at a time, keeping him away from it. Child's play!

He paused a few yards down, looking up. The woman leaned over the rim. The upper portion of her body showed in silhouette, her head seeming to be lighted because of the translucence of the helmet. She looked like an angel on a painted ceiling. The full moon Phobos floated above her head, completing the halo.

She put her hand to her helmet, then flung it out, blowing him a kiss.

Quaid felt a surge of emotion. God, she was beautiful!

But he had business. He waved back, then resumed his downward progress. He realized that he didn't have to use his hands; the reel could be set to pay out the cable at a steady rate. He adjusted it and let go.

Sure enough, he continued down at the same rate as before. This freed his hands for anything else they might be needed for. He relaxed and looked around.

Moonlight illuminated the pit, showing him details he

had not been able to see from above. There were dozens of gigantic vertical pipes rising from the depths, reminding him vaguely of a monstrous calliope. Somehow he was sure they didn't play music! But what *did* they do? They weren't here as a work of Martian art!

There was a vibration at his waist. Something was going wrong with the reel! He grabbed for it, but his clumsy gloves either had no effect or made things worse. The cable uncoiled at a terrifying rate.

Quaid plunged into the bottomless abyss. He flailed wildly, trying to stop himself. His feet lost contact with the wall, and he spun around, seeing the wall, the pipes, and the space between them whirl dizzyingly as he fell.

'Doug!' It was the woman, calling in alarm from above.

He tried to answer, but was too disoriented even to do that. He kept falling, hurtling down into the void, out of control.

'Doug!' her voice came, despairingly, faint in the distance.

The abyss filled with bright white light. Quaid knew it was the end. Somehow he wasn't frightened; all he could do was meet his destiny.

5

2
Lori

Quaid woke, startled. He was in bed, on Earth, quite safe. The bedroom was bathed in morning light. As he re-oriented and his heartbeat returned to normal, he realized that he should have known that his experience wasn't real. He had never been to Mars, so how could he have found himself there, without even questioning it, without knowing how he had come? He had simply popped into existence on the barren surface, and met a girl, and gone into a cave or crevice in the side of a mountain shaped like a pyramid, and down into a huge hole. Did any of that make sense on any rational basis? In the dream he had accepted it, but that was the way of dreams.

Now his mind reviewed it, finding place after place where the scene broke down. All that light from that tiny moon? Well, maybe; how could he know, without being there? But that cable – why hadn't he simply grabbed it and halted his fall? There was no question of his ability to do that; it was attached to him, so he could have circled it at its exit from the reel with his gloved hand, and clamped down, and held on. With his weight only a fraction of its Earth amount, and the power of his arms, it would have been like catching a huge turkey someone threw to him. A jolt, but not impossible. Only the ambience of the dream had made that fall seem inevitable.

Yet a trifling detail bothered him most. *Doug!* the woman had called. That meant she knew him, though he could not draw her name from his memory. Not Mr Quaid, not Douglas, but Doug, cried out with feeling. That feeling summoned a return feeling from him, even now that he was out of the dream, back in reality. She was important to him, more than important; she –

6

Then the rest of it clicked into place. *How had he been able to hear her call* – there in the near-vacuum of Mars' atmosphere? They had not spoken throughout the dream, but there at the end the verisimilitude, the semblance of truth, had broken down.

The bright light at the conclusion – that was *this* light, the light of day on Earth, more intense than that of Mars. Not the brilliance of Heaven or the inferno of Hell encountered at his death, but the ordinary brightness of ordinary day when he overslept. That was a relief!

Yet that voice still tugged at him. That woman . . .

There was someone with him. Quaid blinked and looked.

A beautiful creature was leaning over him. She wore a filmy nightgown that was falling open with a readiness that had to be intentional, to reveal portions of her splendid anatomy. She was not the girl of the dream; she was a stunning blond Amazon. His wife, Lori. How could he have forgotten!

'You were dreaming,' she said sympathetically as she reached forward to wipe the sweat from his brow.

He did not answer, distracted by the clear sight of her full breasts within the hanging nightgown. He had of course seen them many times before, but somehow he never got tired of looking. Talk of impressive architecture . . .

'Mars again?' she inquired solicitously. Her breasts moved as her arm did, as she completed cleaning his face.

He nodded, still upset by the experience, though he was rapidly coming to terms with the current situation. What did the woman of the dream have that Lori didn't? Brown hair, maybe; nothing else. And Lori wasn't exactly wearing a space suit.

Suddenly he realized that the Mars-woman's voice had not been an error in the dream. They had been in space suits, and space suits had intercoms or whatever. He had heard her via his helmet system! It encouraged him to make that connection; it meant that his dream wasn't quite as farfetched as he had thought.

Lori, mistaking his distraction, started to caress him. Her hand trailed down his neck, and she squeezed the muscle of his shoulder. She liked his muscles, and liked touching them; they were a turn-on for her, and he hardly objected to that.

'My poor baby,' she murmured, stroking his pectoral muscle. 'Poor thing, with those bad dreams, those horrible nightmares.' She brought her head down, kissing the crotch of his neck and shoulder in a way that might have been comforting, but was becoming erotic. 'Is that better?'

Her lips were moving across his chest, pausing in the region of the nipple. Her eyes angled up to sight on his face. He didn't want her to stop. 'Mm-hmm,' he said.

Lori resumed progress, working her way down toward his belly. She was trying to seduce him, he knew, to take his mind off the dream, and she was good at it. He was happy to let her continue. If only the woman of Mars hadn't been in that space suit! He could imagine it was her . . .

'Was she there?' she asked nonchalantly.

Oh-oh. Did she have antennae to pick up his thoughts? He felt guilty, thinking of the other woman when it was manifest that Lori was all that any man could desire. But Lori's interest in that other was amusing in its way.

He played dumb. 'Who?'

'You know,' Lori lifted her head, making a contemplative moue. She was playing dumb too, pretending that she couldn't quite remember or describe that other woman. 'The girl with the . . .' She cupped her hands in the universal gesture for large breasts.

He smiled. 'Oh, her.' As if Lori weren't of that type.

But she refused to let it go. 'Well, was she?'

He laughed. 'Amazing! You're jealous of a dream!' The thing was, this did intrigue him, perhaps because it lent some reality to a figure he knew existed only in his imagination.

Lori punched him in the stomach and twisted away. He tried to grab her, but she struggled to get out of the bed. They had always played rough, but not too rough; he never hit her back.

'It's not funny, Doug,' she said, half off the bed. 'Let me go!' Now gravity was helping her; if he let go, she would fall on the floor. 'You're on Mars every night now.'

All too true! 'But I'm always back by morning,' he

8

protested weakly. He realized that there was only so far this could go without turning ugly, because he really did have a secret passion for that nonexistent woman, and Lori was catching on.

He succeeded in pulling her back on the bed. Now Lori occupied his full attention, as surely had been her purpose. They wrestled, and she got her legs around him, squeezing him in a harmless but most interesting scissors grip. He pinned her arms to her sides and tried to kiss her. She turned her head from side to side to avoid his lips.

It was definitely going beyond the game stage. 'Aw, Lori, don't be like that!' he protested, wriggling within her scissors, nudging her where it didn't show. '*You're* the girl of my dreams!'

Lori abruptly stopped struggling. She looked up at him moonily. 'You mean it?' Her scissors relaxed.

'Of course.' And now it was true. Their wrestling had completed what her comforting had started, and now he wanted her very much.

As well she knew. She was, after all, in contact with that region. She entwined him with her long athletic legs, this time not squeezing but embracing, and pulled him in to her. They kissed.

'You are so full of bull . . .' she breathed.

He laughed. 'Well, you know what a bull does with a cow!'

'Cow!' she exclaimed with mock indignation. 'You ever see a cow do this?' She sat up, bestriding him, riding his groin, and hauled off her nightgown. She had the world's finest body, and knew it. 'Or this?' She bounced, her breasts following their own courses while her thighs did special things to his midsection. 'Or this?' She abruptly dropped her upper torso onto him and kissed him savagely. Her tresses slid down around his face and neck, silken smooth, tickling him delightfully.

'No,' he had to admit. 'The cows I know just stand there and wait for it.'

She lifted her head, her eyes glinting with dangerous humor. 'And just how many cows do you know?'

9

'Only one.' He felt her body tense warningly. 'And she's only a dream.'

Lori relaxed. She liked that analogy. He had called the dream-girl a cow, instead of the real one. She resumed her activity. It was certainly true that she didn't just wait for it; she came more than halfway to get it. It was an attitude he liked very well. He put his hands on her buttocks, and felt them tensing alternately, teasing him, daring him to get more than his hands into action.

He rolled her over. She screamed as if being ravished, pausing only long enough to deep-kiss him as he proceeded to the culmination. She did a belly dance, but her abdomen didn't move; it was all internal. Her tongue flicked into his mouth, coordinating with the hidden dance. Oh, yes, she was no cow – but he did feel like a bull, at the moment.

Even so, the picture of the woman of his dreams remained in his mind, and he wished she could be the one with him at this moment. He closed his eyes and tried to pretend that it was the Mars woman he was embracing. He wondered what the hell was wrong with him.

3

Dream

It ended in due course, as all things did. Lori got up and headed for the shower; daintiness was always vital to her, and he had mussed her hair and smeared her lips and done a few other things in the course of having a spectacular time. Lori was Woman-Plus! How had an ordinary Joe like him managed to capture such a creature?

It was not the first time the question had occurred to him. They came from such different worlds. He was a Construction Engineer, Site Preparation Specialist: longhand for the class of low-level laborers who broke up old artifacts to make new ones. In fact, he was a jackhammer jock, just like his dad. It was all he had ever wanted to be and he was proud to follow in his father's footsteps. He was good at it, too, a veritable artist with his machine, working twice as fast as anyone else, but it hardly made him a prize catch for someone like Lori. Oh, he had muscles, and she did like that, but he was no Hi-Q professor or big-bucks executive, he was just a construction worker.

And Lori? Lori was the pampered daughter of an advertising executive. He recalled the day they met, eight years ago. He had been hard at work on the site of an old, glass and steel highrise which was being demolished to make way for a new, plasplex business center. The site was in the financial district, an area Quaid didn't usually see much of, and he had enjoyed the passing parade of nattily attired men and women, late model hovercars, and cleaning droids that kept every surface sparkling. It was an interesting change from his own dingy, decaying working-class neighborhood.

Then he had seen Lori. She had been standing across the street, gazing at him. Even at that distance, he had seen the glint of approval in her eyes as they lingered on his sweat-slicked torso. He had become accustomed to getting the once-over from pretty ladies in expensive dresses, but Lori's look was bolder, and she followed through on it by crossing the street to say hello.

To his unending amazement, they were married three months later. He had insisted that they live on his income for the first few years, but Lori had gradually convinced him to accept her money as his own and they finally left his humble rooms for a spacious, modern conapt in one of the fancier tower blocks. Lori felt right at home, but he was having trouble making the transition. He had taken a lot of kidding about it at work, and he still felt out of place, a working stiff in the midst of society types.

Still, he had no right to complain. The conapt was a marvel. He lay back in bed and gazed at the holoscreen in the ceiling, remembering the erotic holovids he and Lori had made, and how it added that little something extra to have them running while they made love. And he enjoyed the pure, sensual pleasure of giving himself over to the immersion room at the end of a long day, letting its lifters and waterjets turn him and pummel the fatigue from his muscles while the steam rose around him, then relaxing while the airjets blew him dry. The social side of his new life might be giving him trouble, but he found himself getting really used to its physical luxuries.

But above all, he had Lori, her ardor unabated in all the years they had been together. He thought back to the morning's love-making, and a sudden memory of his dream intruded on his thoughts, shattering his contentment. He shook his head, disturbed.

That dream had been too real! He just couldn't throw it off, however foolish it was. And it was incredibly foolish. Why was he, the luckiest of men, dreaming of a fantasy woman when he had Lori? That seemed perverse at best, and crazy at worst.

Lori emerged from the bathroom, her body glistening, and again Quaid wondered what this sleek, elegant rich girl saw in him. With a shrug, he jumped out of bed to take his turn in the bathroom. No time for immersion this morning; a quick shower would have to do. He finished, dried, and got dressed in his work clothes.

He entered the kitchen of their conapt. The lights were already on, programmed to suit his work schedule during the week. He dumped fruit in the juicer and let it whir while he filled the blender with nuts, wheat germ, protein packs, leftover veggies, and a half dozen raw eggs. He added the juice, tapped the blender's controls, and watched it transform the mess into a power shake to end all power shakes. He smiled wryly as he watched. Well, he thought, if Lori loves me for my body, I'll do my best to keep it in shape. He promised himself that he'd do his best to shake off the effects of that damned dream, too.

Lori had showered before him, but was later completing her dressing. His outfit was simple: yesterday's trousers, new shirt for today, boots. Hers might look simple, but it was always a work of art that took time to shape just right. She cared about appearances much more than he did. The mere brushing of her hair took longer than the whole of his preparation.

The news was playing across the room, but he didn't give it much attention. He drank his breakfast and let his gaze stray out the window to the hovercars and traffic runnels and all the little energetic people hurrying to work. In a little while he would be among them. As always. His life would be dull indeed if it were not for Lori – and the truth was, it was pretty dull anyway. He knew himself for what he was: a muscular nothing, with a better life than he deserved, yet not properly grateful for it.

The video newsman continued his spiel. 'On the war front, Northern Bloc satellites incinerated a shipyard in Bombay, starting a fire that swept throughout the city. Civilian casualties are estimated to exceed ten thousand. The Chairman defended the attack, calling space-based weapons the only effective defense against the Southern Bloc's numerical superiority.' There was a brief pause as the camera passed across the carnage. The video news had a real taste for that sort of thing. Quaid didn't bother to look.

13

He imagined the people beyond the window as part of that scene, gassed and dying, struggling to rise and get to their jobs, but falling and clogging the foot runnels. The hovercars veering out of control as the gas caught their drivers, crashing to the lower levels in flames. No, not in flames; today flying craft had safeguards, and, unlike the groundcars, were guaranteed nonexplosive. But they might make pretty wreckages anyway. This city as the site of a war raid: it had its devious appeal.

'Astronomers say they are at a loss to account for six novas,' the newsman continued with an indulgent smile. Everyone knew what characters scientists were! 'It seems that these stars do not fit the pattern of the type. Some stars go nova, and some go supernova, and the mechanisms for these effects are fairly well understood. But in recent years more detailed analysis has revealed that six of the novas simply should not have happened – according to the astronomers.' He smiled again. 'Well, back to the drawing board, boys!'

Yeah, every time the facts didn't fit theory, they just drew up a new theory. Eventually they'd come up with a theory that stuck. Stars didn't go nova for no reason.

'And more violence last night on Mars, where . . .'

Quaid perked up and turned to the video. It was a multi-screen television, the best they could afford, which meant colour but no 3-D. It constituted an entire wall of the cooking-living-dining area of their conapt, and made the tiny apartment seem larger than it was. The screen was divided into many segments, simultaneously displaying several kinds of text and programming: weather, stock market, security monitors for their front door and lobby, a 'baby-sitter' program for any children who might be bothersome, a continuous erotica nook for dirty old men, a shopping bulletin for busy housewives, and an old video-tape channel. Quaid ignored the others without effort; it wasn't just that their sounds were turned down, but that he had the reflex practiced from childhood that enabled every citizen to tune out nine-tenths of what was going on, without effort. Any of the sections could be 'zoomed' to

14

take over the full screen, or any significant portion of it, but this normally wasn't worth the bother; the human eye and mind were the most versatile zoomers. Besides, sometimes different members of a family wanted to watch different segments, and this allowed them to do so without quarreling.

The news footage of the Martian Mine episode occupied the large center portion of the screen. The newscaster narrated in a mini-screen of his own. '. . . an explosion ruptured the geodesic dome over the Pyramid Mine, halting the extraction of turbinium ore, key resource of the Northern Bloc's particle beam weapons program.'

Soldiers in breathing masks roughly handled the miners. It was obvious that the military authority was almost eager for someone to make its day by offering some token resistance. Quaid discovered that his fingers were twitching, as if handling and firing a rifle. That was odd, because he couldn't remember when he had last handled any firearm, if ever.

'The Mars Liberation Front has taken credit for the blast,' the newscaster continued, 'and demanded the planet's full independence from, quote, "Northern tyranny". It claims to be ready to set off further –'

Suddenly the main screen jumped to an environmental window, a broadcast from a supposedly virgin forest that now occupied all the screens on the multi-vision video. It was a beautiful scene, but hardly what he wanted at the moment.

'No wonder you have nightmares,' Lori said, stepping in front, holding the remote control. She was dressed in a smart street suit, ready to go out shopping. 'You're always watching the news.'

Quaid sat down at the table as Lori began buttering bread for her own breakfast.

'Lori, I've been thinking,' he said. 'Let's really do it.'

'Again? I thought this morning's effort would hold you for at least half an hour!'

'No,' he said, impatient with this game.

She realized that he was serious. 'Do what?'

15

'Move to Mars,' he said, fearing her reaction.

Lori took a deep breath, exasperated. 'Doug, please don't spoil a perfectly wonderful morning.'

'Just think about it,' he said. If he could only convince her . . .

'How many times do we have to go through this?' she demanded impatiently. 'I don't want to live on Mars. It's dry, it's ugly, it's boring.'

Quaid looked at a deer sipping at a brook, on the environmental window. 'They just doubled the bonus for new colonists.'

'Of course! No idiot'll go near the place! A revolution could break out any minute!' She fussed with her breakfast, not eating it. She was really upset.

Quaid was upset too. He wished she would consider his dream, instead of disparaging it. She was matchless in bed, but on this subject she was a loss. He controlled his anger, picked up the remote control she had set on the table, and turned the news back on.

He was in luck; the Mars item was still running, 'With one mine already closed,' the newscaster continued, 'Mars Administrator Vilos Cohaagen vowed that troops would be used, if necessary, to keep production at full capacity.' The scene shifted to show a press conference in progress. Quaid recognized the features of the Mars Colony Administrator. Cohaagen was big, almost as big as Quaid himself. He'd have to be, for that job, Quaid thought. Appointed by the Northern Bloc to look after the mining operations on Mars, the Colony Administrator was like a military governor from the imperialist past. He wielded almost absolute power, and his ability to command was evident as he fielded questions from reporters.

'Mr Cohaagen!' a reporter demanded. 'Will you negotiate with their leader, Mr Kuato? He seems to be gathering quite a following among –'

'Nonsense!' Cohaagen said, interrupting him. 'Has anybody ever seen this Kuato person? Can anybody show me a photograph? Hunh?' He waited, but for once the reporters were silent. 'I don't think there *is* any Mr Kuato!' His face hardened. 'Let me make this clear, gentlemen; Mars was colonized by the Northern Bloc at enormous expense. The entire war effort depends on our turbinium mines. We do not intend to give it away just because a handful of lazy mutants think they own the planet.'

Suddenly the windows were back on Environmental. Lori had taken the control and switched again. 'He's right about that,' she said. 'Except that lunatics are crazed by the moon, not Mars. Everything about Mars is crazy!'

Irritated, Quaid tried to grab the control, but she jumped behind the table, laughing.

'Lori, come on!' he snapped. 'This is important.'

She paused, then pursed her lips. 'Kiss!'

Ordinarily he liked her games, which usually involved close contact with her luscious body, and he didn't want to alienate her. He accepted her terms, got up, moved forward, and put his arms around her.

She nestled nicely. 'Sweetheart –' She paused for a threatened kiss. 'I know it's hard being in a new town. But let's at least give it a chance.' Another pause. 'Okay?'

Quaid forced a smile. His last raise had enabled them to move twenty floors up the tower block; which meant moving up the social scale as well. Lori loved it, but Quaid had to admit that, with his working-class background, he was having a bit of trouble adjusting to the 'new town'. At the moment, though, he was annoyed with Lori for distracting him yet again. He really was interested in the news from Mars.

She finally kissed him. She was facing away from the video wall. His hands found hers, behind her back, holding the remote control. While he continued to kiss her, he switched back to the news, and watched it over her shoulder.

Cohaagen was speaking. 'As you might have noticed, we weren't blessed with an atmosphere here on Mars. Not one that's worth anything. We have to *make* our air. And somebody's got to pay for it.'

Lori finally disengaged from the kiss, which had extended beyond her intent. 'You're gonna be late.' Perhaps she was afraid that he really would get worked up

17

for another sexual bout, after she had so carefully put herself together. Her concern was not wholly unjustified.

Quaid released her slowly, as if reluctantly giving up the notion of further interplay between them. His real purpose was to hear whatever remained of the broadcast.

'Right,' the reporter was saying. 'But your prices are extravagant. After a miner deducts the cost of air from his salary, nothing is –'

'It's a free planet,' Cohaagen said firmly. 'If you don't want my air, don't breathe it!'

'Mr Cohaagen,' another called out. 'Any comment, sir, on the rumor you closed the Pyramid Mine because you found alien artifacts inside?' Cohaagen rolled his eyes in exasperation.

'Bob,' he said. 'I wish we *could* find some nice alien artifacts. Our tourist industry could use a boost.' The reporters chuckled on cue. 'But the fact is, it's just another piece of terrorist propaganda, put out to undermine trust in the legally appointed government of Mars.' The news switched back to Earth.

Lori had been nudging him gently but firmly toward the door. Now he yielded to her effort and let her guide him, like a tug with a freighter, to the conapt's exit. She got him to the door and pushed him away.

'Have a nice day,' she said, smiling sweetly.

Quaid smiled, gave her one more quick kiss, and left. He heard the multiple screens, now that he wasn't trying to tune them out, describing the weather, a financial graph, and local security. Well, at least she hadn't put the Environmental back on.

Then, as he passed through the door, something washed over him. It was a mental picture of the sky turning horrendously red, the buildings bursting into flames. All Earth was being destroyed, by a nova! The sun had flared, heating the inner planets, and causing firestorms to incinerate everything. With horror, he knew he was going to die – along with all the rest of his species.

Quaid blinked. The world was normal again. It had been a seizure of imagination, probably triggered by the news item about the mysterious novas. It couldn't happen here, of course; the sun was not the type.

Or was it? The astronomers admitted that stars were going nova that had no business doing it. The astronomers obviously didn't know stars as well as they thought they did! How well did they know the sun?

Not, it was too crazy. He dismissed it, and headed for the elevators.

4
Work

Quaid found himself in the commuter stream he had seen from his window. He hated this, without being certain why; there was nothing inherently wrong about the densely populated foot runnels. Maybe it was just that his dream of Mars lent him an appreciation for the deserted open terrain, where even one other person in sight was significant, especially if it was a lovely woman in a space suit. Here he was constantly jostled by the thronging mass of humanity, breathing the used air of those around him and smelling the industrial pollution that was chronic at these lower levels, no matter what the local publicity ads claimed. Mars, at least, was clean; there was nothing there but red dust and jumbled stones. On Mars, a man could stretch out his arms without banging the snotty nose of the man next to him.

He descended the long escalator which at this hour resembled a rushing waterfall of heads, backs, and shoulders sliding toward the lower levels of the subway station. At the bottom, the stream was diverted momentarily around a small area occupied by a crippled fiddler. Quaid smiled, refreshed by the sight of someone claiming space and attention for himself in the midst of the anonymous morning crush. He paused to slide his ID card into the fiddler's portable credit register. It recorded his donation and he allowed himself to be swept back into the stream again.

He squeezed into a security area. The mass of working folk formed into lines to pass the large X-ray panels. This was a bottleneck, costing him time, but couldn't be helped. There had been so much violence on the mass transit system that measures had had to be taken, and certainly he didn't want to be robbed or killed by some hophead freak on the subway, or be part of a group taken hostage by a nascent revolutionary cult. No metal or weapons-caliber plastics were allowed, unless they were plainly not weapons, and that did reduce incidents of violence somewhat.

Having nothing better to do, he watched the line ahead of him as it turned to pass the panels. Each person lost clothing and flesh to become a walking skeleton, then returned to full human form beyond the panel. He saw an attractive young woman approach, and watched closely as she paraded on the panel, but it was no good; all that showed was her bones, not her bare body. He always hoped that someday something would go wrong, that the X-rays would be diminished just enough to abolish the clothing, leaving the naked flesh. Unfortunately, it never happened; the panels either worked or they didn't, full on or full off. Still, those were nice bones.

His turn came. He passed through, feeling like a stripper on stage. As he passed beyond the panel he glanced back at the line behind him and saw a young woman staring at him, the tip of her tongue playing across her lips, her eyes fixed. She had been trying to see *his* naked flesh! That pleased him, in a minor way. He knew he had good bones too.

What did he care what some strange woman thought? He had a lovely and attentive wife at home, and a lovely and adventurous dream woman on Mars. He didn't need any other affairs. Yet, foolishly, he craved them. At least he craved some way out of this dull existence. Maybe it was adventure he wanted, whether of far travel or of sexual conquest. Anything except this damned daily rat race!

He continued onto an escalator and rode it down to the subway. This was another bottleneck, because there were never quite enough cars to hold all the people crowding in. He was too far back to make the first train that came, and had to wait for the second, which was a good six minutes later. They were supposed to run at three-minute intervals, but they never did; probably some high official was skimming from the transit fund, leaving less money for train procurement and repair. So it was the passengers who paid for it, in extra three-minute delays, helplessly. If he hit one more bottleneck like this, he'd be late for work, and get his paycheck docked.

The train finally came. Quaid squeezed on, feeling like a sardine in a monstrous can. What a contrast to Mars!

Video screens were mounted everywhere, each playing its commercial. It was like the multiple windows of their home screen, except that here it was unremittingly hard-sell. This was a captive market, and the sponsors were merciless. He tried to tune out the nearest screen, but the alternative was to listen to the labored breathing of those packed in around him, and smell their body odors. On the screen a cabbie turned, as if looking at a passenger in the backseat. Beneath the old-fashioned checkered cap was the face of a mannequin. Smiling mechanically, it said: 'Thank you for taking JohnnyCab! I hope you enjoyed the ride.' The commercial faded and another began. His eyes moved there of their own accord.

A happy fellow lay on a round bed, next to a sexpot. He had evidently just made love with her, or was about to. They were under a glass dome at the bottom of the ocean; colorful fish swam around outside. Quaid knew that most of the pretty fish were up near the surface, not three miles down, and that they had better things to do than pose for the eyes of tourists who paid them no attention anyway. Not when there were sexpots to be stroked! But, hell, it was their commercial. It was foolish even to expect realism in a commercial.

'**Do you dream of a vacation at the bottom of the ocean . . .**' the narrator said, in that deafeningly loud voice that advertisers insisted on inflicting on their victims. Quaid winced and tried to nudge away from the screen, but the other passengers refused to give way. They didn't want to be deafened either.

The screen jump-cut to a poverty-level apartment, much worse than Quaid's own conapt, where the fellow of the underwater dome sat alone, surrounded by a towering pile of bills. He looked woebegone.

'**. . . but you can't float the bill?**' the narrator continued from offscreen.

He was scoring there! If Quaid just had the money to move to Mars! That was the real reason Lori opposed it; she knew there was no way they could afford it. Oh, there was the bonus for new colonists, but he knew that was quickly dissipated in moving expenses. There had to be a sufficient cushion, so that a man didn't have to be a miner to survive there. So she made the best of their real-life situation, and he had to admit she did a good job of it, and that he should be grateful. But he was like the poor schnook in the commercial: he longed for a distant planet, instead of the crowded mundane life he could afford. Except that the guy in the commercial couldn't even afford a decent conapt.

The scene jumped again. This time a sophisticated woman was skiing to a stop next to a flock of penguins. She was attractive in her snow outfit, and seemed to be on top of the world – or the bottom of it, as the case might be.

'Would you like to ski Antarctica . . .'

Then the same woman was in an office, surrounded by ten employees, all of them demanding decisions. She looked properly harried. Her hair was mussed, and she no longer looked attractive, just tired. Quaid had seen executive women just like that.

'. . . but you're snowed under with work?'

Despite himself, Quaid was responding to these ads. Antarctica was a long way away, a forbidding, desolate region, similar in its fashion to Mars . . .

'Have you always wanted to climb the mountains of Mars . . .'

Quaid jumped. His attention was abruptly riveted to the screen. There, a sportsman was climbing a rugged pyramid-shaped mountain that looked startlingly like the one in Quaid's dream. Was he imagining this? Was his dream taking over the mundane world, or his perception of it? No, this really was the commercial! It was not himself, Douglas Quaid, in the scene, but a smaller man in a tourist-type space suit, the kind that was made more for comfort than efficiency.

Then the sportsman became an old man creeping up a staircase.

'. . . but now you're over the hill?' The camera pulled

back to reveal the tweed jacket and dignified face of a professorial gentleman, the commercial's narrator.

'**Then come to Rekall, Incorporated,**' he continued, '**where you can buy the memory of your ideal vacation cheaper, safer, and better than the real thing.**' The scene changed to a beach at sunset. The narrator sat comfortably in an odd-looking chair which floated over the water. '**So don't let life pass you by. Call Rekall: for the memory of a lifetime.**' Quaid watched, fascinated, as the Rekall jingle played and a twelve-digit phone number filled the screen.

Quaid was intrigued. He was held in thrall by a foolish dream. That was what this outfit seemed to be selling: a dream, in the form of a memory. Would that be good enough? He knew he needed some way to resign himself to his ordinary life. Maybe this was it.

The commercials blared on, exploring intimate toiletries, supposedly excellent investments, nostril suppositories to denature the pollution, and other products, but Quaid didn't notice. Maybe he had found a way to visit Mars after all!

In due course he arrived at his job. He wasn't late, quite, and soon he was out onsite, doing what he did best. When the demolition execs wanted something broken up fast and well, he was the first man assigned. He never slacked off; he used the work as exercise, building his muscles unceasingly. After all, Lori was turned on by muscle, and maybe the dream woman of Mars was too.

He tried to distract himself from that last thought, focusing his attention on the job at hand. They were in the midst of clearing away one of the old auto factories that littered the landscape. Pollution levels had finally become life-threatening some fifty years ago, as everyone had predicted they would, but it wasn't until people started dropping like flies that anyone had done anything about it.

Fossil fuel-burning vehicles were no longer "regulated" or 'reconditioned'–they had been banned outright, and clean fusion technology, which had been available for years, was finally put to a practical use. The car manufacturers had fought the changeover tooth and nail, but they had finally yielded to public pressure and designed emission-free cars. It was a drop in the bucket, too little almost too late, as far as eliminating pollution went, but it was a start.

The car manufacturers had abandoned their old, outmoded factories in favor of streamlined, wholly mechanized plants in which robots were run by computers. But the detritus of the past remained and it was Quaid's job to get rid of it. This morning he was working on the entrance road leading to the site of the derelict factory. He was hardly conscious of the passage of time as he reduced the roadway to quality rubble.

The thing about working hard was that it took his mind off foolish dreams; he focused exclusively on the job to be accomplished, as if it were the center screen of a truly fascinating video, tuning out all else. There was a certain joy to the breaking up of surfacing; it was as if he were pounding away at the strictures of society that kept him here on dull Earth instead of on some more interesting planet. He was *accomplishing* something.

But now the dream returned, refusing to give up. He tried to ignore it, but it hovered by him. Rekall – was there anything to it?

'Hey, Harry!' he shouted above the roar of the hammer. Harry was a middle-aged jack-jock, with a beer belly and a Brooklyn accent. They'd worked together for a couple of years and Quaid had found him to be a likeable, stand-up kind of guy. 'You ever heard of Rekall?'

'Rekall?' Harry shouted back. Bits of rock fell from his hair as he shook his head. He didn't place the reference.

'They sell fake memories!' Quaid prompted.

Now Harry remembered. 'Oh, yeah,' he said, and bellowed the company's jingle at the top of his lungs. Then he stopped his machine and asked. 'You thinkin' of goin' there?' Quaid took a break, too, leaning on his jackhammer while it hissed in neutral.

'I don't know,' he said, brushing the rock dust from his gloves. 'Maybe.'

'Well, don't,' Harry said firmly.

The bluntness of the reply took Quaid by surprise. Harry obviously knew something about Rekall, Incorporated that the commercials didn't mention. 'Why not?' he asked. If there was something fishy about the place, he wanted to know about it.

Harry leaned closer and lowered his voice. 'A friend of mine tried one of their "special offers". Nearly got himself lobotomized.'

A chill went down Quaid's back. 'No shit . . .' Quaid breathed, raising a hand to his brow.

Harry clapped him on the shoulder and stood to his machine once more. 'Don't fuck with your brain, pal. It ain't worth it.' His jackhammer roared to life, and Quaid revved his, too. He turned back to the work at hand while he mulled over Harry's words. It was good advice, surely. Only a fool would ignore it.

But when he got off work, he went to a phone unit. He ran his finger down a long list of businesses and their office numbers, stopping at Rekall, Incorporated. He wasn't sure yet that he was going to do it, but he was going to find out more. It might be foolish, but it might also be the only way to deal with his dream.

5

Rekall

Quaid paused before the computer console of the building directory before selecting Rekall, Inc. from the list of names. The screen displayed the office's location, but still he hesitated.

Was this the answer? Harry had warned him off, but Harry wasn't subject to chronic dreams of Mars. Mars was an incubus he simply had to get off his back, one way or another. He had either to banish the notion, which was impossible, or go there, which might also be impossible, or find a compromise. This just might be that compromise.

He knew that an illusion, no matter how convincing, remained nothing more than an illusion. Objectively, at least. But subjectively – that could be quite the opposite.

Well, he had an appointment. Within the next five minutes. Now was a point of decision; he had either to go up and be subject to their sales pitch or leave, chickening out. He would have flattened any man who called him chicken – fortunately, none had since he got his adult growth – but now he was accusing himself. He felt the crazy lure of Mars, but also his terror of falling down that mysterious pit. Did he really want to make that dream seem real?

There was only one way to know. Taking a deep breath, he boarded an elevator and made his way to the company's reception area.

The receptionist was a nicely articulated blonde, painting her fingernails by tapping each nail with a white stylus. Red pigment instantly saturated each nail. For a moment she looked bare-bosomed, her breasts sprayed blue, but then the light shifted and he realized that it was the effect of one of those now-you-see-it, now-you-don't variable translucency blouses. Seen from one angle, in one light, she was fully covered; seen from another angle, in other light, she was nude. Mostly she was somewhere between, the effect changing intriguingly as she shifted position. He would have to mention that to Lori; she would probably get a similar outfit for herself.

The woman hid her paraphernalia without embarrassment. She smiled in a practiced manner. 'Good afternoon. Welcome to Rekall.'

Was he doing the right thing? He felt like a schoolboy approaching an adult gambling joint. 'I called for an appointment. Douglas Quaid.'

She checked a list. He was sure this was a pose; he did have an appointment, and there was no one else in the office. She looked up. 'One moment, Mr Quaid.' She spoke quietly into a videophone while keeping an appreciative eye on Quaid, who glanced restlessly at the video travel posters that lined the walls. 'Mr Quaid?' she said. 'Mr McClane will be right with you.'

As she finished speaking, a salesman emerged from an inner ofice.

'Thank you, Tiffany,' he said. He winked at the receptionist, then grinned and offered his hand to Quaid. 'Doug . . . Bob McClane. Good to meet ya. Right this way.' Quaid followed him out of the reception area.

McClane seemed to be a jovial hustler. He was in his mid-fifties, and he wore the latest Martian frog-pelt gray suit. The frogs weren't native, of course; there was no surviving native life on Mars. But imported terrestrial frogs, raised in special Martian farms, had developed unusual characteristics in the reduced gravity and increased radiation, and now there was quite a market for their hides.

McClane led the way into his stylishly decorated office. 'Have a seat, sit down, make yourself comfortable.'

Quaid lowered himself into a sleek, futuristic chair that adjusted itself subtly to accommodate his weight and configuration. This, too, Lori might like to know about; these people were right up with the times.

McClane sat behind his big pseudo-walnut desk. 'Now you wanted a memory of . . . ?'

'Mars,' Quaid said, realizing that the line between doubt and commitment had somehow already been crossed.

But the man's reaction surprised him. 'Right, Mars,' McClane said unenthusiastically.

'There's something wrong with that?'

McClane frowned. 'Enhhhh, honestly, Doug, if outer space is your thing, I think you'd be much happier with one of our Saturn cruises. Everybody raves about 'em and it's nearly the same price.'

Oh. So this was a bait-and-switch operation, to jack him up to a higher price range. 'I'm not interested in Saturn,' Quaid said firmly. 'I'm interested in Mars.'

McClane put the best face on it, his ploy having fallen flat. 'Okay, okay, Mars it is. Now hold on a second while I . . .' He typed on his computer keyboard, and figures came up on his screen. 'All righty . . . our basic Mars package goes for just eight hundred and ninety-four credits. That's for two full weeks of memories, complete in every detail.' He glanced up. 'A longer trip'll run you a little more, 'cause you need a deeper implant.'

More bait-and-switch. 'I just want the standard trip.' Actually he wanted the real thing, but even the fancier memory-trip would be out of his price range.

McClane put on the expression of a reasonable man faced with an unreasonable or slightly ignorant customer. 'We have no standard trip, Doug. Every journey is individually tailored to your personal tastes.'

He was a slippery one! He was going to push up the rates one way or another. 'I mean, what's on the itinerary?'

The man got down to business. 'First of all, Doug, when you go Rekall, you go first class. Private cabin on an Inter-World Spaceways shuttle. Deluxe accommodations at the Hilton. Plus all the major sights: Mount Olympus, the canals, *Venusville* . . .' He leered with the same polish as the receptionist's smile. 'You name it, you'll remember it.'

'And how does it really seem?' Quaid had heard about Venusville, one of the most notorious sleaze dens in the Solar System. He doubted that he would find his dream woman there.

'As real as any memory in your head.'

Quaid did not bother to conceal his skepticism. 'Yeah, right.'

'I'm telling you, Doug, your brain won't know the difference – or your money back. You'll even have tangible proof. Ticket stubs. Postcards. Film – shots you took of local sights on Mars with a rented movie camera. Souvenirs. And more. You'll have all the support you need for your memories. We guarantee –'

'What about the guy you almost lobotomized?' Quaid interrupted. 'Did he get a refund?'

McClane managed not to wince. 'That's ancient history, Doug. Nowadays, traveling with Rekall is safer than getting on a rocket. Look at the statistics.' He scared up a list of statistics and graphs on Quaid's video monitor. They were, of course, confusing in their suddenness and complexity, as they were no doubt meant to be; the client was supposed to be impressed with their number, and be convinced of their validity. 'So whaddaya say?'

He was very fast on the clincher! But Quaid didn't want to be glad-handed into the commitment. 'I'm not sure. If I have the implant, I'll never go for real.'

McClane leaned forward over the desk. 'Doug, can we be honest?'

You mean you've been lying up till now? But Quaid kept his face straight, wanting to see what the next ploy was.

'You're a construction worker, right?' McClane continued.

This character was stroking him the wrong way. 'So?'

'How else are you gonna get to Mars? Enlist?' McClane grimaced, evincing disgust at the notion. 'Face it, pal: Rekall's your ticket. Unless you'd rather stay home and watch TV.'

Unkindly put, but unfortunately accurate. This *was* about the only feasible way to do it, for a construction engineer, site-preparation specialist, jack-jock for short.

Before he could get discouraged, McClane stood, leaned over the desk, and put a hand on his shoulder. 'Besides, think what a pain in the ass a real holiday is: lost luggage, lousy weather, dingy hotel rooms. With Rekall, everything's perfect.'

He was scoring again. Quaid had experienced just those problems, and he hadn't had to go to Mars to do it! 'Okay. It's been my lifelong ambition, and I can see I'll never really do it. So I guess I'll have to settle for this.'

'Don't think of it that way,' McClane said severely. 'You're not accepting second best, Doug. The actual memory, with all its vagueness, omissions, and ellipses, not to say distortions – that's second best.'

Once more, a score. What difference would it make, after he was home from a real trip? All he would have would be the memories and a depleted bank account. The Rekall memories were guaranteed better. Still, there was a niggling doubt. 'But if I know I've been here, to your office, I'll know it isn't real. I mean –'

'Doug, you will never remember seeing me or coming here; you won't, in fact, even remember having heard of our existence. That's part of the package. There will be no contrary indications; everything will point to the validity of your recent experience.'

He was sold. 'I'll take the two-week trip.'

'You won't regret it,' McClane said warmly. He touched a button, activating Quaid's keyboard. 'Now while you fill out our questionnaire, I'll familiarize you with some of our options.'

Quaid started filling out the multiple choice items on his video screen: details of his preferences in many minor things, such as colors of clothing worn, and in some middling ones, such as measurements of approachable women. 'Never mind the options,' he said, becoming impatient with it all.

'Just answer one question,' McClane said earnestly. 'What's the same about every vacation you ever took?'

Quaid didn't care for any guessing games. 'I give up.'

'You. You're the same.' He paused for effect. 'No matter where you go, there you are. Always the same old you.' He grinned enigmatically. 'So what I want to suggest, Doug, is that you take a little vacation *from yourself*. It's the latest thing in travel. We call it an Ego Trip.'

This sounded fishy. 'I'm really not interested.'

But McClane was intent on the sale. 'You're gonna love this.' He straightened up, as if unveiling something special. 'We offer you a choice of alternate identities during your trip.'

This still seemed fishy. What was the point in taking a trip – or in remembering a trip – if it happened to someone else?

McClane preempted Quaid's questionnaire on the video monitor with a list:

A-14 MILLIONAIRE PLAYBOY
A-15 SPORTS HERO
A-16 INDUSTRIAL TYCOON
A-17 SECRET AGENT

'Come on, Doug, why be a tourist on Mars when you can be a playboy, an athlete, a –'

Despite his doubt, Quaid was interested. 'Secret agent – how much is that?'

'Let me tantalize you, Doug. It's like a movie, and you're the star. Thrills, chills, double identities, chases! You're a top operative, back under deep cover on your most important mission . . .' He trailed off.

'Go on,' Quaid said, not wishing to be teased.

McClane sat back. 'I don't wanna spoil it for you, Doug. Just rest assured, by the time it's all over, you'll have got the girl, killed the bad guys, and saved the planet.' He smiled victoriously. 'Now would you say that's worth three hundred credits?'

Quaid reluctantly smiled. McClane's final bait-and-switch ploy had gotten him hooked.

6

41A

There were other routine details that Quaid tuned out in much the way he did irrelevant windows of a multi-screen. It turned out that once the decision was made, there was no need for delay, as this was a purely internal procedure. Internal in the head. A couple of hours, and he'd be back from Mars: it was that simple, as far as his part in it was concerned. McClane had promised that he would have a ready explanation for the lack of missing time; how could he have been at work today, yet be returning from two weeks off-planet? Not to worry; there would be no apparent incongruity. He would keep his memory private, because he didn't want to make his co-workers jealous, and they would not mention his absence, supposing it to have been an embarrassing illness. He would never be inclined to check the actual dates of his trip against the dates of his employment, because his memory had them firmly recorded. A direct challenge, with assembled evidence, would of course turn up discrepancies – but who would want to do that? Not his co-workers, not Lori, who would be relieved to see him get the notion of going to Mars out of his system. She would be notified of what he had done, because she was next of kin and needed to know where the money had gone, but she would go along with it. They would even throw in a bonus for her: a token memory of seeing him off at the spaceport, and being lonely while he was gone, so that she could properly appreciate the impact of his experience. No problems, guaranteed.

In fact, if he remembered any of his visit to this office, he could come in for a refund. There *had* to be no problem, or they took the loss. The system was self-correcting.

Now it was evening, and they were ready. McClane

guided him to another office in the rear of the complex, where there was something resembling an old-fashioned dentist's chair. The chamber looked like a cross between an operating room and a sound-mixing booth. A nurse put a green surgical smock over his street clothes. 'Don't worry, Mr Quaid,' she said as McClane departed. 'This is only to protect your clothing from any staining from the IV. We're not into surgery!'

'IV?' he asked, startled.

'We must put you just a little bit under, Mr Quaid, so that your mind is receptive to the memory implant. It really wouldn't work if you were fully conscious.' She smiled. She was not as pretty as the receptionist, and her blouse was fully opaque, but her smile was pleasant and reassuring.

'Uh, yes, of course,' he agreed, taking his seat in the chair. It was pleasant having a woman fuss over him, any woman, anytime. Lori was good at that, very good. But the one on Mars –

The nurse made sure he was comfortable, placing his arms on the armrests just so and adjusting the headrest. She rolled back his left sleeve and swabbed his forearm with cool alcohol. 'My, you must be a powerful man, Mr Quaid!' she said, noting the musculature of the arm as she dabbed on a surface anesthetic. Most women claimed to be more interested in character than appearance, exactly as most men did, but appearance always got in its innings.

'I'm a construction engineer. A jack-jock.'

'Oho! That explains it! You must be very good at it.'

He knew she was just teasing him along to distract him from her preparations, but he liked it anyway. It was easy to imagine being in bed with such a woman, as he half lay in this supremely comfortable recliner and felt her gentle touch on his skin. He didn't even feel the prick of the needle when he set the IV. He just felt increasingly relaxed as the tube began its flow. He wasn't aware of the nurse's departure and didn't care; he just seemed to float, perfectly relaxed.

A young man entered the chamber. He moved quickly, as if hyperactive. He was thin, with nondescript brown hair and rapidly darting gray eyes, reminding Quaid a bit of a foraging mouse. 'Hello, Mr Quaid,' he said. 'I'm Ernie, your technical assistant. Dr Lull will be with you in a moment. Are you comfortable?'

'Yes.' Indeed he was! Any more comfort, and he'd be asleep.

'I'll just set the "space helmet" here,' Ernie said with a jerky smile as he drew the device out on the end of a metal elbow arm. 'Sort of a joke, that; you see, it resembles –'

'I get the joke,' Quaid said. They were treating him like a child. It was fun when a woman did it, but not when a gawky adolescent man did.

Ernie lowered the burnished metal bowl over Quaid's head. 'This your first trip?'

'Mm-hmm.' Actually, it *was* reminiscent of a space helmet, and he could easily imagine himself stepping out on the barren landscape of Mars with such a device on his head. But it was actually a brain wave scanner, he knew, used to read and modify that portion of his mental activity that related to memories. This helmet was probably worth thousands of credits.

Ernie carefully aligned the complex scientific instrument and locked it in place. Quaid scowled slightly as a strap chafed his head, too snug.

'Don't worry,' Ernie said, adjusting the strap. 'Things hardly ever fuck up.'

Just get on with it, twerp, Quaid thought. He was ready for Mars.

The door opened and a birdlike middle-aged woman entered. She wore a stylish pants suit that didn't do enough for her. Her body was too skinny and her hair too red. This was an artificial woman in the bad sense: she was trying to make herself look competent and successful, and succeeding mainly in making herself look ungainly.

'Good evening, Mr . . .' She paused to check the video chart, obviously at a loss for his name. She found it. 'Quaid, I'm Dr Lull.' She spoke with a Swedish accent, and treated him with an impersonal conviviality that would have grated had he not been sedated.

'Pleased to meet you,' he said insincerely.

The amenities over, Dr Lull donned a surgical smock, then flipped through Quaid's computer chart. 'Ernie, patch in matrix 62b, 37, and –' She looked at Quaid. 'Would you like to integrate some alien stuff?'

'Two-headed monsters?' he asked doubtfully.

She laughed with something approaching actual feeling. 'Don't you keep up with the news? We're doing alien artifacts these days.'

Oh. 'Sure. Why not?' The notion intrigued him. Maybe that was one reason he was so interested in Mars. He hoped to explore, to discover the remnants of some vast lost alien complex, superscience, stun the world with the discovery, bathe in the notoriety of his achievement . . .

Dr Lull tossed the matrix to Ernie. That suggested what she thought of such notions: just a bit of fiction on a cartridge.

'You got it,' Ernie said.

As Ernie plugged in the proper cartridges, Dr Lull fastened straps over Quaid's arms, legs, and torso to hold the rest of him securely in place. This alarmed him slightly; did they think he was going to go into convulsions?

'Been married long, Mr Quaid?' Dr Lull inquired, actually seeming interested. Maybe a woman of her contours was attuned to the notion of being married, having trouble achieving it.

'Eight years.' That surprised him as he heard himself answer. Oh, it was true – but he realized that Lori still looked no older than twenty-five. She had aged hardly a whit; his mental picture of her on the day of their marriage was unchanged from his memory of her session with him this morning. Odd that he hadn't noticed this before. Not that it bothered him; he'd be happy to have her keep her appearance for the next forty years.

Yet even so, that woman of his Mars dream – how old was she? Not out of her twenties, surely.

'Slipping away for a little hanky-panky?' Dr Lull asked, licking her lips. She was definitely interested in the subject; her tone was positive rather than condemning.

Quaid realized that even unattractive middle-aged women had dreams. She was indulging in hers by playing a muted verbal footsie with him, perhaps picturing herself in bed with him just the way he pictured himself in bed with any young and sexy woman he encountered. For the first time he realized that this sort of fancy might be an imposition on the other party, even when unvoiced. At times he had bantered with a young woman, only to have her turn away as if affronted, when he hadn't meant anything by it. Now, picturing himself as the object of Dr Lull's lust – himself strapped down in this chair while she slowly stripped off his clothes and handled him in whatever way might titillate her – he understood the woman's side of it. He did not care to be victimized by her imagination. 'Not really,' he replied shortly.

'All systems go,' Ernie said.

Dr Lull was all business again. 'Good. Then we're all set.' She stepped on a lever, and the back of Quaid's chair lowered to a fully reclining position. 'Ready for dreamland?'

Quaid nodded. It suddenly occurred to him that the helmet might have been reading his thoughts all this time. Did she know what he had been thinking about her? He hoped not!

She reached to the tubing and opened the IV drip. Quaid was startled again; he had thought it was already on! Had all that relaxation been strictly imagination?

'I'll be asking you a few questions, Mr Quaid,' Dr Lull continued, 'so we can fine-tune the wish-fulfillment program. Please be completely honest.'

Not likely! But he was sure he could handle her questions, which wouldn't approach his secret thoughts.

Now he really was beginning to feel the effect of the anesthetic. He wasn't floating, he was sinking. His mental barriers were descending; he no longer cared if she knew his opinion of her.

Dr Lull did not ask a question immediately. Instead she checked his vital signs. She was being careful with his health; that much he appreciated. That business about a poor sap getting lobotomized had bothered him; he didn't want any such accident.

Now she was set. 'Your sexual orientation?

Easy! 'Hetero.' She was just zeroing him in, making sure his reactions aligned with their indications.

She nodded. 'Now take a look at this monitor.'

He gazed drowsily at a vague female outline on a computer screen he hadn't noticed before.

'How do you prefer your women?' she asked. 'Blonde, brunette, redhead, Negro, Oriental?'

'Brunette.' But Lori was a blonde. It was the Mars-woman who was brunette. Still, it was truth – more than he hoped the doctor realized. There was no doubt that Lori was all that a man could ask for. Did his reservation about her stem solely from the color of her hair? He would have to think about that, when he had time to think without being spied on.

He heard soft typing to the side. That would be Ernie, putting the specs into the system. The schematic image adjusted to match Quaid's taste: the woman became brunette, with dark hair, dark eyes, and a slightly olive skin. Not quite like the one in his dream, but he didn't care to have that match perfectly. He wasn't sure why. Maybe it was just that some things were too private to be pro-grammed. Maybe it was that he didn't want his true dream woman distorted by an artificial memory. Let this be some other woman, similar, but not so close as to be confusing. The memory might not be as nice, but caution was best.

'Slim, curvaceous, voluptuous?' Dr Lull asked crisply.

He was really getting sleepy now! That stuff in the IV didn't fool around. 'Volupshus.'

'Demure, aggressive, wanton? Be honest.'

Why shouldn't he be honest? Well, there was a reason, but he couldn't quite recall it at the moment. 'Wanton . . . and demure.' Let them wrestle with that conflicting matchup!

'41A, Ernie.'

So much for conflict! Maybe if he wasn't so sleepy he'd have been able to mess them up a little. As it was, he had spoken true, with someone in mind even though he had thought to keep her a bit removed.

He was vaguely aware of Ernie slipping cassette 41A into his console. The computer image became a schematic version of the woman in Quaid's dream. The likeness was so close it was startling.

Oh, no! Did they know? They couldn't! Yet –

'Boy, is he gonna have a wild time,' Ernie chortled. 'Won't wanna come back.'

Quaid faded out. He was on his way, wherever.

7

Problem

McClane was interviewing another prospective client, a lonely middle-aged woman. These were fairly common customers; women seemed to have more suppressed dreams than men, and to be more depressive. They weren't necessarily poor, either, just tired of being stuck at home while their husbands got all the action. What he offered was ideal for them.

'So you see, Mrs Killdeer, we really can remember it for you wholesale. This will be the best experience you ever had!'

'But there won't be any souvenirs,' she complained.

'Not true,' McClane said earnestly. 'For just a few credits more, we supply postcards, photographs of you at the sights, *letters* from the handsome men you met –'

The videophone rang, interrupting him. Damn! He'd told them not to do that when he was closing a deal. He activated the 'phone and Dr Lull appeared on the screen.

'Bob?' she asked. Her voice was tense. 'You better get down here.'

McClane rolled his eyes in the full view of Mrs Killdeer, as if in league with the customer against the company. It was hardly an exaggeration; good sales were not all that common, and he hated to have his clincher speech messed up. 'I'm with a very important client.'

'Looks like another schizoid embolism,' Dr Lull said.

McClane was shocked. Worse, so was Mrs Killdeer. *She understood the reference!* This was all too likely to cost him two clients: Quaid and Killdeer. What an awful break!

He stood and attempted a reassuring smile. 'I'll be right back.'

But he very much feared she would not be there when he returned. Damn, damn, damn!

40

He strode out of the sales office and down the hall to the rear memory studio. The fools, to interrupt him with an announcement like that, in the hearing of a client! He was going to kick some ass! Did Renata Lull think she could pull a stunt like this and –

But as he entered the studio he pulled up short, his ire forgotten. He stood appalled at what was happening.

The client, Douglas Quaid, had gone crazy. He was shouting and thrashing about in the chair, struggling violently to break the straps that held him down. He was a powerful man – just how powerful McClane hadn't properly appreciated before – and the IV connection was in danger of being separated. Indeed, the whole chair was rocking. What had happened? An adverse reaction to the sedative?

Quaid was like a different person. He wasn't crazed so much as enraged. His eyes were flinty, and his voice was cold and menacing. 'You're dead meat, all of you!' he shouted with perfect clarity. 'You blew my cover!'

Dr Lull and Ernie were cowering against the far wall, trying to keep a safe distance from the struggling man. But McClane had had more experience with cases gone bad; they were more common than he allowed the records to show. Every client was an individual, with different synapses and reactions; there were bound to be some mismatches.

'What the fuck is going on here?' McClane demanded, aggravated. 'You can't install a simple goddamn double implant?!' Politeness was for prospective clients, not for errant employees.

'It's not my fault,' Dr Lull protested. 'We hit a memory cap.'

'Untie me, you assholes!' Quaid roared. 'They'll be here any minute! They'll kill you all!'

Huh? 'What's he talking about?' McClane snapped.

'Stop this operation *now*!' Quaid yelled.

How could the guy be talking so clearly? A reaction-induced berserker might scream and froth at the mouth, but his words would be mostly blasphemy and gibberish.

41

Quaid sounded alarmingly coherent. 'Mr Quaid, please calm down,' McClane said, trying to be soothing. Maybe they could change the mix, get him sedated all the way down, then explore the problem. A memory cap? Who would have expected that!

'I'm not Quaid!'

Multiple personality? That just might account for this, and react like a memory cap, because of the memory taken by the alternate personalities. But Lull should have caught that! McClane nervously walked closer to examine Quaid's eyes.

'You're having a reaction to the implant,' he said, though he was by no means sure of that. Anything to get this thing muscled down so they could work their way out of it! 'But in a few minutes –'

Quaid strained again at his bonds. Suddenly the strap holding his right arm snapped. That arm shot up and grabbed McClane by the throat. What devastasting power the man had!

'Untie me.' Quaid's words were softly spoken now, but the quiet menace was all too apparent.

McClane, choking, tried to pry Quaid's hand from his neck. But even his two hands couldn't loosen the iron grip. Construction workers had strong arms; he had known that. Why hadn't he told them to double the straps? He was going to faint before he could even talk!

Ernie came out of his stasis. He rushed over and tried to wrestle Quaid's arm down, using his full body weight. He might as well have pushed against the branch of an oak tree. McClane felt his consciousness wavering as he struggled unsuccessfully to breathe.

Dr Lull hastily readied a syringe gun and frantically jabbed it into Quaid's thigh. She fired dose after dose of narkidrine, until the man finally released his grip and passed out.

McClane fell to the floor, gagging, the studio and the world reeling. Ernie clung to him, managing to slow his fall.

Dr Lull came over to help. 'Are you all right?' she asked anxiously, putting a hand down to check his forehead.

McClane shoved her hand away and gasped for breath. What a mess this was!

'Listen to me!' Dr Lull said urgently. 'He's been going on and on about Mars.' Now it was evident that she was genuinely frightened. 'He's really *been* there!'

The world slowly ground down and fell into its proper place, but McClane still felt the pressure of those terrible fingers against his throat. He was bruised, for sure, but lucky it was no worse. What a monster! 'Use your fucking head, you dumb bitch!' he rasped. 'He's acting out the secret agent role from his Ego Trip! You should have strapped him securely enough to hold him, so that when he thought –'

'That's not possible,' Lull said coolly. She didn't like strong language, but this time her carelessness had invited disaster.

'Why not?' he inquired condescendingly. She wasn't going to get away with any pseudo-medical jargon to talk her way out of this foul-up!

'We haven't implanted it yet.'

McClane stared at her, his oncoming retort abruptly stifled. 'Oh, shit . . .' Suddenly he was terrified. No implant? And the man had been talking about an actual Mars experience? This was no longer weird, it was dangerous!

'I've been trying to tell you,' Dr Lull said significantly. 'Somebody erased his memory. *The man really has been to Mars!* And that's not all –'

'Somebody?' Ernie cried hysterically. 'We're talking the fucking Agency!'

'Shut up!' Dr Lull slapped him. The stinging blow stunned them all into slience.

McClane tried to think. But how could he think about the unthinkable? The mess they had walked into made a schizoid embolism look like an eyestrain headache. Because it looked like Ernie was right: the memory cap must have been implanted by the Agency. No one else had the technology. And everyone, from heads of state to the lowliest rockrats in the Martian mines, knew that interfering

ing with the Agency's plans could have serious, not to mention fatal, results. He didn't have to be an Einstein to figure out that blowing an operative's cover, even by accident, would qualify as major interference.

The Agency was a semisecret government outfit. Its network was spread throughout Earth and the Martian colony and it was bound by no civilized law. It achieved its goals by any means necessary, although what those goals were and who set them, no one knew for sure. It did indeed have agents like Quaid: brute killers who could be stopped only by others of their kind. The fact that this exposure of one of their agents was unintentional would count for nothing. The three of them could literally be dead meat, exactly as Quaid had threatened. Why the *hell* had he walked into Rekall?

McClane was no killer. But now, horribly, his life was on the line. They could kill Quaid simply by increasing the sedative to lethal level. They could do it right now. But could they get away with it? What would they do with the body? The three of them could hardly move it, let alone get it safely out of here unobserved. Was it bugged? He greatly feared it was – which meant that the Agency would be in motion the moment Quaid's life-blip dropped from some-body's monitor screen. Could they drug him down to near-death, until they got him to somewhere that he couldn't be found? There was *nowhere* he couldn't be found, if they were tuning in on a bug! They would trace his route, and nail Rekall without asking questions. No answer there.

Then it came to him. They didn't have to kill him or hide him! All they had to do was hide themselves, hide Rekall, Inc., from Quaid and the Agency. Divert him from here, erase all memory of his visit here, just as they would have done for the regular treatment. But with a difference –

'Okay, this is what we're gonna do,' he said. 'Renata, cover up any memory he has of us or Rekall.'

'I'll do what I can,' she said nervously. 'It's getting messy in there.'

McClane turned to the frightened youth. 'Ernie, dump him in a cab. Around the corner. Get Tiffany to help you.'

Ernie nodded. He would walk Quaid to the cab and give the cabbie Quaid's home address. It would be hard to track back to the actual point of pickup, and if Dr Lull did her work well, no one would every try. For certain, the Agency hadn't sent Quaid here; he had done it on his own, because of some leakage in their conditioning shield. He had had Mars on his mind – no wonder! If they got him clear of Rekall, there should be no repercussions. If nothing went wrong.

If nothing went wrong. There was the key. But Lull knew that her life as well as his was on the line here; she would do the job right. She did know her trade, as he knew his.

'I'll destroy his file and refund his money,' McClane said, even as his thoughts raced through the details. He got back to his feet and paced the limited floor space. 'And if anybody comes asking . . . we've never heard of Douglas Quaid.'

They all looked at Quaid, sprawled unconscious in the chair. McClane sincerely hoped he never saw the man again.

He returned to the front office. Sure enough, Mrs Killdeer was gone. He no longer begrudged the lost sale; in fact, he was relieved. He had more urgent business to do at the moment. He had to clean up those records, and notify everyone who had seen Quaid that they hadn't, beginning with the receptionist. Actually, he could use her in back, because they couldn't process Quaid properly while he was all the way under, and he might recover a bit too far while they made the delicate adjustments. Tiffany was excellent at pacifying people, especially males; she could help keep the man quiet. Also, that refund – maybe he could null the payment before it was permanently recorded in the main computer system, so that there would never have *been* any payment. That would be much better. No payment, no refund – nothing happened.

If this worked, life would continue much as before. If it didn't, they might all be dead before they realized it. McClane knew he wasn't going to sleep well tonight, or any night this week.

8

Harry

Quaid, befuddled, found himself in the back seat of a vehicle. Rain was beating against the window beside his head. He tried to orient, but his brain barely functioned. How had he come here? In fact –

'Where am I?' he asked of whoever might be within hearing.

'You're in a JohnnyCab!' a cheerful voice responded.

A cab. A car. He had surmised as much! 'I mean, what am I doing here?'

'I'm sorry. Would you please rephrase the question?'

Quaid blinked and looked, swiveling his dull gaze from the wet window to the driver in the front of the cab. It wasn't a man, it was a fixedly smiling mannequin in an old-fashioned cabbie's uniform. Now Quaid remembered: this brand of cab sported the pseudo-human touch, supposing that a fake man was better than none at all. Quaid normally used the verbally programmable, fully automatic cabs, instead of the semiautomated mannequin-interface models. The mannequins tended to be a pain. One reason was because they were prone to misunderstand directions, being relatively unsophisticated machines.

Impatiently, he enunciated carefully: *'How did I get in this taxi?'*

'The door opened. You sat down.'

There was a second reason! They tended to take things with infuriating literalness. Exasperated, he sat back as Johnny raced to beat a red light. Would it make any sense to ask the idiot machine where he was going? Probably not. It was easier to wait until they got there. Meanwhile, maybe his woozy head would clear. What *had* he gotten into? The last thing he remembered was quitting work for the day, and – blank.

In due course the cab pulled up at a place he recognized: his apartment building. So he had been going home! But why so late? It was night now. He had lost hours!

The cab door opened and the mannequin turned its head, piping: 'Thank you for taking JohnnyCab! I hope you enjoyed the ride.' Quail had a strong urge to wipe the manic grin off the dummy's face, but he was feeling too woozy to follow through. He almost welcomed the cold rain that stung him as he stepped out of the cab. It soaked him to the skin, but it also helped him recover his senses somewhat. As he staggered toward the building, a familiar voice called out.

'Hey, Quaid!' The Brooklyn accent was unmistakable. It was Harry from work. Quaid was pleased but puzzled.

'Harry! What are you doing here?'

Harry clapped him on the shoulder and grinned. 'How was your trip to Mars?' he asked.

'What trip?' Quaid pushed his wet hair back from his forehead and returned Harry's grin with a blank look.

'What do you mean, "What trip?" You went to Rekall, remember?'

Confused, Quaid tried to remember. 'I did?'

'Yeah, you did,' Harry said. Quaid fell in step with him and they approached the building entrance together.

Quaid was still uncertain. Maybe he had gone there. They had discussed it briefly at work, and Harry had told him about the lobotomy accident. Then he had – or *had* he? He must have spent those lost hours *somewhere* . . .

'C'mon,' said Harry, 'I'll buy you a drink. You can tell me all about it.' He reached out to take Quaid's arm, but Quaid pulled back. A drink wouldn't help whatever was wrong with his head. All he wanted to do was go home and let Lori look after him. Maybe then he could figure out . . .

'Thanks, Harry, but I'm late,' he said with a touch of impatience.

'Tough shit,' Harry snapped. His face had gone grim, his voice harsh. Before Quaid knew what was happening, three large men in business suits were behind and beside him, hustling him into the building.

47

'Hey!' Quaid shouted. He wasn't sure what was going on, but it scared him and he struggled to break free. Then he felt something. He glanced down. Harry was jamming a gun in his ribs.

'Relax,' Harry said evenly. Quaid stopped resisting, though his heart continued to race. The four men marched him through the lobby and into the emergency staircase that led down to the lower level parking garage.

He had to go. He knew, without knowing how he knew, that they would just as soon knock him out and toss him down the stairs, or worse. He had to recover more of his physical control if he wanted to get out of this alive. When he acted, it would have to be by surprise, and fast, and effective. So for now he kept both his body and his speech slower than it had to be. Let them think he was still doped out. It would be to his advantage in the long run.

'What's going on, Harry?' There was no answer. Thanks to the adrenaline rush, Quaid's head was clearing. His memory was starting to fill in now. He *had* gone to Rekall, and – and what? He had wanted a memory of Mars. He had talked with a man – but the memory faded.

Quaid tried again. 'Are you a cop?' Still no answer. The timing of the attack meant that it had to relate to his visit to Rekall. Maybe someone didn't want him to remember something. But he had gone there only because of his dream of Mars . . .

'Harry, what did I do?' he asked, both afraid and angry. This time he got an answer.

'You blabbed, Quaid!' Harry said angrily. 'You blabbed!'

'*Blabbed*? About what?' Before he had time to decipher the riddle, the goons threw him against a wall and twisted his arms viciously behind his back.

'You shoulda listened to me, Quaid.' Harry's voice was quiet now, but that only made it more menacing. 'I was there to keep you out of trouble.'

Out of *what* trouble. Something to do with a memory? How could a memory hurt anyone? Or maybe it had to do with his dream. No, that was even more ridiculous. Quaid didn't have any answers, couldn't remember enough to even hazard a guess. But it was obvious by now that it didn't matter what he remembered; they were going to kill him anyway. He had thought Harry was his friend. Now he knew he'd been duped. This maneuver had been planned; it wasn't any spur-of-the-moment thing, and Harry was evidently in charge. Which meant that, when he made his break, he'd have to take out Harry first.

'Harry, you're making a mistake,' he said, knowing that if he didn't make his case now, he would never have another chance. 'You've got me mixed up with someone else!'

Harry didn't crack the slightest trace of a smile. 'Unh-uh, pal. You've got yourself mixed up with somebody else.' One of the goons jerked Quaid's arm and he lost his footing. For a moment he thought he was falling . . .

His dream-vision flooded back and suddenly he was sure. Mars *did* have something to do with this! That dream was too real, too persistent! Maybe he really had been there – no, that couldn't be; he had only wanted to go there. He had spent all his adult life on Earth, with Lori. His memory of that was as clear as his notions of Mars were foggy. Still –

There had been this receptionist, with a see-peek blouse and sprayed-blue breasts beneath. 'Mr Quaid, you are a good-looking man, and it spoils your features to become angry,' she said. 'If it would make you feel any better, I might, ahem, let you take me out . . .' No, that wasn't it; he hadn't been angry with her, and she hadn't offered. That must have been a daydream, or an implanted memory. That was the place of implanted memories, of dreams that seemed to have come true in the past. He had wanted a memory of Mars. He had talked with a man – but the memory faded again.

Harry raised his gun to Quaid's temple. His finger slowly tightened on the trigger. He looked as if he was really sorry to be doing this; his eyes were filled with the old this-hurts-me-worse-than-it-does-you look.

Quaid's expression hardened. Like the errant kid in the woodshed, he had his doubts about whose hurt was worse. He was also aware, on another level, that the grouping of

49

men had become perfect. It was time to knock down the dominoes.

Harry had made the classic mistake of holding the gun too close to the target. Quaid's fist came up in a blur of speed and deflected Harry's arm. The gun fired into the stairwell.

Quaid's arm smashed across Harry's neck, crushing his windpipe. Harry hardly had time to collapse, trying to gag, trying to breathe, before Quaid whirled and caught the nearest goon with a sledgehammer fist to the heart. The man was still standing, though dead on his feet, as Quaid leaped at the next. He caught the man's head between his hands and twisted so savagely that there was an audible snap and the face was looking out from the wrong side of the body, the eyes wide-open startled. The last goon had had three seconds to react; he was lurching forward, his gun coming up. Quaid's knee rose to meet his head, smashing the man's nose straight back into the brain. Flat-faced, the goon fell.

A total of five seconds had passed since Harry's finger tightened on the trigger. Four men were dead.

You're slowing down, pal!

What? Quaid shook his head. There was no one there. Just himself and the dead men, gruesomely strewn on the stairs. One of them might have been his friend, once.

He stared in amazement at the bodies. How – what – ?

He looked at his bloodied hands. Were these his? Had they committed this mayhem? It was as if they belonged to somebody else.

He remembered thinking about groupings and dominoes. Then – this.

He gathered his wits. Whatever had happened here, he would get the blame if he remained! He had to get away from this nightmare and safely home.

9
'Wife'

Quaid flew up the stairs and into the lobby, heedless of the other residents in the building who stared as he passed. They let him have an elevator all to himself.

Upstairs, he barged into his conapt, breathless. What a relief it was to be here! But he couldn't rest yet; if there had been one gaggle of goons after him, there might be another, and they knew where he lived.

Lori was inside the holo-console, swinging her tennis racquet in perfect synchronization with a hologram of a female tennis player. The hologram glowed bright red to signal that she'd gotten it right. She smiled as Quaid entered, satisfied with her practice session.

'Hi, baby!' she said.

Quaid darted around the conapt, keeping his head below the window level. He switched off every light in the place, then pulled Lori from the console, and switched that off, too. She looked at him in alarm.

'Some men just tried to kill me!' he exclaimed.

She froze. 'Muggers?'

'No! Spies or something. And Harry from work.' Lori stepped back from him, passing in front of a window. She opened her mouth –

'Get down!' he cried, grabbing her and pulling her to the floor. He covered her with his body so that any bullet would reach him first. 'Harry was the boss,' he explained.

Flabbergasted, Lori drew herself out from under, brushing ineffectively at her crumpled outfit. She seemed to be trying to make sense of it all. 'What happened? Why would spies want to kill you?'

Excellent question! He peeked out the corner of a

window. 'I don't know,' he whispered. 'It has something to do with Mars.'

The magic word! Lori frowned. She was starting to question Quaid's sanity. At this stage, he could hardly blame her. 'Mars? You've never even been to Mars!'

'I know. It's crazy. I went to this Rekall place after work, and on the way home –'

She was incredulous. 'You went to those brain butchers?'

'Let me finish!' But considering what had happened, he couldn't deny that some sort of butchery had occurred. Before Rekall, his life had been normal, even dull, except for that dream of Mars. After Rekall, his life had been confused and just about over. Yet how could even the most realistic implanted memory account for Harry and the goons?

'What did you have them do?' she demanded, worried. 'Tell me!'

'I got a trip to Mars.' That memory had settled into place somewhere during the drive home: not the Mars-memory itself, which seemed to be absent, but his agreement to have them implant it. Something must have gone wrong – but would that have been his death warrant?

'Oh, God, Doug!' She must have thought she had gotten him off the Mars kick; she seemed appalled.

'That's not important. These men were about to shoot me . . .' He trailed off, realizing more clearly what had happened. 'But *I* killed *them*!' It seemed impossible, yet he was sure that *that* memory was real. For one thing, there was the blood on his hands – and now smeared on Lori's tennis outfit too.

But Lori was beyond caring about that, at this stage. She forced herself to be calm. 'Doug, listen to me. Nobody tried to kill you. You're hallucinating.'

'This is real, goddammit!' he exploded. He dashed to another window and looked out.

Lori came after him and grabbed his shoulders. 'Stop running around and listen to me!'

Quaid kept still, glaring at her.

'Those butchers at Rekall have fucked up your mind,'

she told him earnestly. 'And you're having paranoid delusions.'

He held up his bloodstained hands. 'You call this a paranoid delusion?'

She was stunned, evidently uncertain whether to be afraid *for* him – or afraid *of* him.

It was pointless to try to argue with her. He was hardly that certain of the situation himself! He ran into the bathroom, ducking out of the line of sight of the windows. Their conapt was high up, but a good sniper could handle the range, especially if he fired from another building at this level.

Lori waited until the bathroom door was closed and then walked quickly to the videophone. 'Doug,' she shouted over her shoulder. 'I'm calling a doctor!'

His voice came back, muffled. 'Don't! Don't call anybody.'

A faint smile touched Lori's lips as a man's face appeared on the screen. 'Richter,' she breathed. There was something predatory, something hard and cruel in the man's face, but it softened as he heard her whisper his name. 'Hello,' he said. She blew a silent kiss to him.

In the bathroom, Quaid washed the blood from his hands. It had probably come from the goon whose nose he had smashed in – though how he had done a thing like that he still wasn't certain. He knew how to fight, sure: stand up with two fists weaving before the face, and try to get past the other worker's guard to tag him on the shoulder or head. But he had done this with his *knee*. And the others – he had twisted one head just about off, and smashed a larynx. There was no place in clean fighting for that sort of thing. Even if there was – where had he learned it? The sheer speed with which he had acted – instead of a clumsy shoving, he had struck four times, each strike so brutally efficient it appalled him in retrospect. He had been scared, sure, but this had been more like a killing machine.

While he pondered, he finished washing the blood off his hands. He splashed cold water on his face, then glanced at himself in the mirror. He wasn't even scratched! Now it *was* beginning to seem like a fantasy!

But he knew it wasn't. He dried off his face and hands, switched off the light, and opened the bathroom door. For some reason he didn't quite fathom, he stood at the side of the door instead of standing squarely before it, as if to let someone else pass through first.

Tracer bullets ripped into the dark bathroom, smashing the mirror, walls, and fixtures. Glass showered out around him. Quaid dived forward and scrambled into the living area.

The goons were back, another squad! Somehow he had suspected, and his caution had saved his life. They were no longer pussyfooting by shoving him unhurt into a vehicle; they had gotten smart, and were blasting him on sight.

'Lori!' he cried from the floor as he rolled behind the sofa. 'Run!'

The living room was in total darkness, except for the pale rectangles of the windows, beyond which the lights of the city flickered. Quaid moved, his knees making a sound as they scraped on the floor – and bullets tore into the upholstery, inches from his head.

He lurched up and across and dived under the coffee table, rolling silently in a fashion he hadn't known he could do. He froze in place, listening. He heard his assailant moving around, across the room. The gunner was right here, using the darkness for cover!

There had been no answer from Lori. She must have been taken out silently while Quaid was in the bathroom. There would be a separate score to settle for that, if she had been harmed! But first he had to save his own life.

In the darkness he felt his features hardening into a familiar expression. His memory might be blank, but he realized that this was not the first time he had been under fire. He knew how to handle it.

He fetched a pillow from the couch, noiselessly. Then he tossed it across the room.

Tracer fire blasted the pillow.

Quaid launched himself. He leaped over a chair at the source of the tracers, again moving with a speed and surety that amazed him.

He made contact. Bullets were fired wildly, scoring on the wall and ceiling. Then he got the gun away and it skittered across the floor.

Already he was working on the assailant. He pounded a shoulder, a leg, trying to get the range on the struggling figure in the darkness. Then he scored on the torso and heard the pained grunt as the other person's breath whooshed out. The gunner was small, depending on speed rather than strength. He applied a quick chokehold with one arm, just tight enough to keep the other subdued, and reached for the light switch on the wall.

The light came on. Quaid blinked, his eyes adjusting. He looked at the person he held.

It was a woman, her fair tresses in disarray. In fact, it was Lori.

He was astonished – and devastated. His *wife* had been gunning for him? How could this be?

'Lori . . .' he began.

She stomped on his foot. Even through the shoe, it was effective; pain flared. For a moment his grip on her relaxed.

She spun a sharp elbow into his face, forcing him to pull back, but not to release her entirely. She turned, bracing against his arm, and pummeled him with a rapid barrage of chops and punches to chest, neck, and face. She knew what she was doing; there were no dainty slaps, but well-aimed and surprisingly strong blows that were doing damage. In fact, they could have knocked out a lesser man. Only his greater mass and conditioning protected him; he automatically tensed his muscles and turned his head, resisting the strikes and causing them to slide off without full effect.

Dazed more by the identity of his attacker than by the blows themselves, Quaid did not retaliate. How could his lovely, loving wife be doing this? Just this morning, she had been so soft and sexy, her hands so gentle and evocative! Had it been a strange man, he would have countered almost before the first blow landed. But against Lori –

But she had only been warming up. Now she had proper working room. She wound up for the coup de grace. This one would not be avoided or resisted.

He punched her in the stomach. The blow was powerful rather than fast, and she was light. He had pulled his punch somewhat, still loath to really hurt her. Also, he had been shaken by her violent attack on him, and for the moment weakened. The effect of the drug had not yet worn off entirely, which made it worse. Even so, the punch launched her all the way to the kitchen.

She kept her feet, by no means downed. She was in better condition as a combatant than he had ever suspected. In fact, it seemed that there was a whole lot about her that he hadn't known. But how could *she* be in on this conspiracy to kill him? She wasn't even interested in Mars!

He staggered toward her, knowing that he had to put her down and question her. It had never occurred to him that she would know anything about this astonishing situation, but now that he knew she did, he had to learn whatever she knew.

Lori grabbed a carving knife from the holder on the wall. Now she stalked him, moving with more confidence than he did. He retreated, realizing that he was up against no amateur.

He looked around for her gun and spied it on the floor across the room. He started toward it, but she intercepted him, deftly slicing his reaching arm. He tried to dodge aside and make for the gun again, but she whipped the knife across his chest, opening a thin gash. She kept him at bay, tagging him whenever he focused on the gun instead of on her, but wasn't able to make a lethal score on him. He was becoming a mass of shallow wounds and dripping blood.

He feinted toward the gun once more, with his left hand. She stabbed at the arm, inflicting another injury – but was caught by his right fist. It was a solid blow to her jaw.

Lori fell back, stunned. Quaid quickly picked up the gun and aimed it at her. '*Talk!*'

She remained stubbornly silent. He shoved the gun barrel in her ear. He meant business, and it showed. The hard alternate personality had taken over again. 'Why is my own wife trying to kill me?'

'I'm not your wife,' she said.

He cocked the pistol. Lori panicked.

'I swear to God! I never saw you before six weeks ago! Our marriage is just a memory implant – *aggghh!*' Quaid grabbed a handful of hair and yanked her head back. How could she claim that eight years of marriage hadn't existed? He *remembered!*

He remembered the way she had sauntered across the street that first day. He remembered their wedding, the startling contrast between his father's humble finery and her father's stylish Martian frog pelt-tux. He remembered their wedding trip as vividly as though it had happened yesterday; the ride on the transcon zaptrain, the suite in the expensive hotel where they had been catered to by a veritable fleet of service droids. It had been the first time he'd slept on a gelbed, the first time he'd tasted Venusian champagne. They'd sipped it from crystal flutes grown in zero-g on one of the space stations. He could still see the strange shape of the crystal, feel it in his hand, taste the sparkling blue wine.

He thought back to the first few years they had spent together in his old neighborhood. Lori had looked as out of place as a lunar diamond in a trash recycler, and he recalled how happy she had been when he finally agreed to move to the new conapt. He could never forget that night of celebration . . . How could Lori say that none of that had happened? He *remembered*.

Yet she had tried to kill him, and it had been no accident of misidentification. She knew who he was and wanted him dead. That suggested there was something in what she said.

'You think I'm an idiot?' Quaid said bitterly.

Lori's gaze and posture indicated that she thought exactly that. She seemed to have become a cold bitch, as different from the loving woman as Quaid was from the killing machine that seemed to be taking over his body. Her tennis outfit was in ruins and there would be a bruise on her face, yet she seemed haughty rather than humiliated.

'I remember our wedding!' he said.

'It was implanted by the Agency,' she said flatly.

'And falling in love?' Though now he realized that he did

not truly love her. He *remembered* loving her, but somehow he had a truer feeling for the woman of Mars. Oh, Lori was a lot of fun in bed, but that wasn't the same. This preposterous notion was beginning to make sense!

'Implanted.'

'Our friends, my job, eight years together. I suppose the Agency implanted that too?

'The job's real,' she said evenly. 'But the Agency set it up.'

'Bullshit.' Quaid pushed Lori away, but kept the gun trained on her. He tried to remain skeptical, but his certainty was beginning to erode. This explanation resolved too many little – and big – mysteries. Her disparagement of his dream of Mars – because he was supposed to be kept away from Mars? Harry's effort to steer him clear of Rekall – because he wasn't even supposed to remember Mars? There was a whole lot here that he still didn't understand, but at least this gave him some ideas to work with. He had been distracted by the life he thought he had – a wife like Lori, a friend like Harry – so that he wouldn't recall the life he might really have. It was as if the old structures had to be torn down before new and more solid ones could be built. Lori spoke, confirming some of his suspicions.

'They erased your identity and implanted a new one. I was written in as your wife so I could watch you, make sure the erasure took. Sorry, Quaid,' she said, her tone belying any regret. 'Your whole life is just a dream.'

He slumped against the wall. The fact that it was starting to make sense didn't make it any easier to take. Before it had been only a dream that bothered him; now his whole life had become a dream. 'If I'm not Doug Quaid, who am I?'

She shrugged. 'Beats me. I just work here.'

How callous could she be? Yet her attitude supported her statement. Her love for him had been the pretense: this was the reality.

Quaid pulled himself up from the floor to sit in a chair. He rubbed his forehead, trying to decide how to react. The realization that his memory-life was only a pretense did not restore his real life; that remained blank. He had no idea where to go or what to do. His foundations had been knocked out from under, and he was still falling. What kind of a landing would it be?

Lori suddenly became much friendlier. Her face softened, and her figure lost its indifference. She became more like the woman he had known.

'I'm gonna miss you, Quaid,' she said. 'You were the best assignment I ever had. Really.'

'I'm honored,' he said, distrusting this. She had shown him convincingly enough how little she truly cared for him; what was she up to now?

He took her by the elbow and pulled her with him, the gun still at her head, as he looked out the window. He was alert for any false move on her part; she would not knock aside the gun the way he had knocked Harry's gun. He didn't even need to watch her directly; he could sense her motion. Where were the others? He was sure they were out there, somewhere. Though he could not remember any details, he knew the nature of these things: operatives did not work alone. They always had interlocking networks, the one covering the back of the other. He might have set them back momentarily by killing four, and by nullifying Lori, but that was no victory, only a foiling of two of their ploys.

'You sure you don't wanna . . . ?' she asked. 'For old times', sake?' She reached out to him affectionately.

His gut twisted with the irony of her words. If what Lori was telling him was true – and he was beginning to believe it was – then he and his whole world were strangers. If he had no past, how could he have a present? Quaid wasn't a man given to deep reflection; he was a man of action. When the Mars dream had surfaced, he'd gone to Rekall to do something about it, or tried to, at least. But what could he do about this? What action could he take to regain the life he had lost?

For now, at least, it was a moot point. He had to figure out a way to survive the goons before he could begin to search for the missing pieces of his identity. He looked out a second window, more to focus his mind than his eyes. He knew the goons would not be visible out there. In fact, if they were there, they'd soon take him out with a snipe-scope. He had to act swiftly. But how?

59

Lori withdrew her hand. 'It's not like we're strangers, you know. If you don't trust me, you can tie me up,' Lori said, tugging at her décolletage to show more breast.

'I didn't know you were so kinky.'

'It's time you found out.'

What was she up to? He knew she wasn't interested in sex with him. He turned back to her – and caught her looking at the video screen.

Uh-oh.

One square of the screen was a security monitor showing the lobby of the apartment building. Four agents were entering an elevator. The evident boss was enormous, solid, and looked vicious, like an attack dog trained by repeated beatings.

Quaid glared at Lori and pressed the gun to her head. 'Clever girl,' he said through his teeth.

'You wouldn't shoot me, Doug, would you?' she asked, maintaining her friendly and somewhat helpless pose. 'Not after all we've been through.'

He hated to admit it, but she was moving him. He didn't want to hurt her, though she had certainly tried to kill him. 'You're right, Lori. Some of it was fun.'

She smiled. 'Yes, it was, Doug. If you want, we can –' He was not that much of a fool. He knew he had scant time. 'Who are they?'

'Who?'

'Don't make me do something I don't want to do.'

She dropped the pretense. 'The big one's Richter. He's as mean as they come. His partner is Helm, not much better. Look, Doug, I confess I tried to distract you. It's my job. But I can help you avoid them, if –'

He lowered the gun and touched her breast. She smiled encouragingly, inhaling. Suddenly he raised the gun and clubbed her on the head, knocking her out.

'It's been nice "knowing" you,' he said, surprised by his own action. His other self had taken over again, doing what was required. Well, he hoped it knew what it was doing, because he certainly didn't!

10

Subway

Quaid raced down the corridor, past the other conapt doors, avoiding the elevator. He heard it rising, slowing; that was the goon-squad, for sure! If they saw him, he was dead. He had the gun, but they would have ten times his firepower. He ducked through an EXIT door barely before the elevator door opened.

He held his breath and flattened himself against the wall, listening. He heard them boil out and charge to his conapt: one, two, three, four. How he could count them with such certainty by the thudding of their feet he didn't know; he must have had very special training, somewhere, sometime, back in the erased portion of his memory. Maybe it was like the man who tallied a herd of cows accurately at a single glance; he counted the legs and divided by four. No joke, in this case; he could hear only the footsteps, which out-numbered the men walking them.

Four – the same number he had seen on the monitor. That meant they had left no man below to intercept him. That was another tactical error on their part. But what could you expect of goons? They weren't true professionals, just hirelings whose brains were dispensable.

Good enough. He got moving again, having paused only a few seconds, and resumed breathing. He bounded down the stairs, taking several at a time, down around the endlessly twisting squared-off spiral that went to the street level. It was easier to climb a stair two or three steps at a time than it was to descend it the same way, but he evidently had training for this too. He virtually sailed down, four, five, six at a time, bounding like a ballet dancer, touching the rail for guidance. He did have the technique for it, and this was good, because he had a long way to go.

One reason he had taken time to question Lori when he knew the goons were on the way up was that he knew how long it would take them to arrive. Even the fastest elevator could not cover two hundred storeys in an instant. The elevator *was* fast, a virtual rocket, but limited by the acceleration normal residents could handle, even when set on 'Priority'. So there had been time.

But now he had to cover those two hundred levels himself, fast. Thanks to his technique, he was traveling at top running speed. Straight down, it would have been a two-thousand-foot fall; as it was, it was just about a mile of stairs. Could he cover a mile in five minutes? He'd better, because it would take the goons maybe one minute to ascertain that he had fled, maybe two more to catch a swift DOWN elevator, and three more to make it to the ground floor. Six minutes max – less if they got a break on the elevator schedule. He would have no more than a minute's head start on them, with luck, and maybe none with no luck. So he bounded down at a seemingly suicidal rate. It would be suicidal *not* to!

Once he got to the first level, he knew he could cut though the building and scramble down the slanted roof that sheltered the sunken delivery port. That would shave more time off his route to the subway. So this was it for him: his escape not from fire or some other routine emergency, but from assassination. Five floors, ten, fifteen – he lost count, and it didn't matter, because all that counted was the first.

One minute! he thought. *Give me one minute's head start, and they'll never find me!* which meant six minutes for them. Would they be stupid enough to dawdle longer at the conapt? Pray that they were!

Richter led the way into the conapt. His face contorted with rage when he saw Lori lying unconscious on the floor. He hadn't wanted her to take this assignment, important as it was for her – their – advancement in the Agency. He had warned Lori that the man called Quaid was dangerous, but she had simply teased him for being overprotective. Well, she wasn't teasing now. He knelt beside her, gently trying to bring her around.

'Lori,' he called softly. 'Lori!' Her eyes fluttered open and she groaned as she touched the bruise at her temple. 'You all right?'

She nodded gingerly. 'Sorry,' she said weakly. 'I guess I blew it.'

'What's he remember?'

'Nothing, so far.'

Helm had produced a small tracking device and touched a button, activating it. He held it up and turned around in a searching pattern. Suddenly a red dot started to blink as it swept past the window. He kept it pointing in that direction and pushed another button.

Now the tracker's little screen came to life, displaying a three-dimensional plan of the building from the point of view of this spot. It was as if it were a model made of transparent glass. Down near the bottom, the blinking red dot was moving in a crazy spiral, like a poisoned fly. He was going down the stairwell, and making damn good time.

Suddenly, the dot left the building altogether. Richter crossed to the window, with Helm close behind. They spotted Quaid running down an inclined rooftop toward the Commons. 'Shit!' Richter exclaimed. 'The subway! Go! Go!'

Helm and the other two agents bolted for the door, but Richter remained behind. Silently, he pulled Lori to her feet and into his arms. It had been too long since he'd held her and only God knew when they'd get the next opportunity.

'Pack your stuff and get out,' he said, pulling away from the embrace.

'What if they bring him back?' Lori asked as he headed for the door.

Richter paused in the doorway. He turned, and Lori was frightened by the look in his eyes. 'They won't,' he said. He turned abruptly and was gone.

Quaid breathed a silent sigh of relief as he made it safely to the subway station. He had had his one-minute start, maybe more. What had the fools been doing up there, making time with Lori? If so, he owed her a vote of thanks, ironically, though he was sure it wouldn't have been voluntary on her part. He was sorry he had had to knock her out, but it had been the only way to keep her from sounding the alarm before the goons even got there. He hadn't loved her, though he had liked her, and wouldn't have hurt her for the world – before this business broke. She had seemed too good to be true, and now he knew that she *was* too good to be true. She was just on an assignment. Six weeks – no wonder his eight-year memory of her hadn't changed! It was actually a six-week experience.

He had thought his life dull. It sure wasn't dull now! But at the moment he would gladly have traded to have it back. At least he would be safe, instead of fleeing for his life, with no notion where he was going or who he was. If he had it to do over, he'd stay the hell away from Rekall, keeping his eyes and ears open and quietly investigating his situation, until he knew enough to act without bringing the goons down on his head.

People were staring at him. Quaid slowed down, glancing occasionally over his shoulder. It was better to be lost in the crowd, if the goons weren't right on his tail. How close were they? He had hoped for a minute's start and gotten it, but he knew they wouldn't just let him go. He had to catch a train to nowhere and lose them completely.

Naturally the minutes passed before the train came. He waited beyond the security area, not wanting to commit himself before he had to. Three, four minutes – how long could this hold? He was a sitting duck here! He had gotten a break by escaping the building, but the luck was turning the other way now.

Then he heard the train. He was going to make it! He headed for the entry passage.

He realized that he'd better get rid of the gun; it could be traced, and might have a marker in it they could orient on. Certainly it couldn't pass through the security area, so he couldn't get on a train with it.

He glanced back one more time – and saw Richter and

company run into the station. Damn! Another thirty seconds and he'd have been clear!

His plan changed instantly. He stayed in line, but kept the gun. What did an alarm matter when the killers had spotted him? He stepped past the panels.

He glanced at the little monitor screen facing the customers in line. He was a walking skeleton, and the gun in his bony hand was glowing bright red! The alarms wailed and red lights flashed. Guards sprang forward to intercept him. There was nothing careless about this security section!

He couldn't run yet, because of the people ahead of him in the narrow channel. He had thought they would clear out when the alarm went off, but they were confused and standing still. Meanwhile the guards were rounding the screen, their own guns glowing red.

Could he go the other way? On the monitor his skeleton stopped and turned, echoing his indecision. He saw Richter and Helm coming. That was worse!

There was no way out, forward or backward. He turned to the side, jumped the guide rail, and charged the X-ray panel itself. On the monitor his skeleton loomed suddenly larger; then he crashed through his own skeletal image, shattering the screen. There was screaming from the ladies in the station.

That got him out – but not to the train. He had not escaped the goons. Where next?

His hidden other self took over. He sprinted forward, dodged around a crowd of gaping commuters, and vaulted down a staircase. It would take him to the trains traveling at right angles to the ones here, on the next level down. But he still didn't know where he was going. He could catch a train, sure – but to where?

Richter and his goons arrived at the head of the staircase. He consulted the tracking device. The flashing red dot that was the quarry appeared on the screen, moving steadily downward. Richter panned the device, checking the surroundings. Near the bottom of the staircase were several UP escalators.

The quarry would take one of those, trying to sneak back to the street level and lose himself. He wouldn't want to take a train, because he had nowhere to go. So instead of chasing after him and being just too late, they could surround him. Then he'd really have nowhere to go. It was a messy job; it was awkward as hell trying to take a man out in a public place. But soon it would be done and they would disappear.

He signaled for everyone but Helm to continue on the samel level. 'Go, go, go,' he bellowed, and to Helm: 'You, come with me.' They dashed down the stairs after Quaid.

Quaid reached the bottom of the stairs and looked warily around. No goons. He ran forward, saw an escalator flowing up, and headed for it. Still no goons. But he didn't trust this. At any moment they would come charging around a corner, guns blazing. Determined to take him out – because he dreamed of Mars? No, because he wasn't who he thought he was.

None of this seemed to make much sense. He needed time to work it out, to explore every last corner of his fragmented memory and pull out anything that was there. Maybe he'd discover he was a criminal who – but no, they wouldn't have given a criminal a nice conapt, a decent job, and a woman like Lori. Unless they were keeping him on ice until the time came to testify at a big trial. Yes, that just might make sense. They didn't want him remembering prematurely because he might go back to his pals instead of testifying against them. That would explain why Lori, who as it turned out hadn't cared for him at all, had been so actively friendly. It had been her job to keep his mind occupied. Or his pecker. Same thing, they had figured. They might have been right, but for his Mars dream-girl.

He was on the escalator now, riding the stairs up. He glanced behind, seeing nothing but routine citizens. Where were the goons? They should be here by now!

He glanced forward – and there they were! Four agents arriving at the top landing, looking below. He tried to shrink down, hiding amidst the commuters, but he was too big to manage it. His only hope was that they wouldn't see him before he got close enough to –

They were peering down, checking the whole region. THEY SAW HIM!

There was no pause, no call for surrender. They simply started shooting.

Quaid feinted to the side. An unlucky commuter caught a door-piercing bullet in the head. He fell backward into Quaid. His face was gone.

There was screaming as the others realized what was happening. All the commuters crouched on the stairs, trying to get out of the line of fire. That left Quaid exposed, the only one standing.

He couldn't duck down like the rest; they'd riddle him in seconds, now that they had him spotted. Indeed, his other self had no intention of allowing it. He was already in motion, mounting the escalator, using the faceless body as a shield. His gun was in his hands, firing up at his enemies. One, two, three, four – and the four goons went down in order, each holed by a single bullet.

Quaid didn't know who his other self was, but he was beginning to like him. That man was a survivor!

He was safe now, for the moment. He could get out of the subway station and –

A bullet zinged by his ear. From behind! He twisted to look back. There were Richter and Helm running up to the escalator, firing as they went. Now they were on it, climbing over the prostrate commuters, still firing. If they had paused to take proper aim, Quaid would have been dead before he knew they were there.

Quaid heaved up the corpse he had been using as a shield, turned, and hurled it down at the two agents, bowling them over. Then he charged the rest of the way up the stairs. He reached the landing and ran down the hall.

He had maybe a ten-second lead if those were the only ones on his tail. Where could he go? On up and out to the street? There might be more goons posted at the exit. If he made it, he'd still be right in the area; they'd be casting around for him in cars and maybe aircraft. He couldn't go back to his conapt; Lori would report him immediately, if she didn't shoot him first.

That left the subway trains. They went all over the city and to outlying points, making connections everywhere. The agents couldn't cover every exit in the entire subway system! So if he could make it onto a train without them following, his ten-second lead should become a ten-minute lead, and he could be out of the city before they had much notion where he was.

His body already knew this. It was pounding down the passage, heading for another train. He tucked his gun into his pants; he was now inside the security area, so it wasn't setting off any more alarms.

He came to the landing where there was a train. The last commuters were just squeezing on. He sprinted along the platform, which was mercifully clear at the moment, and for the train.

The last commuter boarded. The departure signal sounded. The door closed.

Quaid made a flying leap and squeezed onto a car at the last second, beating the closing doors by a hair. He had made it! He stumbled, trying to avoid bumping into the other passengers. He was doubled over, but managed to keep his feet.

Bullets shattered the glass of the door just above him and plowed the far side. Richter and Helm had arrived! Had he been standing upright –

'Get down!' he shouted at the other passengers, knowing what was coming.

The train started moving. A series of windows shattered. The passengers decided to take his advice. They ducked down as well as they were able.

The train picked up speed. Quaid peered out a window-hole. He saw Richter and Helm watching, disgusted, as the train left the station. He had beaten them – for now.

He turned to find the other passengers staring at him. He realized that he was covered with blood from the corpse he had used as a shield. Well, he was not about to offer them any explanation. The less they knew about him, the better for him – and them. Richter seemed to have no compunctions about his methods; if he thought any other person knew where Quaid was, he would force that person to talk at gunpoint – and then maybe shoot him anyway.

He avoided their glances and oriented instead on the commercial on the nearest screen. It was a huckster, standing in front of a spaceship. 'Don't settle for pale memories! Don't settle for fake implants! Experience space travel the old-fashioned way on a real-life holiday you can afford.'

The travel agency's answer to Rekall! Quaid shook his head and sighed. He wished he could take them up on it. Because one thing that hadn't changed, in this almost-complete demolition of his life-style, was his fascination with Mars. He still wanted to go there, one way or another, and to find that brunette, if she existed.

Did she exist? All he could do was hope that she did. His tangible life with Lori had become illusion; maybe his dream of the other woman could become real.

11

Help

Richter and Helm strode angrily out of the station and stepped through the rain to their car. Richter was fuming. They had lost the quarry after all, and then gotten nabbed by the subway security men because their guns had set off the alarms again. They had had to show their IDs to get out of it. That would look bad on the records. Not to mention the four additional lower-echelon agents lost. That made eight total, plus a civilian or two. What a smell that would make for all concerned! The first takeout had been bungled by Harry, obviously a duffer who shouldn't have been assigned in the first place. But this time it was Richter himself, and he would get no credit for just about succeeding. 'Just about' was just about good enough for a demotion!

He hated the man who thought he was Douglas Quaid. He had never liked him. There was something about him he didn't trust, but Cohaagen just couldn't see it. He'd promoted the sonovabitch, for Christ's sake! Richter snorted with disgust.

But he hadn't started hating the bastard until Lori had been assigned to play the role of his 'wife'. After all his Beauty and the Beast jokes, that had been almost too much to bear. And now that the man had eluded and humiliated him, that hate had festered into something white hot and barely controllable. He would see the man's brains splattered across the landscape before he was done, and it still wouldn't be enough. If he was lucky, maybe he'd get the chance to see the man sweat before he died.

They climbed into the car. Helm took the driver's seat, Richter the passenger seat, where the equipment was. The rain on their clothing quickly steeped the interior with its pollution, contributing to his foul mood.

The dashboard was filled with elaborate tracking devices, electronic maps, and communications equipment. Richter furiously turned knobs and punched buttons, trying to get a reading on the quarry. Damn it, the tracking was supposed to be continuous; what was fuzzing it? Was the equipment glitching? Guess who'd get the blame if a bad tracker let him down! He knew Cohaagen didn't see eye-to-eye with him on this procedure, and if the man got a pretext to take him off the case –

The radio came to life. 'Six beta nine, we have a transmission from Mr Cohaagen.'

Richter looked at Helm and groaned. Think of the devil!

But he couldn't avoid it. 'This is Richter. Patch it through.' He wiped the rain from his face and smoothed his hair, though it didn't do much good. Modern science was wonderful, but at the moment he wished they hadn't invented a way to set aside the limitation of lightspeed, making virtually instant communication between planets possible. Then Cohaagen would not be able to second-guess him on this mission, while a chase was in progress.

The video monitor lighted, flickering, then showing a grainy image of Cohaagen's face. The man was neither as handsome nor as well spoken as he was on broadcast interviews, no surprise. He fixed on Richter, scowling. 'What the fuck are you doing, Richter?'

Richter put on an ingratiating smile he knew fooled no one; it wasn't meant to. 'Trying to neutralize a traitor, sir.' *And that's the correct term! Chew on that, sir!*

Cohaagen's scowl expanded into open anger. 'If I wanted him dead, I wouldn't have dumped him on Earth!'

Richter smoothed out his own features, playing the obsequious underling, again without any concern for belief. 'We can't let him run around, Mr Cohaagen. He knows too much.'

'Lori says he can't remember jack shit.'

'That's now,' said Richter. 'In an hour, he could have total recall.'

'Listen to me, Richter.' There was static on the line, but not enough to blot out Cohaagen's words. 'I want Quaid

71

delivered *alive* for re-implantation. Have you got that? I want him back in place with Lori.'

Over my dead body, Richter thought. It was all he could do to keep himself from tearing the video monitor out of the dashboard and hurling it from the car.

'Did you hear me?' Cohaagen demanded. Richter reached over and twisted a dial, causing the reception to break up. It would be impossible to tell from the other end what had caused the disruption.

'What was that, sir? I couldn't hear you.'

Cohaagen glared. 'I said xtr+b . . . lsw . . . rojwf . . .'

Richter intensified the interference, deliberately preventing himself from hearing Cohaagen's orders. Helm gazed impassively out the windshield into the rain, affecting not to be aware of anything. He didn't like having the quarry slip the noose any better than Richter did.

'Hello?' Richter said. 'We've got sunspots. I'm switching to a different frequency.' How glad he was that such transmissions were unreliable when anything happened on the solar scale!

A blinking red dot appeared on the console tracking device. Helm nudged Richter, and Richter nodded. They had locked in on their man.

'Mr Cohaagen, are you there?' Richter continued. 'Hello? Hello?' So polite, with a touch of perplexity: the recording would show that he had no idea that his orders had changed.

With a contemptuous twist of the dial, Richter ended the transmission. Cohaagen wouldn't be able to prove anything; interplanetary signals were notorious for interference. A price was paid for violating light-speed. There had been just enough genuine interference to cover his tracks.

Richter allowed himself a small, grim smile. He turned to Helm. 'Fuckin' asshole. He shoulda killed Quaid when he had the chance,' he said. Now he, Richter, would do it instead, with pleasure. They had locked on to the quarry, and no sunspots, real or fake, would interfere.

Helm gunned the car into traffic, splashing water on

commuters walking out of the subway station. Their protests carried faintly, music to Richter's ears. He put a hand up over his shoulder and hoisted one finger, signaling them, though he knew they couldn't see inside the car. The gesture gave him satisfaction anyway. Too bad he couldn't show the same signal of respect to Cohaagen.

Quaid had decided not to go too far. They would be expecting him to flee the city, so would be racing to cut off the exit points. Therefore he remained close – but not too close. His alternate self had deserted him; it manifested only when immediate, effective action was required, such as killing several men in several seconds. He was on his own, and that satisfied him for now.

He got off the train a few stops down and went into a lavatory. He looked a mess, all right! He slopped water across his face and hands and dabbed at the worst of the stains on his shirt, though not much could be done about that. He had a bright idea, squatted, scraped his fingers along the floor near the wall, and got a good load of dirt on them. He rubbed this into the shirt, covering the remaining bloodstains. Now he looked mostly filthy, like a tramp, not like a refugee from a slaughterhouse. It would have to do. He combed his hair back and assumed an expression of dullness, as if he were just a tired laborer returning from a hard day in the sewer.

He boarded another train, trying to make it difficult for the goons to trace his route. But he couldn't do this forever; he needed to get into some other region. For that he needed money.

He paused at a money vendor near the end of the subway line and got as much cash as he dared: enough to pay for a plane to another continent. The transaction would be traced, and in minutes the goons would be on his tail again; that was why they hadn't cut off his ID card already. But though he lacked the deadly expertise of his hidden self, he did have some native cunning. Instead of going to the airport, he caught the next train back toward the center of town, and rode almost to where he had started. That should catch them by surprise. He hoped. They might figure that he wasn't counting on the ID tracer, and was innocently going his way, and wouldn't do anything unpredictable. He hoped again.

He got off and took an escalator up. He emerged from an archway marked SUBWAY onto the ground floor of an ancient 1980s shopping mall which had degenerated into a barrio street scene, complete with bars, flophouses, pool halls, pawnshops, and massage parlors. The mall was crowded with kids on skateboards and bikes, and there were even bums sleeping in doorways. It was like stepping into the past, and he almost felt nostalgia. Life must have been simpler before the planets were colonized!

This was the ideal place to hide. He spied a fleabag hotel across the mall. Cash would be accepted there without question, and he wouldn't have to show his ID. He'd be able to rest, and wash out his shirt, or maybe pick up other clothing at a secondhand outlet. He was catching on to survival as an anonymous fugitive.

The coast was clear, as it were. He resumed progress and entered the hotel.

Helm drove the car rapidly through the rainy streets.

'Hey, man,' he said. 'I bet you're glad Lori's off *that* case.' Richter's jaw tensed, but he kept his eyes on the tracing device.

'It's just a job,' he said shortly.

'Well, I sure wouldn't want Quaid porking *my* girl.'

Richter snarled. His hand shot out and he grabbed Helm's ear, twisting it painfully. The car swerved. 'You're saying she *liked* it? Is *that* what you're trying to say?'

Helm struggled to control the car and to avoid having his ear ripped from his head. 'No, no, of course not!' he said through gritted teeth. 'I'm sure she hated every minute!'

Richter gave Helm's ear another cruel twist and then released it. Flushed, he turned his attention back to the tracking device, which zoomed to a more detailed map section. 'Circle twenty-eight. Top level,' he said without expression. And then he smiled. The old Galleria . . . Of course. Quaid thought he could hide by dodging back into the slum.

'Know something?' he asked Helm. 'I think he hasn't caught on that he's bugged.' But he was, all right. Indeed, it had been that bug that first alerted them to Quaid's visit to Rekall. The alarm had sounded when the man had gone off his normal route, and they had made a quick trip there to question the Rekall staff and dispatch them.

Helm skidded the car around a corner, keeping his eyes on the road and rubbing his ear.

Quaid went to his hotel room. It was about what he had expected, which wasn't much. It was separated from other chambers mainly by plasterboard. If he cared to listen, he could hear what was going on in nearby compartments: the clinking of glasses, a shrill argument, an all-night poker game, the thudding of heavy sex, and plenty of video noise. That made this the perfect place to hide in.

But he had no sooner closed the dirty curtains at the window than the phone rang. He didn't answer. But it bothered him: why should anyone be calling here? Was it for last night's tenant? In which case maybe he'd better answer it, and try to pretend to be that man, in that way concealing his own presence. Still –

On the fourth ring he stepped to the side of the screen so he couldn't be seen and hit the ANSWER button. He didn't speak. If they asked for a name, he'd use that name. He peered slantwise at the screen, staying clear of its pickup.

All it showed was a man's hand blocking the lens. Well, that was another way to do it!

'If you want to live, don't hang up,' a gruff male voice said.

This didn't sound like a wrong number! Quaid stood still, not hanging up, but also not speaking.

'They've got you bugged,' the caller said. 'And they'll be busting down the door in about three minutes unless you do exactly what I say.'

Quaid, staying clear of the pickup, searched his clothes for the bug. Like a damned fool, he had never thought of that!

'Don't bother looking. It's in your skull.'

Quaid looked around, spooked. 'Who are you?' His identity was obviously no secret from this caller.

'Never mind. Wet a towel and wrap it around your head. That'll muffle the signal. It's not a strong one.'

'How'd you find me?' He had to assume that this was a friend and not an enemy. Why should an enemy warn him?

'I'd advise you to hurry.'

Quaid saw the sink on the other side of the room. He walked in front of the videophone to get there. There seemed to be no point in hiding now.

'That'll buy you some time,' the caller continued approvingly. 'They won't be able to pinpoint you.'

Quaid felt like a fool, but he wetted a large towel and began to wrap it around his head. He managed to form a clumsy turban, though it dripped down the back of his neck.

Helm guided the car, homing in on the signal generated by Quaid's bug. The tracking device changed from a detailed map to a general map of the area. The blinking light grew dim.

Richter stared. 'Shit!'

'What is it?' Helm asked.

Richter fiddled with the tracking device and whacked it a few times. 'We lost him!' How the hell? Maybe he was taking a shower. Richter knew that water could mess up the signal. He clenched his fists in his lap. He wasn't a patient man by nature, but he could learn. Quaid couldn't stay in the shower all night, and when he came out . . .

Helm kept driving.

Quaid rewrapped the wet towel, making a better turban, but it still dripped down his neck.

'That's good enough,' the caller said. 'Now look out the window.'

Quaid went to the window and cautiously pulled aside the curtain. He peeked outside. This was no skyscraper; he was not far from the pavement.

'See the phone booth by the bar?' the caller inquired from behind him.

76

He looked across the limited landscape and located the bar, then the booth. A mustachioed soldier of fortune was looking right back at him, holding up a doctor's satchel.

'This is the bag you gave to me,' the soldier said.

'*I* gave to you?'

'I'm leaving it in the booth,' the soldier continued. 'Come get it and keep moving.'

Quaid saw the man begin to hang up. 'Wait!'

The soldier paused. It was evident that he wanted to keep moving, too. 'What?' he asked impatiently.

'Who are you?' He needed to know the name of this mysterious ally. Everyone he had trusted had turned against him. This man might be the only friend he had left. Quaid had to know who he was.

The soldier hesitated, then spoke abruptly. 'We were buddies in the Agency back on Mars. You asked me to find you if you disappeared. So here I am. Good-bye.'

'Wait!' Quaid said desperately. 'What was I doing on Mars?' But the phone had gone dead and the soldier had left the booth. Quaid pounded the window-sill in frustration as he watched the man walk quickly away. Yet what he had told Quaid was invaluable. If he had belonged to the Agency, and left it –

But he had no time for conjecture now. He dashed out of the hotel room, holding the wobbly turban on his head.

Richter and Helm circled the mall in the car. The rain continued unabated, stinking worse than ever. Richter banged the tracking device, but it didn't help. He's here, Richter thought. I can smell him. He whacked the device again. The interference continued.

Helm made no comment. He just kept driving.

Quaid ran out of the hotel. He looked for the soldier of fortune, but the man was gone. Damn it! Maybe the stranger had saved his life and maybe he hadn't. Could he trust him? Suppose he had been safe in the hotel room, and this had smoked him out to where the goons could gun him down? That didn't seem to make a lot of sense, but then very little of the past day did.

But he was forgetting the satchel. Maybe that would answer some of his questions. He started for the phone booth and was dismayed to find that an old lady had beaten him to it. She had the satchel in her hand.

'Excuse me, ma'am,' he said. 'That's mine.'

The old lady regarded him sourly. 'I don't see your name on it,' she snapped.

Quaid took hold of the satchel and pulled it gently. 'Someone left it for me.'

The little old lady refused to relinquish the bag. 'Let go!' she hollered.

Quaid pulled a bit harder. 'Please, ma'am. I need it.'

'Find your own bag!' she replied, clutching the satchel to her chest with all her strength. 'You should be ashamed of yourself, you big bully!' A few bystanders had gathered, to enjoy the free entertainment.

Quaid was at a loss. He didn't want to hurt the woman, but he needed that bag. He jerked it forcefully from her grip, nearly losing his turban in the process.

'Excuse me, ma'am,' he apologized. 'I'm sorry.' He turned on his heels and ran. The little old lady's voice echoed after him.

'Fuck you, asshole!'

From a doorway, the soldier of fortune watched. He held his breath during Quaid's awkward struggle with the elderly woman, and sighed with relief when Quaid gained the bag and ran off. They had been through a lot together, on Mars and Earth both, and the man who was now known as Quaid had saved his life more than once. In fact, it had been that man who had first brought him into the Agency. At the moment, the soldier wasn't sure whether that had been a blessing or a curse.

He thought of how the Agency had changed since he had been recruited. It had originally been formed to oversee the diverse intelligence-gathering groups of the Northern Bloc. Its mission was to keep the spooks in line and ensure that they did not become too powerful for the Northern Bloc government to handle.

Then Vilos Cohaagen had been appointed Head of the Agency. Under his leadership, the Agency had not only acted as watchdog on the other groups, but had gradually absorbed them. The cooperation it received from a wide variety of law enforcement bureaux was deceptive. They cooperated with the Agency because, to a greater extent than anyone imagined, they *were* the Agency. Cohaagen had the imagination to see what could be done with such a network and, more important, he had the political savvy to make it grow invisibly. No one questioned his actions because no one noticed them. By the time they realized what he'd done, it was too late.

Cohaagen had used the Agency to gather a vast amount of dirt on key people in government. His file on the Chairman was especially damaging. When the time was ripe, he had used the dirt to win his appointment as Mars Colony Administrator. Cohaagen knew that whoever controlled the Martian turbinium mines controlled the Northern Bloc, *all* of the Northern Bloc, not just a few powerful politicians. Without turbinium to fuel their weapons, the Northern Bloc would be forced to surrender.

The Chairman knew this too, but he also knew that Cohaagen would have to resign from the Agency in order to take up his post on Mars. The Chairman thought that by sending Cohaagen to Mars and naming a successor to head the Agency, he would regain control of it and neutralize Cohaagen.

The fool. The Agency's new leader had been Cohaagen's puppet. For all intents and purposes, it was still under Cohaagen's control. And now the turbinium mines were his, as well.

As long as he could hold them. The soldier of fortune smiled. Cohaagen might be an effective Agency Head, but he knew nothing about running a colony. He was so intent on political intrigue that he ignored the welfare of the people on Mars, especially those who worked in the mines. When they protested their deteriorating living conditions, he cracked down on them without mercy. But his terror-tactics were backfiring, creating the revolution that now threatened to halt turbinium production and undermine Cohaagen's quest for power.

The soldier of fortune shook his head. He was not a politician. He had no interest in matters of state. But, unlike many of the thugs who had recently been recruited, he did have a strong sense of personal honor. The things Cohaagen had ordered him to do to suppress the revolt on Mars were not honorable. He was a skilled professional, not a petty sadist. He wanted out of the Agency and he wanted out fast.

His duty to the man called Quaid done, he could continue to effect his carefully planned disappearance. He had made a promise and he had kept it, at great personal risk.

Now he could lose himself, his promise fulfilled. He sauntered casually into a side street, trying to act like an ordinary pedestrian, but he was nervous. He knew that the Agency was after his friend and would stop at nothing to nail him. He had helped a buddy, as he knew he must, but if the act were ever discovered, it would alert the Agency and put his own disappearance in jeopardy. That was why he had to conceal his identity; the less known about him, the better.

Cruising around the Galleria, Helm saw someone who looked familiar. He nudged Richter and pointed. Richter, too, recognized the man. His eyes condensed to points. What the hell was Stevens doing here? Hadn't he and the quarry been buddies back on Mars? Were they in on this little game together? Richter would soon find out.

Helm cut the car into a parking space. Swiftly and silently they got out, stalking the man.

Stevens left the inner circle of the mall, his eyes darting nervously into the dimness before him. He turned his head briefly to see if he was being followed – and walked straight into the arms of Richter and Helm. Helm grabbed him and smashed his head against a wall, then landed a few solid kicks to his ribs and kidneys. Stevens slumped on the sidewalk.

'What're you doing here, Stevens?' Richter asked. 'Visiting your old pal Quaid?'

'What are you talking about?' Though dazed, Stevens recognized Richter, the Agency enforcer, the kind of thug that gave the organization a bad name. Stevens leaned on one hand, propping himself up as best he could, but he knew that he was doomed.

'Do I have to explain?' Richter raised his foot and brought it down on Stevens' widespread hand. Stevens screamed as the bones in his fingers snapped. Helm shut his mouth with another well-aimed kick.

'Where is he?'

'Can't say,' Stevens mumbled through blood and broken teeth. 'Classified.' Evidently, the ploy with the towel had been successful, and they had lost the quarry. Let him stay lost. Stevens didn't intend to take his friend down with him.

Richter ground his heel into Stevens' hand. The pain jolted straight up his arm to his shoulder.

'You can tell us, Stevens,' Richter said soothingly. 'We're on the same team.' He bounced casually on Stevens' mangled hand.

'Okay, okay!' Stevens wheezed. 'Just call Cohaagen; get clearance.' Furious, Richter stomped on Stevens' shin, cracking it against the edge of the curb.

'Are we clear yet? Hunh?' he taunted.

Stevens rocked in agony. He knew he couldn't take much more. Suddenly he felt a faint flutter of hope. Helm's attention had been diverted by something; he elbowed Richter and pointed.

'There he is!' Richter peered into the distance and saw Quaid walking past a JohnnyCab stand on the far side of the mall. He had something white wrapped around his head and was carrying some sort of bag. Richter smiled malignantly. Yeah, Quaid was holding the bag, all right.

Gun in hand, Helm took off in pursuit, but Richter lingered, looking down at Stevens' crumpled form.

Bending slightly, he tapped Stevens on the shoulder. The man looked up, into the barrel of Richter's gun.

A shot sounded.

12

Johnny

Quaid had the satchel, but he still had nowhere to go. He walked down the street in the rain, no longer noticing it. He hoped the bag had what he needed, whatever that was. It seemed like a very slender thread on which to hang his life.

Suddenly, he heard a sound that had of late become all too familiar: someone had fired a gun. He supposed it wasn't *that* unusual in this neighborhood, but he'd been through too much already to take it for granted. Looking for the source of the sound, he saw two men racing toward him. They were too far away for him to see who they were, but he didn't wait for introductions. He turned and plunged into a waiting JohnnyCab, ducking down and trying to hide his head.

Johnny turned to the backseat and smiled his patented smile. 'Welcome to JohnnyCab. Where can I take you tonight?'

'Just drive!' Quaid snapped. 'Quick!'

The mannequin paused, then spoke with the same friendly tone. 'Would you please repeat the destination?'

Quaid glanced back through the rear window. The two men were close enough now for him to make out their faces. They were the two goons who had been after him at the subway station. They must have traced him here despite the towel!

'Anywhere!' he exclaimed, still looking back. 'Go! Go!' He saw Richter draw some heavy artillery and aim it. 'Shit!'

Johnny did not move. Neither did the cab. 'I'm not familiar with that address,' he said.

Now Helm had his own gun out and was taking aim. They were still half a block away, but those guns looked like young cannons from here.

'McDonald's! Go to McDonald's! Now!' Richter and Helm started firing. Still the cab didn't move.

'There are fourteen McDonald's franchises in the greater metropolitan area. Please specify –'

Enough was enough. Quaid knew that if he didn't get moving in seconds, he'd be done for! He grabbed the mannequin and wrenched it from its moorings, dragging the thing into the backseat and taking the steering wheel with it.

Bullets shattered the back window. Quaid wished briefly for the old days, when all vehicles were required to use shatterproof glass or plastic. He leaned over the driver's seat and reached awkwardly for the joystick on which the steering wheel had been mounted. The cab lurched forward.

Johnny's head spoke: 'Please fasten your seat belt.'

Without the steering wheel, Quaid barely had control of his vehicle. How was he going to manage?

As well as he had to, he thought grimly, as bullets whizzed past his ears. He gunned the engine and tried to maneuver the sensitive joystick into a left turn down a side street. Another window shattered and he jumped, sending the cab into a spin. He was flung to one side as the cab turned in a neat circle.

Richter and Helm poured on the gunfire. Windows exploded around Quaid as he tried to regain control of the cab. He jerked the joystick in the opposite direction – and it broke off in his hands!

'Shit!' The cab stopped spinning and sped onward, leaving Richter and Helm behind. For a moment Quaid thought he was in the clear. Then he glanced through the windshield.

He was headed directly for a concrete wall.

'Prepare for a collision,' Johnny said calmly. 'Prepare for a collision.'

Quaid felt hysterical laughter fighting its way out as he struggled to reach the nub of the joystick, but it was quickly replaced by sheer terror. The car was completely out of control and the wall was getting closer by the second. A crash was unavoidable. He opened the door to jump to safety.

Then he remembered the satchel! Clinging to the doorframe with one hand, he reached back into the cab and hauled the satchel from on top of Johnny's smiling face.

'Prepare for immediate impact,' Johnny said, unperturbed.

Quaid leaped! This, too, his body knew how to do; a stunt that might have killed an amateur hardly bruised him, as he tumbled clear and rolled down an embankment, hanging on to the satchel as if for dear life. Seconds later, the cab smashed into the wall and exploded in flames.

Quaid was safe, for the time being. But Richter would soon be after him again, when he discovered there was no corpse in the JohnnyCab. Quaid had to lose himself better than he had before, and stay lost.

He climbed to his feet and disappeared into the darkness.

Richter and Helm pulled up short as the cab exploded. The rain was still coming down, but it could do little to extinguish the great gouts of flame that flared from the ruined vehicle.

They gazed at it, catching their breath while savoring the destruction. All kinds of mayhem were nice, but fire had its own special appeal. Helm started forward, but Richter held him back.

'Not yet,' Richter said, offering Helm a cigarette. 'I like my meat well done.' He lit his own cigarette, then turned to watch the barbeque.

Meanwhile, below, Quaid was climbing over a fence, satchel in hand, unobserved. This was the industrial section of town. He headed into the comforting concealment between two brick buildings. With luck the goons would be distracted by the smashed cab above long enough, and would lose his trail entirely. He ran on, gaining confidence. Now he needed to find a private place, out of the dreary rain, to check the satchel. He put a hand to his head, holding the ragged turban in place; he was lucky he hadn't lost that during his encounter with the wall!

Helm had gone for the car and radioed for backup. Now he, Richter, and four other agents watched as two firemen foamed the smoking wreck and searched for remains. One of the firemen backed out and crossed over to Richter.

'Nobody home,' he said, with a shrug.

Richter and Helm looked at each other in amazement.

'Maybe he burned up,' Helm said.

Then the other fireman called out from the wreckage. 'Wait a second! I've got something!'

Richter and Helm approached eagerly as the fireman dragged a charred form from the foam. It was the smoldering remains of the mannequin driver. The ghastly head turned.

'Thank you for taking JohnnyCab,' it said brightly. 'I hope you enjoyed the ride!'

The quarry had slipped the noose again! Enraged, Richter smashed his fist into the Johnny head, cracking its jaw and shutting it up. He grimaced and drew his hand back quickly. The damned thing was hot!

An agent ran over to him. 'We picked up a reading at the cement works,' he said. 'It's weak, but it's him.'

'Move!' Richter shouted.

13

Hauser

Quaid zigzagged through the industrial complex, trying to stay out of sight while exploring for a suitable building. He wanted something that was deserted but not too obvious as a hiding place.

Quaid had been in such places many times on the job. He was familiar with the acrid smell of chemical waste leaking from rusting drums; the sight of tangled, outdated machinery; the oily orange and green scum floating on the surface of each puddle. He knew better than most people how many factories had closed down since the war with the Southern Bloc had heated up. With the big money going into weapons manufacture, the production of ordinary items had all but ceased.

It meant little to the wealthy, such as those in Quaid's new tower block. The luxuries they craved were supplied by small, specialized 'boutique' factories. Now, as in the past, the rich were getting richer and the poor were getting screwed. The abandonment of the larger industrial centers had meant shortages and deprivations for the average person. It had also made it that much harder for people to find jobs: the new defense plants were almost entirely mechanized.

No wonder so many people were emigrating to work in the Martian mines. Not only were huge bonuses offered, but job security as well. It looked pretty likely that the demand for turbinium would continue to increase for a good long while.

Turbinium was a rare resource, unknown on Earth, but relatively common on Mars, a key ingredient in the particle beam weapons program. Exactly what it was and how it was used was classified information; it wasn't even listed in most reference works, but it was known that the Northern Bloc's space-based weapons system depended on it. The stuff was more valuable than diamonds and as long as the war continued, miners would be needed to wrest it from the Martian soil.

Quaid stopped in his tracks as he spotted a likely hiding place: a large, delapidated factory building in which he was sure he could find a hiding place.

Later it would be scheduled for demolition, to make room for a new parking garage, but right now it was deserted. The windows weren't even locked; there must be nothing in here worth stealing.

He climbed through a window and finally out of the rain, ducking his head to avoid getting the turban knocked askew. He found himself in a cavernous industrial ruin. Water dripped through holes in the roof. Ideal!

He wasted no time. He set the satchel on a corroded assembly-line apparatus and removed the contents, hoping feverishly that they would somehow tell him something about his true identity. Maybe then he would understand why those thugs were trying to kill him.

There were packets of Martian money: lots of it. He whistled to himself as he flipped through the red banknotes. Since Martian currency was valid on Earth, just as Earth credits were valid on Mars, this would solve any financial problems he might have. But at the moment it wasn't what he needed. He needed something to save his life.

The next items proved to be of more interest. There were two ID cards. One, made out to someone named Brubaker, held a photo of a face that matched his own. His hands trembled with excitement. Was his real name Brubaker? Was Brubaker the man those thugs were after? He scanned the other ID. The photo was that of an overweight, many-chinned woman of indeterminate age. She had to be someone important to him – why else would her ID be in the satchel? He stared at her face, searching within himself for any spark of recognition. Could she be a relative? His mother? A girlfriend? It was no good. The face meant nothing to him. Pushing back a surge of disappointment, he continued to empty the satchel.

There was a weird sort of surgical instrument sealed in clear plastic. Well, the satchel looked like a doctor's black bag, so maybe this was to make it look more authentic. He could claim to be a specialist of some kind.

There was a strange rubber mold. He held it up and saw that it was an elaborate, head-covering mask with some kind of electronic gadgetry embedded in it that made the mouth move and changed its expression slightly. It matched the woman's face on the ID. So it had to be a disguise, with identification to back it up. Beneath the mask were yards and yards of a slimy, plastic fabric; part of the disguise, he hoped. He'd need more than a mask – even a fancy job like this one – to transform himself into the woman pictured in the ID.

He delved deeper. There were only a few items left. He pulled out a package of candy bars.

He peered at them, surprised. No, they really were garden-variety candy: Mars bars. Someone must have had a warped sense of humor. Still, they did remind him that he was hungry. Were they safe to eat?

There was a pair of strange galoshes. Huh?

He delved again, and came up with a combination wristwatch and numerical pad. He examined the little instrument, touching one of its buttons.

Suddenly he was startled by the appearance of a dangerous-looking man. The man was staring at him from the shadows about thirty feet away.

There was no time to think. Quaid drew his gun and fired. The man simultaneously aimed and shot at Quaid.

Who was going to drop? Quaid felt no injury, but that could be deceptive. A man could be severely injured and never feel it until he had dealt with the one who had given it to him. He couldn't examine himself until he knew what the other was going to do.

The other man seemed to have the same idea. Guns extended, they held each other in check.

Quaid took a step forward. So did the man, stepping into the light. He wore a crude floppy turban on his head.

Quaid was astonished. The man was himself! Or rather, a mirror-image hologram, of extremely high fidelity.

He walked toward the hologram, which of course matched him step for step. Quaid raised an arm; the holo raised an arm. Quaid made a sudden movement, as if trying to catch the other off-guard, the way they did in the old joke routines. The holo wasn't fooled.

The watch! He had touched a button, and the image had appeared. He touched it again. The holo-man disappeared with a *bzzzt*.

This could be a nice device! If Richter came gunning for him . . . yes. He strapped the watch onto his wrist, careful not to touch the button again.

Helm drove slowly through the abandoned industrial district. The two of them were directing searchlights onto the buildings from the roof of the car. So far, all they had spied was rain-soaked desolation.

Richter spoke into his radio. 'Any sign of him?'

There were four agents in two cars on other streets, paralleling Richter's car. 'I heard a gunshot at the old Toyota plant,' one reported on the radio.

Ha! 'Meet me at the loading dock,' Richter said. It was an odds-on bet that was their quarry. Maybe he had shot a rat for food, or one of the starving hounds that roamed the region.

Quaid shooed away a rat that was trying to get to his Mars bars. That was a good sign, actually; the rats were canny, and wouldn't go for poisoned food.

There was one more item in the satchel. He brought it out: a miniature videosdisc player/TV set. There was a disc in it, which meant there might be a recording for him. That was what he needed most: information. He set down the player so that its screen faced him, and turned it on.

His own face, minus the turban, appeared in close-up. It addressed the camera. 'Hello, stranger. This is Hauser. If things have gone wrong, I'm talking to myself – and you've got a wet towel wrapped around your head.'

Quaid jumped, touching the turban.

Hauser laughed heartily. He had an air of complete self-confidence. Well, it was nice to know that someone thought he knew what he was doing. Quaid tore open a Mars bar and ate it while he listened.

'Whatever your name is, get ready for a big surprise,' Hauser continued, becoming serious. 'You're not you. You're me.'

Quaid chomped on his bar. 'No shit,' he said staring at Hauser's face.

Richter's car converged with the other cars at the gates of a huge abandoned factory, topped by a decaying 'TOYOTA' sign. Richter checked the tracking device, which registered a pale glow. 'Bingo!'

Inside, Quaid continued watching the little screen with rapt attention. He was finally getting somewhere!

'All my life I worked for the Mars Intelligence branch of the Agency. In other words, I did Cohaagen's dirty work. Then a few weeks ago I met somebody – a woman. And I learned a few things. Like I've been playing for the wrong team.' Hauser sighed and looked guilty. 'All I can do now is try to make up for it.'

Quaid threw a piece of his candy bar to a persistent rat. It was foolish, but he felt some sympathy for any creature who had to hide out in a place like this, hated and hunted by man. The rat picked up the morsel and scurried away.

Hauser tapped on his head. 'There's enough shit in here to fuck Cohaagen good – and that's what I'm planning to do. Unfortunately, if you're listening to this, he got to me first. And here comes the hard part, old buddy; now it's all up to you.'

Quaid chewed, not so sure he liked this idea. If his image on the screen knew what he had been through so far, and thought that was the easy part . . .

'Sorry to drag you into it, but you're the only one I can trust,' Hauser said apologetically.

★

Richter sprang up a set of stairs, leading Helm and four agents inside the building, out of the rain. This time there would be no subway passages, no elevators or trains for the quarry to use for escape. This time they would nail him. Richter wanted to hear the bastard scream before he died.

Two rats came back, looking for handouts. News traveled fast, in this rat race! Quaid grinned briefly. What the hell! He tossed each of them a chunk of candy. Now if he could only get rid of the human rats who were after him this readily . . .

'First things first,' Hauser said on the screen. 'Let's get rid of the bug in your head.' He tapped his head right between the eyes. 'Take the thingy in the plastic bag – ' He held up the bag, exactly like the one Quaid had. 'And stick it up your nose.'

Up his nose? What joy! But probably better than a bullet in the head, which was what that bug would summon.

He opened the plastic bag and removed the surgical instrument. It looked like the metallic tentacle of an alien.

He pressed the plunger. Out came an inner tentacle with a tiny grasping claw. He thought of a snake striking from a hole in the wall, catching something and dragging it back into the wall. Up his nose?

'Don't worry, it's self-guiding.' Hauser said reassuringly. 'Just shove real hard – all the way up to your maxillary sinus.'

Quaid remembered an ancient joke: *'When my dog misbehaves, I give him a steak.' 'But surely he likes steak!' 'Not up his nose, he doesn't!'* That dog wouldn't like this torture instrument up his nose either. But Quaid had a steak, er, stake in it: his life.

It had to be done. Gingerly, he stuck the instrument up his nose and started to push. He grimaced with the pain. He could handle regular pain, as of clobbering his fist into a wall, but there was something peculiarly discomfiting about an intrusion deep in the nose. It wasn't just the snot; it got perilously close to the brain, up in there. He pictured one of those rotary drain cleaners, worming into the pipe, set to chew up any obstruction. But the obstruction here wasn't a jammed turd, it was his nasal tissue!

'And be careful,' Hauser said from the screen. 'It's my head too.'

No shit! Quaid warily sat down and continued the procedure. The metal snake was indeed self-guiding; it seemed to know where it was going. All it needed was thrust. Damn, he hated this!

Richter and his men fanned out inside the cavernous factory, commencing the search. They used small but powerful flashlights. They were quiet, but rats and pigeons fled from their path. Richter hoped that wouldn't give the quarry warning; he wanted to catch the man by surprise. For one thing, that might save some lives. He had to give that to him: eight agents taken out in one day, by a man who literally didn't know who he was. It spoke well for Agency training! Too bad they couldn't afford to train them all that way!

Grimacing horrendously, Quaid shoved the instrument farther in. It moved the last painful distance up his nose. He pressed the plunger.

There was a crunch of cartilage, and the pain was forgotten. It was replaced by blossoming agony. Quaid reeled, feeling faint. *Would* a bullet have felt worse? It would have been faster, anyway!

'When you hear the crunch, you're there,' Hauser said encouragingly.

Gee, thanks for telling me that, Doctor! Quaid leaned back against the wall and rested, with the alien tentacle still wedged up his nose. He felt blood trickling through the sinus cavity, somewhere in there, like boiling brine percolating through cold limestone caves. Oooooh, suffer! His nose felt so swollen that it seemed his eyes must be pushed to the sides of his face, like those of a frog.

Meanwhile, Hauser was still talking. He walked into a close-up on the screen. 'Now this is the plan. Get your ass to Mars and take a room at the Hilton. Flash the Brubaker ID.' There was a flash shot of the fake identification in the satchel. 'That's all there is to it. Just do what I tell you, and we can nail the sonovabitch who fucked us both.' Hauser's tone became more personal. 'I'm counting on you, buddy. Don't let me down.'

The TV turned itself off. Quaid was left in the dark, overwhelmed by more than the pain.

He had gotten his information. He was, or had been, Hauser, a Mars Intelligence agent. That explained his special abilities with hands and guns. An agent was a cleaned-up name for killer, in the name of the mission. He had been on the wrong side, and now was on the right side, so his former pals were now his enemies.

But if they had caught him after he changed sides, as obviously they had, why hadn't they simply killed him? Why go to such extraordinary trouble to set up a man they would consider to be a traitor on Earth, with a doll like Lori and a decent if dull job? He had thought it could be to protect him until he testified about something, but it seemed to be his enemies who had set him up like this. That knocked the sense right out of it. So there was still a hell of a lot he didn't know.

Well, at least he knew where to find the answers. He took a deep breath, took hold of the tentacle, and yanked it from his nose. It came out, streaked with blood and mucus, while the agony flared again.

Dizzy with the pain, he looked at the glistening silver pea held in the gory little claw. So this was the bug! His first thought was to throw it away, but then he had a better notion.

He unwrapped the towel from his head and used it to mop the blood from his hands and face. Then he fished out a Mars bar. He had no appetite at the moment, but didn't need it.

He saw rats in the shadows. The word had spread again: free food. Well, he was in an obliging mood, though his nose felt as if it had been crushed in a big rattrap. 'Get in line, fellows,' he murmured to the rats. 'I want every one of you to have an equal chance.'

BEEEEP! A bright red dot flashed on the tracking device. 'I got him!' Richter exclaimed. He led the agents through the factory at a run.

Quaid began to repack the satchel. He was about to add the videodisc device when flashlight beams cut through the dusty air. He dropped the machine and ran toward a pile of rubble as a hail of bullets saturated the room. Whoever was firing was taking no chances. Quaid vaulted silently from the window and ran as fast as his legs could carry him.

Richter and his men swung left and right like heat-seeking missiles. The tracking device showed the quarry's exact location. The fool must have forgotten how to mask the signal, if he had even been aware of it. Maybe he had done something to interfere with it without realizing, and now was doing something else.

'He's moving,' Richter said. 'In here!' He sprinted through a door, into the designated room.

Something moved. They unleashed a firestorm of bullets that tore up the room.

The shooting stopped. Suddenly it was very quiet. There was no body in sight. *What the fuck?* Richter checked the tracking device.

The red dot was there, moving. There was a sound, loud in the silence.

'There!' Richter cried.

The automatic rifles fired another burst. A tin can flew up, riddled.

He checked the tracker again. The red dot was moving away. 'No, there!' He pointed under a stalled assembly line.

They ran along the line, firing under the belt.

Still no body – and still the dot was moving on the tracker, just beyond the place they had fired at last. Did the man have nine lives?

There was a skittering sound, moving across the floor in the darkness. They fired at the sound, blasting into a pile of junk.

Richter passed his light over the pile. Quaid's body was not there.

He looked at the tracker again, puzzled. The flashing dot clearly indicated that Quaid was directly in front of them. But he wasn't. There was only the junk.

Richter slid his light beam over the rubble, and illuminated –

A terrified rat, with a fragment of a Mars bar wrapper in its mouth. The tracker was pinpointing the rat.

Now he caught on. The asshole had fed the bug to the rat, maybe in the candy. They had been chasing the rat, while the quarry got away.

They had been outmaneuvered – again.

Infuriated, he blasted the rat to smithereens.

As a red haze of fury cleared from his eyes, Richter became aware that Helm was standing beside him, holding the remains of the videodisc player. It had been hit by a stray bullet and now squawked like a broken record. Richter slowly turned his head and watched a static-ridden snippet of the recorded message on the cracked screen.

Only a small shard of the disc remained, but there was enough to recognize Hauser's voice saying: '. . . Get your ass to Mars *squrtrk* Get your ass to . . .'

14
Ship

Helm drove again. Richter, fuming, composed himself for a formal report. He set the videophone on RECORD and watched as his own image appeared on the screen, as if it were a reflection.

'It's not looking good,' he said. 'He remembers all his field techniques, and he's been getting help from, get this, Stevens, and God knows who else.' He grimaced, in the manner of a good man beset by incompetence; let Cohaagen make of that what he would. 'I put all spaceports on highest alert, but if he doesn't turn up by takeoff, I'll grab the first shuttle and be waiting for him on Mars.'

He pressed a button. The disc reversed, then replayed: '. . . waiting for him on Mars.'

Good enough. He ejected the videodisc, turning to an agent in the back seat, and handed him the disc. 'Beam this to Cohaagen, *after* I'm gone.'

The man nodded. He didn't need to know why the message was being handled this way, he just had to follow orders. By the time Cohaagen tried to countermand, it would be too late.

Richter intended to nail his quarry, no matter who stood in the way, even if it was his boss.

Through the moving windshield wipers he saw the spaceport coming into view. Well, one thing about going to Mars: it would get him out of this fucking rain! Mars was dry, desert dry; there would never be any rain there.

Next day Richter strode through the empty lounge section of the vessel. Several security guards rushed to keep up with him. The space cycler vibrated and rumbled in preparation for takeoff.

97

'We've looked everywhere,' a security man said. 'Baggage, the galley –'

'Staff quarters,' the second security man put in.

'What about the landing gear housing?' Richter asked tersely.

The two security men looked at each other. Obviously this had been overlooked.

'I'll check it out,' Helm said. He headed down some stairs.

Richter passed a porthole. Through it he saw the complex engines and wings of the space cycler. It was a heavy-duty passenger craft, slower but more comfortable than the shuttles. Tourists were fussy about things like acceleration and free-fall, though it was more efficient to accelerate quickly and then coast. Anything for the damned tourists!

He continued on into the cabin area. In this section, each cabin contained a transparent sleeping capsule. Regular passengers usually chose to spend the entire trip sleeping in the snug confines of their capsules. Most tourists, on the other hand, set the capsules to varying sleep-wake cycles, so that they could enjoy the company of other passengers and view at least some of the glories of space through their exterior portholes. The cabins also had interior portholes and, fortunately for Richter, most of the passengers hadn't opaqued the glass yet.

The captain of the ship charged up, confronting him angrily. 'Not again?! Security's been through here twice!'

Richter ignored him. He walked on down the aisle, looking through rows of portholes at the faces of passengers who presented themselves for inspection. He came upon the back of one's passenger's head. He slammed his fist on the porthole. The startled passenger turned and faced the window.

'Nobody's gotten on or off,' the captain said. He was obviously fed up with this, but powerless to stop it.

Continuing to ignore the Captain, Richter came across a few opaqued portholes. This was more promising! He flung open the doors. None of the passengers was Quaid.

'We're over two hours late!' the captain protested. When

Richter made no reply, the captain had had enough. He spoke quietly into a radio unit on the wall. 'Start the engines. We're leaving.'

Not till Richter gave the okay! He continued checking capsules.

A hugely fat lady waddled from the back of the ship toward the front. She carried several packages. As the captain hung up, she squeezed past him. Her vanity was such that she even wore high heels, though they jacked her up to above the height of most men and did absolutely nothing for her sausagelike legs.

'Excuse me, madam,' the captain said with forced civility. 'You'll have to return to your capsule.'

'Where's my cabin?' the lady wheezed, shoving a boarding pass in his face.

'Number nineteen. Straight ahead.'

'Thank you.' She waddled on down, taking her time.

The engines, responsive to the captain's directive, revved up more noisily. Richter emerged from one cabin and pushed the fat lady out of the way, disgusted by the brief contact. 'What's that noise?'

'We're taking off now, or we'll miss the lunar sling,' the captain said. 'You're welcome to come along for the ride.'

'You can't take off until I say!' Richter said. 'Security takes precedence over schedule!'

'Really? I shall have to recheck the manual. Now I suggest that you take one of the vacant berths if you don't want to handle the acceleration on the floor here. We have sealed the entry port.'

Richter realized that the captain was pulling the same deal on him that he had pulled on Cohaagen. He would be unable to prove that the captain didn't know that security took precedence, and by the time he got hold of the space manual it would be academic: they would be in space.

He glared at the captain, about to say something acid. Helm rushed up. 'I checked the landing gear. It's clean.'

The captain collared a passing stewardess. 'Charlotte, show these gentlemen to some cabins,' he said briskly. Then he headed to the fore.

'Right this way,' the stewardess said, smiling prettily.

Richter had to follow her, grinding his teeth. His only consolation was that he was sure that Cohaagen was grinding his teeth with even more anger.

Richter and Helm went with Charlotte toward the rear. The captain moved on toward the cockpit in front. He passed the fat lady, who was still struggling to climb into her upper berth.

'Where's my cabin?' the fat lady asked.

'This is it, ma'am,' the captain said patiently. 'You've found it.' He shook his head as he got past her. It had been a long day.

Richter, glancing back, smiled briefly. He was glad that the captain had his problems too. Served him right.

Charlotte showed them to their capsule. She smiled without a trace of guile, which meant she was a professional in her capacity as Richter was in his.

What did pretty stewardesses do in the long hours of travel, in their time off? Maybe it would be worth finding out, as long as he was stuck here. She could be a useful ally, because she interacted with all the passengers. If he asked her to report anything odd, it just might help him a lot.

Richter put on his most charming smile, as hypocritical as Cohaagen's own. 'Thank you, miss,' he said. 'Perhaps we shall see more of each other soon.'

Her smile congealed, as if she had just spied a tarantula in her purse. 'I doubt it, sir,' she said, beating a hasty retreat.

Damn!

The fat lady hurriedly locked the door and opaqued her porthole. 'Where's my cabin?' she asked, though there was no one else there.

She put her hands up, took hold of her ears, and pulled. As she jerked, her face split in the middle. The skin peeled away from the nose on either side, taking with it the fat cheeks and chins.

Underneath was the face of a man. It was Douglas Quaid.

He drew the artificial face the rest of the way off. Even the hair was fake, and the small earrings. As it came free, it sprang shut, resuming its original aspect, somewhat deflated.

'Where's my cabin?' the face asked querulously. 'Where's my cabin?'

He held it in his hands and poked at it with a finger, but it kept talking. 'Where's my cabin?'

Annoyed, he slammed the face against the wall. It was quiet.

He relaxed. Then, after a beat, the face spoke again. 'Thank you.'

He had to smile. At least the mask had done its job, fooling the goons.

He didn't bother to remove the dress or the layers of foam-filled plastic that rounded out his slim shape into the gargantuan proportions of the fat lady. He was quite comfortable in it and, besides, he didn't want to be caught on board without his disguise. He had already decided to ride out the trip in stasis and he would pull the mask back on after takeoff. There was no sense taking chances.

As he leaned back in his capsule, he stared down at the most remarkable feature of the outfit Hauser had provided. The galoshes were covered with thin, flexible holograms, which gave the illusion that he was wearing sturdy high heels, though inside, his heels were flat on the bottom. This had the effect of subtracting three inches from his height, because people allowed for the height of the heels. He was still one big, tall figure of a woman, but able to pass. He would have to be careful never to let his knees show, though, because his calves would seem shortened. There wasn't much to worry about in that department, however; his dress came down almost to his ankles, effectively hiding his legs.

There was more he was hiding. Realizing that he would need a gun, but that he wouldn't be able to smuggle it aboard a subway, let alone a spaceship, he had shopped at a blackmarket outlet for a special one. It was made entirely of plastic and other nonmetallic materials, guaranteed to set off no alarms. Plastic could be made as hard as metal, as its bullets showed, and bullets used plastic explosive for their detonations. Such guns had been outlawed for decades, but could be had – for a price. This one was even fancier: it disassembled into camouflaged parts. The buttons on the fat lady's dress, the decorations on her shoes, the combs in her hair – everything served some other purpose, so that even a physical inspection would not betray its larger nature. The gun would be a job to assemble, but it could be a lifesaver. Just so long as he didn't need it while he was in costume!

Actually, now that he passed the boarding check, he could assemble the weapon and keep it ready in his purse. Then when he reached Mars he could disassemble it into a few major components and stash them in his purse and the spaces in his galoshes. Mars didn't have the fancy X-ray sensors Earth did; it depended on routine physical inspection, which he understood was cursory. So he could sneak the gun by, and put it together again quickly thereafter. He would have to rearrange his clothing to make it hang together without some of its buttons, but women were known to change outfits all the time. It would be all right, as long as he didn't encounter any tornadoes. There really was small likelihood of that, on almost airless Mars.

The engines' roar increased. The vessel shook violently. These clunkers were lucky if they didn't shake themselves apart during takeoff! He hurriedly strapped himself into his bunk as the ship heaved itself up.

He leaned back, relaxing. It was the only way to handle acceleration. Now he could sort out his slowly recovering memories, aided by what he had learned last night. So he was Hauser, a turncoat agent with a conscience. He liked that. He had seen enough of Agency methods to know that he didn't want to be associated with it. But what was the secret he knew that made him so dangerous to them? That remained blank. Why had they gone to so much trouble to keep him alive and healthy, despite having to detail a crew to keep watch on him and keep him pacified? They must have wanted him for *something!* But that, too, was blank.

At least he was on the way to Mars, where the answers were. To Mars, where the woman of his dreams was. He was now certain she existed. He had dreamed of her because he remembered her, on a level suppressed by the implant that had rendered him into Quaid. Somehow some of that memory had leaked, giving him a desire to return to Mars and an image of the woman. If he could find her, he could find the rest of his past.

He would also have to deal with Cohaagen. Hauser had told him that, and it rang true. He would not be allowed to live if Cohaagen and his deadly minions remained free.

The acceleration pressed him back, making breathing labored. He found himself thinking of three things: smashing Cohaagen, loving the Mars woman, and something else of overwhelming significance. But it wouldn't come clear. Not yet.

He oriented on that third thing, knowing that in it lay the key to all the rest. It was – it was what he had been going after when he was with the woman, when he fell into the pit. It was there, under the ground of Mars. But what was it? Its physical aspect was only part of it. There was so much more . . .

He lost the thread. He let it go for the moment and pulled the curtain aside to gaze out the porthole. He imagined himself turning ghostlike, a hologram, flying through that port and out to pace the ship, then around to see the fiery, noisy exhaust of the engine. He zoomed right into it, until all his world was blazing red. If only he could burn away the whole of his false existence, and recover his real identity, and know what it was that haunted his deepest mind, that was so significant as to change the fate of a world . . .

15

Spaceport

It was dark and silent. Then Phobos, the larger of the two potato-shaped moons of Mars, floated into view. It was about seventeen miles long, thirteen across, and twelve deep, which was pretty small as moons went, but still about twice the size of its companion, Deimos. It was as ugly as a barren rock could be, hardly more than a fragment torn from some larger body and frozen in its irregularity. But it was an excellent spot for a rendezvous, because it was solid without having any significant gravity of its own.

The space cycler came into view, closing on the moon. The ship looked tiny in comparison, a mere speck. Then, above the two, was the huge red mass of Mars, so large in proportion that only its arc showed. Yet Mars was one of the smallest planets, barely over a tenth the mass of Earth. How perspective changed things!

Quaid, aboard the small shuttle, watched Phobos and the space cycler recede. The other passengers paid no attention, bored with this as they had been with the rest of the journey out. All they wanted was tourist trophies and the gaming tables. But he was fascinated. The riddle of his life was here, and not just in the people here. There was something about the landscape of Mars . . .

The shuttle thrust up, closing the distance. Gradually Quaid's orientation altered, until he no longer saw the planet as above, but as below. That was a bit more comfortable.

The shuttle crossed the landscape, ragged and pocked by craters of every size. Quaid was locked into it, unable to tear his eyes away. This was almost like his dream, only, only –

He shook his head. It just wouldn't quite come. What had been done to his memory was like a thick rope wound around his body, tight, chafing, giving only a little in places, hurting him when he struggled. He needed more than just his thoughts to free himself.

The terrain was violent, as befitted the planet named for the god of war. He saw part of the enormous equatorial canyon called Valles Marineris, the better part of three thousand miles long, dwarfing Earth's Grand Canyon. In some sections its walls had collapsed, evidently washed out by flooding. Mars had once had water on its surface, a lot of it; now that water was locked in buried ice, in virtual glaciers under the dust and sand of the surface. No one was sure just how much water there was, if it could only be released, or what might lie below it. He saw the three great shield volcanoes sitting atop the Tharsis ridge. He knew this region; it was coming back to him as he gazed down at it! But where was the thing buried deeper in his memory? It had something to do with the ice . . .

Now the shuttle approached the peak of Olympus Mons, some fifteen or sixteen miles high according to his memory, a magnificent mountain unlike any other in the Solar System. It might have seemed odd that a planet much smaller than Earth had a volcanic mountain much larger than any on Earth, but this was because the gravity was less, and the mantle of the planet did not constantly shift. On Earth such a structure would have been brought down long ago by the forces of gravity and weather, and the shifting mantle tended to cut volcanoes off from their sources before they could do much.

The retro rockets fired for the shuttle's vertical descent. On the boulder-strewn plain of Chryse, the spaceport roof opened up, revealing a landing pad inside. The shuttle dropped into the spaceport, and the roof closed over it. Such mechanisms were necessary because the air of Mars was far too thin to permit external unloading.

Quaid, in the guise of the fat lady, exited with the tourists. He showed his passport, the one provided by Hauser in the satchel, and an official seal stamped down on it. MARS FEDERAL COLONY/CONFEDERATION OF NORTHERN

NATIONS. No one was really checking the papers; Mars wanted both tourists and colonists, and so kept the red tape to a minimum. That meant that a person could normally be processed through within a couple of hours.

It would be better, of course, if they got it down to two minutes. But bureaucracy was incapable of that. Even if there was only one little bag to check, containing no more than a Mars candy bar, that justified an hour's delay. On other planets, where they didn't care about making a good impression, it would justify four hours' delay, and more if the victim fussed. Bureaucrats were little tyrants in their domains, never able to understand why visitors didn't like them.

Fortunately, the Mars gravity made standing in line easy. Even a fat lady like him could handle it.

In the Immigration Hall of the spaceport the travelers were queued up in three long lines, waiting to be processed by the three immigration officers on duty. Why didn't they have a dozen officers there, doing other chores between ships? Richter smiled knowingly. Because that would be too efficient. Visitors needed to feel the power of the bureaucracy, which was demonstrated by wasting their time. He approved of this. It was right that civilians be constantly reminded who had control.

He looked around. An imposing picture of Cohaagen hung on the front wall, greeting all visitors. Soldiers stood ready, armed, in case anyone should think of protesting. He remembered seeing a video about the ancient days, when the Nazis added vicious attack dogs to the lineup, and loosed them if anyone gave them a pretext. Lovely!

He saw the fat lady standing in line behind a mother with a baby slung over her shoulder and his lip curled in disgust. Thank God, Lori never gained weight! The thought that he would see her soon raised his spirits even more.

An escort of soldiers appeared. They shoved people aside to make room for Richter and Helm, who were escorted to the front of the nearest line. As they passed, they jostled the fat lady, who was playing cootchy-coo with the smiling baby. Richter recoiled at the touch.

Two agents in suits approached, greeting Richter and Helm like VIPs. Well, why not!

'Welcome home, Mr Richter,' the first agent said enthusiastically. 'Mr Cohaagen wants to see you right away.'

Richter walked past the two, hardly deigning to notice them. 'What the fuck is that?' He pointed to graffiti on the wall: KUATO LIVES. A painter was in the process of cleaning it up.

'Things have gotten worse,' the agent said tightly. 'The rebels took over the refinery last night. No turbinium going out.'

Richter and his entourage proceeded down the hallway. He was disgusted. The last thing they needed was messages from the mythical leader of the Mars Liberation Front! It was enough of a pain dealing with that traitor Hauser without running afoul of imaginary characters. The worst problem with nonexistent folk is that they couldn't be killed.

'Any news about Hauser?' he asked, reminded of his mission.

'Not a word.'

Bothered about something he couldn't quite nail, Richter paused and looked back at the patiently waiting people. He saw the baby playing with the fat lady's hair. The fat lady had rearranged her outfit, but it still didn't do a thing for her. Then the baby pat-a-caked the woman's face with some force, not knowing its own strength.

'Where's my cabin?' the fat lady asked incongruously.

Richter focused on her, vaguely disturbed. Was that the only thing she knew how to say?

The fat lady opened her mouth, seemingly horrified. The baby laughed.

Oh. She was doing it for the baby. Richter turned away, dismissing his concern. The entourage had almost exited the Immigration Hall.

'Where's my cabin?' the fat lady asked again.

Richter stopped and turned again. Suddenly his vague concern was clarifying into a sharp suspicion. Was it possible?

The fat lady was evidently trying to stifle herself, holding her face as if it were talking without her volition. The baby laughed and laughed at this exhibition. The other people were looking at her now, including the soldiers, who found her behavior strange but not dangerous. Women did tend to get soppy about babies; it was one of the annoying things about them.

Then the fat lady looked his way. She locked eyes with Richter.

Now he knew! 'That's Quaid!' he rasped. 'Stop him!'

The fat lady broke from the line and ran to the front, moving with surprising alacrity for her size. She opened her face, which peeled away on either side.

The soldiers were shocked, thinking she had some kind of loathsome disease. She charged them, and they almost fell over each other getting out of the way, not wanting to be infected. That enabled her to run away from Richter.

Richter scrambled after Quaid, drawing his gun, but couldn't get a shot. The damn lines of stupid people, now scattering across the hall, ruined any decent line of sight.

Another soldier pulled a gun at close range to the fugitive. But Quaid swatted his arm, shoved him into another soldier, then smashed a third soldier in the face. Richter would have admired the man's finesse if it hadn't been so important to nail him. Agency training sure showed!

But Quaid couldn't stay clear for long. He was confined to the spaceport, and the people were clustering at the sides of the hall. In a moment he would be a fair target.

Quaid ran down a corridor. Now, there was a mistake! He had lost his interference. Six soldiers were racing after him, and Richter and Helm after them. They'd corner the rat in a moment!

There was a large window by an intersection. Through it the barren Martian landscape could be seen. It was near-vacuum out there; the man couldn't escape that way!

Quaid was about to dodge around a corner, but a young soldier blocked the intersection. Quaid tossed the deflated mask to the soldier, who caught it instinctively. The mask snapped together and said, 'Get ready for a big surprise.'

The soldier gaped – and the mask exploded!

The explosion shattered the window. It fragmented outward, driven by the pressure of the Earth atmosphere.

This created an instant tornado, as the air funneled out. The spaceport was depressurizing in the manner of a balloon let go. Everybody grabbed onto anything handy and hung on for dear life.

The idiot! Richter thought. They had just about cornered the rat, and Quaid had to pull a stunt like this! Now they were all in trouble.

He saw Quaid grab the railing around an open staircase leading down. Trust the man to be able to handle this better than most! He was going to haul himself away while the soldiers were helpless.

One of the soldiers who had been closest to the window was sucked through the aperture into the near-vacuum. Quaid's clothes and padding were sucked off his body and followed the soldier out the window. Quaid was left in the short-sleeved shirt and rolled up trousers he wore under the costume, and with the ludicrous high-heeled shoes. And clutching his purse, yet!

An immigration officer struggled to a control panel and managed to activate the emergency alarm.

Metal barriers started sliding down in sequence, covering all the windows and doorways to the left, the right, behind, and ahead. SQQRRCHANG! SQQQRRCHANG! SQQQRRCHANG!

Good! Not only would that stop the loss of air, it would trap Quaid inside, so they could finish the job. No careless bullet would smash any of those barriers!

He saw Quaid looking frantically around. *Yeah, look, you shit! You're cornered now! And I'm the one who's going to –*

A barrier started to lower over the staircase passage nearest to Quaid. SQQQRRRRR!!!

Quaid pushed off and rolled under just before –

CHANG! He was through.

No! Richter thought, anguished.

A metal sheet slammed over the shattered window. Had

the system had any brains, it would have closed that one first and saved them all a hassle.

The tornado instantly dissipated. Now the tourists had breath to scream, gaspingly. Fuck them!

Richter sprinted to the staircase barrier. 'Open it! Open it!'

'I can't,' the nearest soldier said. He was a young twerp, obviously inexperienced. 'They're all connected.'

Frustrated and furious, Richter backhanded him across the face with his gun.

16

Venusville

The noisy, old-fashioned train, probably a refugee from a condemned twentieth-century New York subway, pulled out of the station and entered a dark tunnel. Outside were clattering sounds and flashing lights, as if the thing were about to fly off the tracks and smash into a pillar. That, combined with the crowding, created a feeling of anxiety.

Quaid looked around, alert to potential danger. He wasn't exactly well dressed at the moment; he had barely been able to hang on to his purse when his unsecured clothing got blown off. He was doing his best now to make that purse seem like a package. But no one seemed to notice. Blasé Mars natives (anyone who had been here more than a year was a native) were talking among themselves, and he overheard snippets of conversations.

'While you were gone,' one Martian said, 'Cohaagen raised the price of air.'

'Again?' her companion asked, resigned. 'That's the third time in the past two months.'

'Yes, and meanwhile our pay stays the same.'

Interesting, Quaid thought. They never mentioned the price of air when they offered the sizeable bonuses to potential colonists from Earth.

The woman was speaking again, in a lowered voice. 'And did you hear about the Hamiltons?'

'I noticed that their place was dark last night.'

'And the night before, and the night before that.'

'Gone on a trip?'

'You could say so,' the woman said with a knowing smile. Her voice became scarcely more than a whisper and Quaid strained to hear her. 'We'll see how long the Administrator lasts when all of his workers have "gone on a trip".'

Quaid followed the woman's eyes as she looked pointedly at the posters that plastered the interior of the car. The posters proclaimed a huge reward for the capture of the mysterious leader of the rebel forces, Kuato. The name was spelled out in large, clear letters.

But there was no picture.

Here was something else that got short shrift in the emigration brochures. Quaid had had no idea that the Mars Liberation Front had such a broad base of support. The newscasts made it sound as though the rebels were just a few, disaffected troublemakers. Yet they had the obvious approval of the ordinary-looking, middle-class couple on the train. It certainly didn't sound as though Vilos Cohaagen was universally beloved. Hardly surprising, if he was gouging the populace for the very air they breathed. He filed the information away for future reference.

Red light flooded the car. The clattering diminished as the subway emerged onto the surface of Mars. Quaid peered out the window at the weird landscape, drinking it all in. It was barren, it was awful, but it was the land of his dream!

He crossed to the other side of the car as the reverberations faded. He stared, fascinated, experiencing a rush of emotion.

There was the pyramid-shaped mountain of his dream! There was a mining facility on its side. His dream was real! The things in it really were here on Mars!

After a moment he turned and tapped the nearest Martian on the shoulder. 'Excuse me. What's that?'

The man glanced at him, then out the window. 'You mean the Pyramid Mine?' Then he saw Quaid staring fixedly at it. 'I used to work there, till they found all that alien shit inside. Now it's closed.'

Alien artifacts? Then that, too, was true. He *had* been there, and his dream was a true memory, not idle fancy! But if he had fallen in, how could he have survived unscathed? Unless the fall had been broken, and he had taken a bash on the head that gave him amnesia. But that wouldn't explain why others wanted to kill him, or why Hauser wanted to get even with Cohaagen. He still knew far too little!

'Can you visit?' he asked, rapt.

'Ha. Can't get within ten miles.'

So there was some secret there. Why were they keeping people away? Certainly they weren't going to keep *him* away! One way or another he would get there, and unravel his past.

And find his woman.

The Pyramid Mine was as impressive from another angle, as seen from the hall leading to Cohaagen's office. Richter stared through the glass wall at the mining complex, wishing that he rated a stunning facility like this. He entered the office and faced the back of Cohaagen's chair across his desk.

'Mr Cohaagen,' he said. 'You wanted to see me?'

Cohaagen swiveled around in his chair. He smiled silently for a moment. 'Richter,' he said finally. 'Do you know why I'm such a happy person?'

Because you're the top man, Richter thought, with subordinates to chew out. He let none of this show through the dutiful expression on his face.

'No, sir,' he said respectfully.

'Because I've got a great fuckin' job,' Cohaagen said calmly. 'As long as the turbinium keeps flowing, I can do anything I want. Anything. Nobody's looking over my shoulder. Nobody cares how I live. Nobody gives a shit if a few Martians have to suffer.' He paused.

'I'll tell you the truth,' he continued. 'I wouldn't trade places with the Chairman.' It was difficult for him to keep a straight face. He had the Chairman by the short hairs and he knew it, but it wouldn't do to give that kind of information to Richter. No, the masquerade would go on. For the time being.

Besides, there was nothing funny about the rebel situation. They were causing him more trouble than he had expected. If they weren't stopped . . . No. It wasn't a thought worth considering. He *would* stop them.

He stood, leaning forward, his hands on the desk. 'In fact,' he continued, 'the only thing I ever worry about is that one day, if the rebels win, it all might end.'

Suddenly Cohaagen exploded in fury, pounding his fist on the desk. The fishbowl that graced one corner jumped. 'And you're fuckin' making it happen! You disobeyed my orders! And then you fuckin' let him get away!'

Richter's face remained impassive. There was no way Cohaagen could prove that his radio transmission had gotten through, so there was no way he could prove Richter's insubordination. They both knew that.

'He had help, sir,' Richter said evenly. 'From our side.'

'I *know*,' Cohaagen said impatiently.

'But I thought . . .' Richter could not conceal the surprise in his voice.

'Who told you to *think*?' Cohaagen snapped. 'I don't give you enough information to *think!*' He shook an index finger in Richter's face. 'You do what you're told! That's what you do!' Cohaagen resumed his calm demeanor. He opened a drawer and withdrew a small box. He gently shook some flakes into the fishbowl on his desk.

'Now let's get down to business,' he said in reasonable tones. 'Kuato wants what's in Quaid's head and he might be able to get it. Rumor has it that the geek is psychic.

'Now I have a little plan to keep this from happening. Do you think you can play along?'

Richter wanted to push Cohaagen's head into the damned bowl and let the fish eat his face, but 'Yes, sir' was all he said.

'Great!' said Cohaagen, looking up from the fish with a beaming smile. 'Because I was just getting ready to erase you.'

Quaid stepped from the subway station and emerged into the dazzling downtown section of Chryse Planitia. This was where sophisticated, wealthy people conducted business. The beautiful public square overlooked the spectacular Pyramid Mine. There was a great deal of airspace here, and the geodesic dome was clean.

In fact, this was the kind of place where he would like to be, even if he didn't have his past to recall. It might be crowded in the subway, but it would never be crowded in the great outdoors of Mars! Not only was Earth crowded all over, it was also polluted, while here –

But he couldn't dawdle. There were agents on his trail, and they would catch up to him all too soon. He needed to disappear into his assumed identity.

He looked around and spied the entrance to the Hilton Hotel. He walked inside.

It was as fancy inside as outside. This was truly a paradise for tourists!

He approached the desk, where a clerk sat at a computer terminal. The clerk looked up and smiled with recognition. 'Oh, Mr Brubaker. Nice to have you back.'

Well now! Hauser had really set this up well! 'Nice to be back,' he said.

'Would you like the usual suite?'

'Of course.' This was almost too good to be true. Of course it wasn't true, technically, being an assumed identity. But where identities could be set up, they could also be tipped off to enemies. He would play along, yet keep alert.

The clerk checked the monitor. 'Hmm. Seems you left something behind on your last visit.'

Quaid tensed. He had left a slew of murderous goons behind! But also his memories, and his woman.

The clerk walked to the mailboxes and returned with a sealed manila envelope. He handed this to Quaid. 'There you go.' He studied the monitor. 'Now, that'll be suite two-eighty in the blue wing. The key-card will be ready in just a minute.'

The clerk turned away to encode the key-card. Quaid tore open the envelope and pulled out a sheet of red paper folded into a small square. He unfolded the paper and found an advertising flyer for a bar. The Last Resort, in Venusville.

Oh, yes, the notorious sleaze den, a magnet for tourists. There was a Marsville on the planet Venus too, with a similar reputation.

He focused on the flyer. It contained a drawing of a naked girl. On the back was a handwritten message. 'For a good time, ask for Melina.'

Surreptitiously, Quaid took a hotel pen and scribbled 'Melina' under the written message. The hair on the back of his neck prickled as he saw the handwriting matched.

This was a message intended only for him. He thought of the woman of his dreams. Was it possible? No, of course not. Yet –

Before he knew it, he was on his way out. As he opened the door, he glanced back. The desk clerk was turning back. 'Here's your key, Mr Bru –'

Then the man realized that he was speaking to emptiness. He looked surprised.

The door closed behind Quaid. He emerged at the front of the hotel and stepped toward the cabstand.

A black man in an outfit reminiscent of the ancient jive era approached him. The man looked to be about forty. 'Need a cab, man? I'm Benny, and I'm what you want.'

Quaid nodded toward the first cab in line. 'What's wrong with that one?'

'He ain't got six kids to feed.'

Quaid saw the driver of that cab was a punk in his twenties. That wasn't any more appealing than Benny. He nodded.

'It's right around the corner,' Benny said eagerly.

As Quaid followed to the bootleg cab, the punk cabbie saw his fare being stolen. 'Hey!' he protested. Then he realized that it was no use. 'Asshole!'

Mars wasn't much different from Earth, after all! But for the kind of business Quaid might have here, with agents on his trail, a scoundrel cabbie might be better than a legitimate one. Benny wouldn't be eager to turn him in to anyone, and probably knew the back alleys of Mars as well as anyone did.

As he approached the dilapidated cab, a huge explosion ripped through the upper level of the Pyramid Mine. Windows shattered and Benny was thrown to the ground as alarms began to sound. Quaid managed to keep his footing, barely.

Benny staggered to his feet, slightly dazed.

'Welcome to Mars,' he said wryly. Suddenly soldiers

were everywhere, shooting at unseen rebel forces who returned fire. Benny lifted the gullwing door of the cab hastily. 'Let's get out of here, man.' Quaid climbed in.

Benny quickly pulled into traffic and then seemed to relax.

'What's all the trouble about?' Quaid asked, craning his neck to watch the smoke rising from the mine.

'Oh, the usual,' Benny said nonchalantly. 'Money, freedom . . . air.' He changed lanes. 'So, where to?'

'Venusville.'

Benny gazed at him. 'How's that again, man?'

Quaid pulled out the flyer. 'Venusville.'

Benny shook his head. 'Man, *this* is Venusville! The upside part of it, anyway.'

'Then make it the downside part of it.'

'Oho! You know what you want!' He put the car in motion. 'Any special – ?'

'The Last Resort.'

'Mister, you can do better than that!'

'That's the address I have.'

'Right, man!' Benny agreed dubiously. He guided the car toward the edge of town.

Quaid took this opportunity to shuck the clumsy galoshes. He wore his own shoes underneath. Two segments of the plastic gun were nestled in the toes of the galoshes; he stuffed these in his pockets, then added two more segments from his purse. He didn't want to carry that purse around anymore; he would ditch it somewhere along the way. He was just glad that he had been able to hang on to everything that counted when the window blew out at the spaceport.

Soon they entered one of several big tubeways that crossed the chasm separating the two sides of town. Ah – now it was coming clear! The slum section was on the other side of the tracks, as it were.

'First trip to Mars?' Benny inquired conversationally, in much the way an updated JohnnyCab mannequin might. If he had noticed Quaid's business with the galoshes and purse, he was too discreet to mention it. Tourists could have peculiar ways.

117

Quaid was staring out the window, still distracted by the view. Such colossal mountains, rifts, rubble-strewn plains; the perfect desolation, yet enthralling too. He could look at this stuff for hours, for days! Yet that wasn't the half of it. He had dreamed of Mars, longing to travel there. Now he was here, and he was fascinated by it, but the longing remained. For his real identity, and for the woman, and for something else. But try as he might, he never quite got the whole picture. It was as if under all his superficial concerns lay a deeper one, like basalt under topsoil, signifying some horrendously significant past event that he ignored at his peril. As if the matter of whether he survived were inconsequential, compared to what the buried layer meant.

He came out of it, realizing that the cabbie had spoken to him. 'Mm-hmm. Well, no . . . Sort of.'

Benny absorbed that. 'Man don't know if he's been to Mars or not,' he muttered.

Quaid realized that it did sound confused. But it was true. Someone in his body had been to Mars before, but Quaid himself had not. When he recovered his memory, then he could claim to have been –

He shook his head. The more he learned, the less he seemed to know for sure.

The tubeway emptied into a plaza in the poor section of town. The contrast with the affluent neighborhood was shocking. The upside had broad, clear streets and lovely views; this downside had grim, claustrophobic streets tunneled into the mountainside. It was in perpetual night. There were dim street lamps, but the only natural light flowed through a distant archway. This was not because of a change in the hour: the Mars day, coincidentally, was about half an hour longer than Earth's, and so easy to adapt to that most people hardly noticed the difference. It was because of the subterranean nature of the city. This was like living in a mine. It was no pun to call this the shady neighborhood.

People moved listlessly under low ceilings. A significant proportion of the population, if what was visible was typical, was deformed in some way. Quaid shuddered.

All the buildings were dilapidated and covered with signs and graffiti. Psychic parlors seemed to be quite popular. Numerous WANTED posters advertised a reward for Kuato, and like the ones on the train, they had no pictures. Kuato, the fabled leader of the Mars Liberation Front. Quaid could see how the denizens of a place like this could long for liberation! If they put their hope into a nonexistent figure – well, maybe that was better than having no hope at all.

Something almost floated to the surface of his mind, but it slipped away before he could catch it. Did he know something about a way to liberate Mars? Liberate it from what? The fact was, poverty was endemic; there was plenty of it on Earth too. There was no magic wand to wave to free the downtrodden masses of Mars.

Or was there? He saw soldiers patrolling the streets in pairs. The hostility between them and the people was palpable. Could there be a way to get these poor folk out of the dark ghetto and into the sunside? To provide enough daylight land for all of them?

He shook his head. He was no social worker. As long as domes were required to provide livable atmosphere, the common folk would be captive to those who built and controlled the domes. It was just the way Mars was.

The cab gained on an attractive woman with a sexy walk, seen from behind. She held a small child by the hand.

'Not bad, eh?' Benny inquired.

Quaid had to concede that even this hellhole had its bright spots. As they passed the woman, he turned around to see her face.

She was horribly deformed. Her child had the same congenital defect.

Darkness and poverty weren't the only afflictions here! Quaid turned to Benny. 'Tell me something. Why are there so many . . . ?'

'Freaks?' Benny supplied helpfully. 'Cheap domes, man. And no air to screen out the rays.'

Oh. No doubt the material of the domes, when properly placed, screened out harmful solar radiation while admitting the good part of the light. But a cheap dome would simply let it all through. Mars was farther from the sun than Earth was, so the light was less intense, but it still had harmful components. On Earth the ozone layer served to filter out a lot. There had been trouble when man's carelessness had depleted that ozone, and nothing had been done about it until the skin-cancer rate quintupled. That finally got the attention of the politicians, and they started listening to the scientists who had been screaming warnings for decades, and put in motion programs to restore the ozone. It had been expensive, and had taken time, and the job was still being done, but the cancer rate was dropping. Here on Mars, it was evidently more than cancer; it was genetic damage. That was a tyranny that not even an enlightened social system could alleviate. It was inherent in the conditions of the planet.

If only there *could* be one simple, universal answer! One change that would solve all the problems of the powerless. But that was dreaming, and not sensibly.

The cab parked in front of The Last Resort. It was a seedy dive, even by the standards that obtained here.

'You sure you wanna go here, man? You're liable to catch a disease.'

A sensible caution! Quaid did not find the place very appetizing. Yet where was he to look, if not where the confusing message had hinted?

Maybe it made sense. If the wrong person got the envelope and saw the ad and came here, looking for the promised good time, he would get disgusted at this point and give it up. But the right person would not be dissuaded. So it was a good way to couch the message.

'I know a much better house down the street,' Benny offered. 'The girls are clean, the drinks aren't watered, and – '

'The boss gives kickbacks to the taxi drivers,' Quaid finished.

Benny turned around and pleaded guilty with a broad smile. He had a mouthful of bad teeth, including two gold caps, one with a crescent moon design, the other with a star. 'Hey, man, I got six kids to feed.'

Quaid handed him a large tip. 'Take 'em to the dentist.'

Benny got excited as he counted the money. Quaid opened his door and got out. By the time Benny looked up, he was walking away.

'Hey, man!' Benny called after him. 'I'll be waiting for you. Take your time. Benny's the name.'

Yes, he remembered. Quaid turned part way to wave the cabbie on, then entered The Last Resort. He hoped he wasn't making a bad mistake.

17

Melina

Quaid stopped just inside the door and cased the joint. It was evidently a low-class whorehouse for miners. Girls walked in and out, picking up clients and bringing them upstairs. The flyer had suggested no less – and no more.

He sat at the bar next to a couple of miners. The matter-of-fact bartender came over and waited for Quaid's order. The man was big enough and ugly enough to warrant prompt attention; he probably moonlighted as a bouncer.

'I'm looking for Melina,' Quaid said.

Immediate suspicion clouded the man's face. 'She's busy. But Mary's free.'

Mary, a sexy, well-built prostitute, appeared from nowhere and approached Quaid. 'Not free,' she purred. 'Available.'

He looked at her. He noticed that she had three full breasts, prominently displayed in a special bikini top. For any man who got his main kicks in that department, here was extra measure! But he remembered Lori, illusory though his marriage to her had turned out to be, and knew he would have been spoiled for this even if sex had been his object. 'Thanks. I'll wait.'

'Earth slime,' she said. It was the type of response he had expected.

Then she farted and oozed over to another potential customer. That Quaid hadn't expected. Maybe he hadn't had enough experience with this type of place.

He returned his attention to the bartender. This time he pressed a red banknote into the man's hand.

The bartender became less unfriendly. 'Thing is, pal, Mel's real picky. Kinda sticks to her regulars.'

If the woman could afford to be picky in a place like this, she had to be very special! 'Get her. She'll like me.'

With some trepidation, which Quaid noted with interest, the bartender called toward a table near the stairs. 'Hey, Mel.' There was a pause, as of someone ignoring the call. 'Melina.'

Quaid looked in the direction the bartender was calling. A woman sat at a table with some miners, laughing uproariously. She perched on the knee of a sullen, unshaven fellow, her back to the bar. One of the miners, facing the bar, saw the bartender trying to get Melina's attention. He signaled her, and she turned around.

Quaid was stunned. *She was the girl of his dreams!*

'She's with Tony,' the bartender murmured. 'Fair warning, mister: if you don't like to fight . . .'

'Some things are worth fighting for,' Quaid replied.

'Then take it outside. My employer values his furniture.'

Melina's laughter had faded abruptly and her face registered shock. Her eyes darted to those of the miner across the table, then returned to Quaid's. She made a decision. She rose from Tony's knee and sashayed over to the bar. Quaid stood, waiting for whatever came. He knew already that he had made an invaluable contact – but what was its nature? This woman resembled his dream-vision only in appearance. There was little dignity in the cheap, seductive smile she gave him as she crossed the room.

'Well, if it isn't the human hard-on,' Melina said. She stepped into him and gave him a wet and sloppy kiss. Then she ground against him, feeling his muscles under the shirt. 'Still bulging, I see.' She looked down. 'Ooo. Whatcha been feeding it?'

He realized that this was a public place, while anything between them was private. They couldn't say anything here – if there was anything to say. So he played along. 'Blondes.' Literally true; Lori was a blonde.

'I think it's still hungry.' She pulled him toward the stairs. As they passed the miners at the table, Tony stuck out his leg to block their way.

'Where do you think you're going?' Tony demanded.

'Relax, Tony,' Melina said. 'There'll be plenty left for you.'

Tony wasn't satisfied. He grabbed Melina's arm and pulled her onto his lap. 'I was here first!' He turned to Quaid. 'Take a number, pal.'

Quaid gripped Tony's wrist and leaned in close. 'This ain't a bakery.'

Tony looked as though he was ready to try the question.

'George,' Melina said with exasperation. 'Talk some sense into this ape.' The miner across the table sat back in his chair. He looked relaxed and confident.

'Ya got some place to go?' George said reasonably. 'Give the big guy a break.' Reluctantly, Tony let go of Melina's arm. Then Quaid let go of him.

'Knock yourself out,' Tony said gruffly.

Melina rose and resumed her progress toward the stairs. Quaid followed, keeping a wary eye on Tony and the rest of the room. If any agents appeared – He lost his train of thought as he looked in surprise at the woman coming down the stairs.

She was a midget. Her head came no higher than Quaid's waist and she was attired only in a push-up corset. She eyed Quaid with interest.

'Thumbelina, honey,' Melina said. 'Take care of Tony, will ya? He's got ants in his pants.'

The midget nodded, but kept her eyes on Quaid's pectorals. 'You need any help, holler,' she said with a suggestive smile.

In the upstairs hallway, Melina glanced back at him. Her seductive leer promised a good time ahead. She pulled open one of the doors that lined the hall and let him enter the room first.

Melina carefully pulled the door closed, turned to Quaid – and slapped him. 'You bastard!' she bit out. 'You're alive! I thought Cohaagen tortured you to death!'

'Excuse me,' Quaid said, taken aback.

Her tone of voice and bearing were completely different. The cheap whore had vanished with the closing of the door. This was suddenly an intelligent and motivated woman, who even in her rage carried herself with a certain dignity. Quaid didn't know what to make of this abrupt reversal.

'You couldn't pick up a goddamn telephone? You never wondered if *I* was all right? You weren't just a tiny bit curious?'

Quaid was at a loss for words. He liked this woman a thousand times as well as the one in the barroom, but he understood her no better than the other. He just looked at her innocently.

Melina's anger seemed to have been vented. The pressure was off now. She gazed at him, her expression changing again, her mood opaque.

Suddenly she flung her arms around him. She kissed him passionately. Quaid remained baffled, too surprised to cooperate very well.

'Oh, Hauser – thank God you're alive!' she cried. So she did know him! How else would she have known that name? He made a halfhearted effort to pull away from her embrace. He hadn't come for this, yet he did desire her.

'Melina . . . Melina . . .' Was that really her name? It seemed to fit, yet his memory did not leap. His heart pounding, he summoned the strength to push her away. 'Melina!'

She paused, flushed and panting. 'What?'

'There's something I have to tell you . . .'

She waited, curious. Quaid continued with difficulty. 'I don't remember you.' That was an over-simplification, but it would have to serve. His dream image was just that: an image, without substance. He didn't know this woman at all, any more than he knew Hauser. Had he really been out on the barren surface of Mars with her, exploring the Pyramid Mine?

Melina's breathing had returned to normal. She looked confused. 'What are you talking about?' she asked.

'I don't remember *you*. I don't remember *us*. I don't even remember *me*.'

Melina gave a short laugh, not really believing him. 'What, you suddenly got amnesia?' she said. 'How'd you get here?'

125

Now they could get down to business. 'Hauser left me a note.'

Melina obviously didn't take him quite seriously. 'Hauser? *You're* Hauser.'

'Not any more.' She looked at him with puzzlement. 'Now I'm Quaid. Douglas Quaid.'

A grin spread over Melina's face. 'Hauser, you've lost your mind.'

'I didn't lose it. Cohaagen stole it. He found out that Hauser switched sides, so he turned him into somebody else.' Quaid shrugged. '*Me.*'

Melina regarded him suspiciously. 'This is too weird.'

'Then he dumped me on Earth,' Quaid went on, 'with a wife and a lousy job and –'

'Did you say *wife*?' Her eyes flashed. 'Are you fuckin' *married*?'

Quaid realized that he'd put his foot in it and scrambled to cover his tracks. 'She wasn't really my wife,' he said lamely.

'Oh, how stupid of me.' Sarcasm dripped from her voice. 'She was *Hauser's* wife.'

'Look,' Quaid said hastily. 'Let's forget I said wife.'

'No!' Melina was furious. 'Let's forget everything! I've had it with you! I've had enough of your lies!'

'Why would I lie to you?' He was exasperated. He was so close to filling in the empty spaces in his memory and it looked as though he'd never get any closer.

Her voice became icy. 'Because you're still working for Cohaagen.'

'Don't be ridiculous,' he said shortly. It was a mistake. She practically spit in his face.

'You never loved me, Hauser! You used me to get inside.'

'Inside what?'

Now she was even more suspicious. 'I think you better go.' She got off the bed.

That was the last thing he wanted to do, and not just because of her sex appeal. 'Melina, Hauser needs me to do something.' He pointed to his head. 'He said there's enough in here to nail Cohaagen for good.'

126

'It won't work!' she snapped. 'I'm not falling for it this time.'

'Help me remember,' he said, standing.

He stepped forward, but she stepped back. 'I said get out!'

'Melina!' he pleaded. 'People are trying to kill me!'

She bent to reach under her mattress. Quaid found himself staring down the barrel of a huge automatic pistol she swiftly brought up. 'Really?'

He studied her steely eyes. There was no hope there.

Damn! This wasn't just a loss of information, it was personal. He had found the woman of his dream, and she hated him.

With a sense of deep loss, he backed out of the room. As he closed the door Melina gave up the struggle to hold back her tears. She had been a fool to believe that Hauser had ever loved her.

He had joined the rebel cause, proclaiming that he had seen the errors of his ways and wanted to help the poor people of Mars throw off the yoke of Cohaagen's oppression. She had doubted his sincerity from the start. Cohaagen must have had a very low opinion of the rebels to think that he could plant a spy among them so easily. She had never let Hauser come anywhere near Kuato.

She had spent a lot of time with Hauser, though, in her role as watchdog for the Resistance, and while her mind had retained its initial mistrust, her heart had eventually betrayed her. The man was intelligent, amusing, and magnetically attractive, and he had claimed to be in love with her. Before she could stop herself, she had found herself falling in love with him. She wept with anger at herself now. How could she have let it happen? A rebel, in love with an Agency spy? It was obscene.

When he had disappeared, she had tried to dismiss him from her mind and heart. She had tried to lump him in with all the other turncoats and weasels in Cohaagen's employ.

She had failed. When she had seen him in the bar, the old feelings had crowded in again. She knew he was trying to prey on those feelings. He was trying to use her again with his ridiculous story of amnesia and memory implants. It was an insult to her intelligence and she resented it, bitterly, but what could she do? She knew, deep in her heart, that she loved him still.

In the barroom, Benny had his hands all over Mary, who was fending him off expertly but without real conviction. 'I said I'm available, not free,' she reminded him.

'I'm not asking for freebies, honey,' he protested. 'It's more like a commission.'

Then he saw Quaid walking down the stairs, despondent. 'We'll pick this up later,' he promised.

He rushed to intercept Quaid by the door. 'Hey! That didn't take long.'

Quaid scowled at him and walked out.

Quaid stepped into the dense crowd in the plaza, taking pains to avoid the soldiers, who seemed to be everywhere. Benny scrambled to keep up.

'Ever make it with a mutant?' Benny asked.

'No.'

'I know these Siamese twins,' Benny said. 'Man, you won't know if you're comin' or goin'.'

'I'm not in the mood,' Quaid said. The thought poured salt on the wound. How great it could have been, *should* have been, with Melina! Yet how could he convince her of his feelings when he couldn't remember anything about their relationship?

Benny was still dogging his heels. 'How 'bout a psychic?' he said. 'You wanna get read by a psychic?'

Could she tell him how to make it up with Melina? Fat chance! 'Where's your cab?' Benny pointed across the street. Quaid sighed. 'Bring me to my hotel.'

Benny shrugged as they drove out of the dark slum and entered the bright, sunny tubeway. He had done his best.

Somehow the brightness didn't do a thing for Quaid's spirits.

18

Edgemar

Quaid relaxed cautiously in his room at the Hilton Hotel. It was tourist-room night, which was not the same as Mars night. The half-hour-added length of the Martian day might not seem like much of a problem to the workers here, but tourists fresh from Earth could get all out of synch. So each room could be set to whatever rhythm and particular time the occupant wanted. Quaid hadn't bothered to reset it from the time the prior occupant had left it. After all, he was a fresh tourist too. Thus it was night in here, while still late afternoon outside.

Cohaagen's minions still hadn't come after him. Had he truly given them the slip, or were they waiting till the time they thought he would be asleep? After their several unsuccessful attempts to kill him, they might have learned caution. More likely they just didn't want a big messy scene here in the tourist district of Mars. They might succeed in taking him out, but if it cost them a bad tourist season because travelers would be afraid of getting murdered in their hotel rooms, it wouldn't be worth it. So maybe he was safe, for the moment – and maybe he wasn't. He would take precautions when he slept, setting up a dummy in the bed while he slept elsewhere, just in case.

But his mind really wasn't on survival at the moment. It was on Melina. What should he have done to make it right with her? He was now assured that she was the woman of his dream, for a setup would have played along with him, pumping him for information while she had supposedly spontaneous sex with him, then signaling the goons to come. Instead she had thrown him out. That convinced him, painful as it was to take. So maybe he had played it right after all, because now he knew he could trust her – if only he could get her to trust him.

Well, he would sleep on it. Maybe he would dream again, and the dream would be of her, and show him how to approach her. Meanwhile he would try to relax. He had eaten, perhaps foolishly: he had loaded up on more Mars candy bars, and a package of vitamins, just to keep things balanced. It wasn't that he was a freak for candy, but it made him feel closer to Hauser, and he hoped that he could get close enough to remember something vital. He wasn't any more of a psychologist than he was of a social worker, but it seemed to him that the more he immersed himself in the things associated with Hauser, the more likely he was to trigger some additional insight into the man. Such an insight could save his life, or give it more meaning.

He turned on the video. The room didn't sport a wall-sized screen, as Mars didn't have much of a consumer industry, but it was possible to adapt to the smaller set.

An in-house documentary about – what else? – Mars came on. There were boring images of black rocks in the red desert. The same sort of scene had fascinated him earlier in the day, but now that he had blown it with Melina, anything that didn't look like her was dull.

'The first evidence of an alien presence on Mars was not uncovered until forty years after the first manned expedition,' the narrator said, off-camera. 'When glazed sand provided proof of visitations by nonhuman travelers.'

Quaid lay on his bed in the dark hotel room, bathed in the pale blue glare of the screen and the pale red glare from the skylight. This should really interest him, he knew, but the image of Melina's angry face pretty much blotted it out. With her by his side, eveything about Mars was wonderful; without her, the allure was gone.

He changed the channel. The face of Vilos Cohaagen filled the screen and Quaid sat up to watch more closely. Cohaagen was delivering a speech from his office.

'Tonight, at 6.30 P.M., I signed an order declaring martial law throughout the Mars Federal Colony. I will not tolerate any further damage to our mineral export operations. Mr Kuato and his terrorists must understand that their self-defeating efforts will only bring misery . . .'

Quaid regarded the face of his enemy. Why was Cohaagen declaring martial law? What was the point? With the power of Administrator and with the Agency at his fingertips, it seemed ridiculously redundant. But that was the way of politicians. As long as things *appeared* to be aboveboard, they could continue with all the dirty work they pleased below decks.

The news report changed. Here was something else they never mentioned to earthlings considering emigration to Mars.

The scene was of an airlock in which four shackled prisoners were standing. The air was being slowly let out of it. It was evident that the prisoners knew this, and were helpless.

'Francis Aquado, defacing public property,' the announcer said. 'Judith Redensek and Jeannette Wyle, resisting arrest. Thomas Zachary, treason.'

The depressurization continued. The prisoners gasped, suffocating. Their mucous membranes bled. Their eyes bulged. The camera focused on each in turn, the close-ups showing all the detail a sadist could desire. This was obviously death by torture. Not only was it evidently standard, here, it was so firmly established that it was done openly, televised for a mass audience. That said something ugly about the nature of the audience. On Earth, at least, the dirt was usually swept under the carpet.

The screen went dark. He had turned it off involuntarily. He held his lead, lost.

If the penalty for defacing public property on Mars was an agonizing death, that meant that anyone who made graffiti was doomed if caught. If an innocent person was arrested on a trumped-up charge and resisted, that resistance became grounds for execution. Treason might be no more than stating an objection to such policies. He was already guilty of them all! He hated Cohaagen, and he had in effect defaced public property when he resisted arrest, because he would be blamed for the broken spaceport window. There was no doubt he was guilty of treason, because already he condemned the government of Mars. If there ever appeared before him a magical button labeled ABOLISH MARS GOVERNMENT, he would push that button in an instant. But the chances were that the Mars government would catch him first and push the button marked ABOLISH HAUSER/QUAID.

Yet there was supposed to be a secret locked in his head that could blow it all wide open. If he could just remember it!

He was startled by a knock at the door. He froze, on the alert. Would the goons knock?

The knocking was repeated. 'Mr Quaid . . .'

He hesitated, then decided to answer. After all, the goons would probably just have broken in, or fired bullets through the door. 'Yes?'

'I need to talk to you – about Mr Hauser.'

Quaid had used neither name at this hotel. He was registered under the name of Brubaker. That meant that this was no routine caller. The voice seemed familiar, though, and Quaid squinted with the effort of trying to place it. It was no good.

He couldn't take a chance. He got out his gun and cocked it. The first thing he had done, once he got private, was to assemble it from the various segments stashed in his pockets, which had in turn been assembled from the various items of apparel that its components seemed to be. He approached the door very carefully, from the side. 'Who are you?' he demanded.

'Dr Edgemar,' the muffled voice came. 'I work for Rekall, Incorporated.

'It's difficult to explain,' Edgemar said. 'Could you open the door, please? I'm not armed.'

Quaid opened the door, carefully, ready to shoot. An unthreatening intellectual in a tweed jacket stood there. Seeing him, Quaid finally knew where he had heard the voice before. It was the narrator from the Rekall commercial he'd seen on the subway, back on Earth. The commercial that had triggered this whole chain of events.

Quaid trained the gun on the man and glanced down the hall.

'Don't worry,' Edgemar said. 'I'm alone. May I come in?'

Quaid pulled the man roughly into the hotel room and closed the door. He frisked Edgemar, but found no weapon.

'This is going to be very difficult for you to accept, Mr Quaid.'

'I'm listening,' Quaid said tersely.

'I'm afraid you're not really standing here right now.'

Quaid could not repress a chuckle, though he was tense. 'You know, Doc, you could have fooled me.' Which might be exactly what the man was doing! So far he had mentioned neither Cohaagen nor Melina – and Quaid would not be able to trust him anyway. He could claim to be from Melina, to lull Quaid and get him to go along peaceably into the trap Cohaagen had set. But this ploy was interesting, even in this nervous situation. What could Cohaagen stand to gain by convincing Quaid that he was somewhere else? It would be easier to *send* him somewhere else – such as to hell, riding on a bullet through the brain.

'As I was saying, you're not really here,' the man insisted. 'And neither am I.'

Some delusion, if the doctor shared it with the patient! Quaid squeezed Edgemar's shoulder with his free hand, verifying its solidity. 'Amazing. Where are we?'

'At Rekall.'

Quaid's cockiness wavered. Could this be making sense? He had gone to Rekall, and suffered severe disorientation. In fact, his world had collapsed, making him a hunted fugitive.

'You're strapped into an implant chair,' Edgemar continued. 'And I'm monitoring you at a psycho-probe console.'

'I get it – I'm dreaming!' Quaid said sarcastically. 'And this is all part of that delightful vacation your company sold me.' Only no prepackaged dream would have included that scene with Melina, where instead of fulfillment he had received a painful setback. Only reality did that kind of thing to a man!

'Not exactly,' Edgemar said, not bothered by Quaid's attitude. Doctors learned early not to be moved by their patients' reactions. 'What you're experiencing is a free-form delusion *based* on our memory tapes. But you're inventing it yourself.'

That made Quaid pause. Suppose the tape had Melina scheduled as a joyful reunion, but his cynical mind was not able to settle for that? So his suspicion became *her* suspicion, in the dream, and she rejected him? He had heard that a person's mind could do that; it was called transference, or something. He could have ruined it himself!

Still, he didn't buy it. 'Well, if this is *my* delusion, who invited you?'

'I've been artificially implanted as an emergency measure,' Edgemar said without hesitation. Then, gravely: 'I'm sorry to tell you this, Mr Quaid, but you're experiencing a schizoid embolism. We can't snap you out of your fantasy. I've been sent in to try to talk you down to reality.'

'And "reality" is that I'm not really here?' Quaid asked.

'Think about it, Mr Quaid. Your dream started in the middle of the implant procedure. Everything after that – the fights, the trip to Mars in a first-class cabin, your suite at the Hilton – these are all part of your Rekall package.'

'Complete and utter bullshit!' Quaid said, beginning to fear that it was not.

'What about the girl?' Edgemar asked evenly. 'Brunette, buxom, wanton *and* demure, just as you specified. Is that "bullshit"?'

'She's real,' Quaid said. 'I dreamed about her before I ever went to Rekall.'

'Mr Quaid, can you hear yourself?' Edgemar asked persuasively. 'She's real because you dreamed her?'

'That's right.' And indeed, he believed it, not expecting the doctor to understand.

Edgemar sighed, discouraged. 'Perhaps this will convince you. Would you mind opening the door?'

Quaid jabbed his gun into Edgemar's ribs. '*You* open it.'

'No need to be rude.' The man straightened his shoulders and walked to the door. Quaid shadowed him, ready for anything as the man opened the door.

Anything except what he saw.

Lori stood on the threshold!

Quaid did his best to absorb this extra shock. Lori was beautiful, in exactly the kind of wanton and demure outfit he liked, showing more breast than she seemed to be conscious of, her face evincing a trace of color where he had hit her with the gun, by the eye. He was abruptly sorry about that; he had never hit her before.

Lori put on a brave face, almost like holding back tears in front of a sick child. There was not the slightest indication that she had ever been anything other than Quaid's adoring wife. 'Sweetheart . . .'

But she had blasted away at him with the gun! She had tried to knock him out, and to kill him with a kitchen knife. His scratches from those slices were still healing. She had become seductive only to distract him while she watched Richter and Helm approach on the monitor. She had told him how their entire relationship had been implanted, except for the past six weeks. Sweetheart?

God help him, he wanted to believe her! If this was a dream, then her attack on him had never occurred, and she really was his adoring woman.

'Please come in, Mrs Quaid,' Edgemar said.

Hesitantly, Lori entered the room. Her hips still moved in that way that used to drive him crazy. And still did. He might not love her, but he sure as hell didn't hate her either!

Then why would he have cast her as such a villain in his dream? To make a pretext to get rid of her so he could go after his Mars woman? That made ugly sense. A crazed mind – he could not afford to do that in reality!

Neither could he afford to trust her! Quaid pulled Lori to him and roughly frisked her. Even in this he hurt, because his traveling hands verified just how good her body was. He had caressed that body so many times, and had had such delight in it. How could he doubt her now?

'I suppose you're not here either,' he said gruffly. He was coming across to himself as boorish, but what choice did he have? One mistake meant disaster.

'I'm here at Rekall,' she said.

Quaid laughed and pushed her away. But he was hurting inside. If only she would break, and curse him, and say she hated him! Then he would feel justified in treating her like this, whether this scene was dream or real.

'Doug, I love you,' Lori said, her large eyes moist.

'Right. That's why you tried to kill me!' He had to maintain the pose, covering his awful doubt.

'Nooo!' she protested, breaking into tears. 'I would never do *anything* to hurt you. I love you. I want you to come back to me.' Her despair was heartbreaking.

'Unbelievable,' he muttered. But his certainty was shaken. It would be so easy to take her in his arms . . .

'What's unbelievable, Mr Quaid?' Edgemar asked. He assumed a reasonable tone. 'That you're having a paranoid episode triggered by acute neurological trauma? Or –' Now his voice was derisive. 'That you're really an invincible secret agent from Mars who's the victim of an interplanetary conspiracy to make him think he's a lowly construction worker?'

Quaid's certainty, such as it was, was being further undermined. The recent events he had experienced certainly did seem nonsensical now! The things that didn't make much sense – how better to explain them than as the product of a slightly deranged dreaming mind?

Edgemar looked at him with great sympathy and kindness. 'Doug, how many of us are heroes? You're a fine, upstanding man. You have a beautiful wife who loves you.'

Lori beamed at Quaid with pure affection.

'You have a secure job with a bright future,' Edgemar continued. 'Your life is ahead of you, Doug.' He frowned benignly. 'But you've got to *want* to return to reality.'

It did seem to fit together. Quaid was almost convinced. Certainly he had wanted to be an adventurous hero, but this adventure had pretty well turned him off that sort of thing. He had wanted a beautiful woman, and in fact Lori was that. So her hair wasn't dark – was that cause to throw her away? Considering the way Melina had treated him . . .

'What do I do?' he asked.

Edgemar opened his hand, revealing a small pill. 'Take this pill.'

'What is it?' Quaid was not so dull as to miss the fact that an imagined pill could not do anything the imagination couldn't.

'It's a symbol. A symbol of your desire to return to reality,' Edgemar explained. 'Inside your dream, you'll fall asleep.'

And wake up in reality? That had happened before, when he had fallen down the alien tube on Mars and woken in bed with Lori. That had its appeal! He picked up the pill and contemplated it. He could appreciate the rationale: in life a person took a pill to get well. In a dream he took one to *want* to get well. The effect could be similar.

'You should know, Mr Quaid, that Rekall will provide you with free counseling for as long as you need it. In addition, if you sign a release, we'll agree to a large cash settlement.'

'How much?' The question was automatic, though he hardly cared. The larger question was whether he wanted the reality he had known on Earth or a continuation of this crazy-quilt adventure on Mars. The answer should have been obvious, but the memory of Melina, and the hint of something else, something so important that –

'A hundred thousand credits. Maybe more.'

Lori brightened, becoming hopeful. 'Think about it, Doug. We could buy a house.'

Instead of the conapt on the two hundredth floor. That, too, had its appeal. Maybe a vacation in an undersea dome.

'Of course,' Edgemar said, 'this all hinges on your taking the pill.'

On the verge of succumbing to their logic, Quaid grew suspicious again. Why should it all hinge on his taking the pill? Why couldn't he merely declare, 'I'm through with dreaming! I want to return to reality and Lori!' and be there? On rare occasions he had had what he thought was called lucid dreaming, where he came to realize that it was a dream, and could control it somewhat. Generally when that happened, though, the dream lost its substance and he woke. So instead of hauling in a lucid sexpot, he woke with a hard-on and nowhere to put it. That had been back when he was a teenager, before Lori. Still, the principle was there: if he couldn't break out of the dream without the symbol, why should it work *with* the symbol? Why were they so eager for that symbol?

'Let's say you're right.' Quaid said. 'This is all a dream.' He raised the gun to Edgemar's head. 'Then I can pull this trigger, and it won't matter.'

He started to pull the trigger. Here was a test that meant something. If this was not a dream, Edgemar would be exceedingly eager to avoid this test!

'Doug, don't!' Lori cried.

But Edgemar remained preternaturally calm. His eyes and voice expressed his unselfish concern for his patient. 'It won't make the slightest difference to me, Doug, but the consequences to you would be devastating. In your mind, I'll be dead. And with no one to guide you out, you'll be stuck in permanent psychosis.'

Was it possible? Psychosis was a disease of the mind. Could his own act determine which way his mind went? Would shooting Edgemar be his decision to avoid reality, rather than any tangible act to embrace it, such as taking the pill?

'Doug, please let Dr Edgemar help you!' Lori pleaded.

His finger on the trigger, Quaid was torn with doubt. He knew he could do it, and splatter the doctor's brains. But did he *want* to? If that meant that he was locking himself into a dream of violence and uncertainty and frustrated love?

'The walls of reality will come crashing down,' Edgemar said. 'One minute you'll be the savior of the rebel cause, then, next thing you know, you'll be Cohaagen's bosom buddy. Until finally, back on Earth, you'll be lobotomized.'

Quaid was totally demoralized. It had to be true: if he really was in a semicoma back on Earth and could not be brought out of it, they would lobotomize him. There was no point in maintaining a vegetable. It was uneconomic. A lobotomized man might not be very creative, but he could handle a jackhammer. So he had better guess right; it was disaster to go with illusion, either way.

'So get a firm grip on yourself, Doug,' Edgemar said firmly. 'And put down the gun.'

Hesitantly, Quaid lowered the gun. If this was a dream, and he shot someone, he would die (or be lobotomized: same thing) instead of the other person.

'That's right. Now take the pill, there you go . . .' Edgemar paused as Quaid's hand slowly took the pill. 'And put it in your mouth.'

Quaid put the pill in his mouth. It tasted exactly like a pill. But of course it would, in a dream as well as in reality.

'And swallow,' Edgemar continued, as if talking a blinded pilot down to a landing.

Quaid hesitated. Edgemar and Lori watched with great anticipation.

'Go ahead, Doug.' Lori said.

But he was racked with indecision. Suppose this *wasn't* a dream? Then the pill might be – in fact, probably was – a knockout dose, or even lethal.

Then he saw a single drop of sweat trickle down Edgemar's brow.

His Hauser-reflex took over. Abruptly he swung his gun at Edgemar and fired.

The plastic explosive in the plastic gun sent the plastic bullet straight through the man's head. Blood splattered in a dense circle on the wall.

Then the bloodstain exploded, blasting Quaid backward through the air. A big hole appeared in the wall. He had guessed wrong! His dream world was crashing down, exactly as Dr Edgemar had said it would!

Then he struck the far wall and sank to the floor, dazed. Four Mars agents stormed through the hole in the wall and grabbed hold of him.

But this wasn't the end of the dream! This was the confirmation of the Mars reality! They had not attacked him before because they were trying to catch him alive, to find out what he knew. When the pill didn't do it, they burst in to grab him physically. It was perfect sense!

Reassured, he started to fight back. They were trying to handcuff him, but he elbowed a jaw, dislocated a shoulder, and shoved and kicked his way out of their grasp. He pulled clear of an agent who was holding his foot. They weren't using guns, they were trying to wrestle him down!

Hands touching the floor for balance, he staggered toward the door. He was about to get away, and to hell with the dream!

But there was someone before him. He looked up. Lori blocked his path. Oh, okay. He started to move again – and her foot smashed his face.

He staggered, hurt more by her antipathy than by the blow. He didn't want to strike her again! It had been bad enough back on Earth.

He had paused only momentarily, but that gave the others time to grab him and restrain him. He tensed, ready to heave the ones on his arms into each other, headfirst.

Then Lori kicked him in the testicles, and the planet went up in pain. He stopped resisting; there was nothing but the agony, and her treachery. She had said she loved him!

As if from a distance, somewhere beyond the radius of pain, he heard her talking. 'That's for making me come to Mars. You know how much I hate this fucking planet!'

No, he didn't. He had thought it was just a pose to discourage him from wanting to go there. Evidently not everything about her had been an act.

The agents cuffed his hands behind his back. He was helpless. Then Lori kneed him in the face, knocking away most of the rest of his consciousness.

Vaguely, he felt himself being dragged to the door. Lori had done him one favor at least. She had finally convinced him of her true feelings toward him. He would never again be deceived by her. Not that he was likely to get the chance. His consciousness faded out.

Lori spoke into a wireless videophone.

'I've got him,' she said, smiling as Richter's face appeared on the screen.

'Bring him down,' said Richter.

Lori puckered her lips in a silent kiss. 'Ciao.' The transmission ended.

19
Escape

Outside the Hilton Hotel, Richter and Helm waited in a
car. Richter clenched his fist with satisfaction. He'd rather
have killed the man, but at least Lori had been able to take
him alive, satisfying Cohaagen's order.

'Take the service elevator,' Richter said. 'We'll meet
you.' Already Helm was piling out of the car. Richter
followed him, and they ran inside the hotel.

Quaid came blurrily awake. He was being dragged to a
service elevator. Two guests and a bellboy with a luggage
cart stood to the side, not interfering. He must have been
out only a few seconds – just long enough for his balls to
settle down to a bearable level of agony.

They propped him up while waiting for the elevator. He
stared at the floor, offering no resistance, just trying to get
more of his consciousness back. His eyes focused on
something nice. After a moment he realized that it was
Lori's legs. Too bad her heart didn't match the quality of
her body!

He also noticed that she wore an ankle sheath, with a
knife. There was no doubt now that she was a pro! How
could he ever have been fooled by her?

The elevator doors slid open. There was a burst of
gunfire.

Huh? Had they shot him after all? He didn't feel
anything.

Then the agent in front of him fell. The man's face was a
study in surprise. Quaid hadn't been killed – the agent had.
What was going on?

Then a woman ran out of the elevator. She had legs as
good as Lori's and a fuller bosom, and long dark hair.

Then, as his gaze made it to the face, he was amazed. It was Melina!

Melina whirled, her gun blazing. In a moment she had mowed down the remaining three male agents, whose hands were occupied with Quaid. She managed to miss Quaid himself. Either he was lucky, or she was an excellent shot.

Lori dropped to the floor, swung her legs, and swiped Melina's feet out from under her. The gun went flying. Lori grabbed Melina's hair and yanked back so hard she almost broke the woman's neck. She wound Melina's hair around her fist, anchoring the head, and smashed her face into the wall. Once. Twice. Three times. Melina stopped fighting. Quaid knew the feeling, having just experienced it himself.

He squirmed over the pile of agent corpses. His hands locked behind his back, he wrested a gun from a dead hand. The agents had guns, they just hadn't been using them on Quaid. This time.

Lori pulled her knife from the ankle sheath. She lifted it high, preparing to plunge it into Melina's heart. But she paused a moment.

Melina's eyes came into focus. She saw the blade poised above her.

That was what Lori had been waiting for. She evidently knew who Melina was: his dream-girl. She wanted Melina to see it coming. Maybe she also wanted Quaid to see her do it. She was out to hurt him any way she could, and she had found the perfect way.

'*Don't!*' Quaid cried. He wasn't pleading, he was warning.

Lori turned and saw that he had her in the sights of his pistol. But she also saw that he was contorted, with his hands cuffed behind his back. Could he fire accurately from that position?

Lori's manner changed, in the chameleonlike way she had. She evidently knew the answer to the question of his accuracy! 'Doug . . .' she breathed. 'You wouldn't hurt me, would you?'

He kept the gun aimed at her.

Lori lowered her knife and brought her hands together innocuously. 'Be reasonable, sweetheart. We're married.'

Yes, so it had seemed, once. But he knew better now. Much better. His gun did not waver.

Lori subtly pulled the knife into the throwing position, holding the tip of the blade. He had no doubt of her ability to hurl it exactly where she intended. He had become her primary target.

'Consider this a divorce,' he said gruffly.

Lori swung her arm back for throwing.

Quaid fired. The bullet struck her in the forehead. The knife dropped from her hand. Then Lori dropped.

He might have let her go, even after her attempt to kill Melina. He hated to kill women. But she had proved her nature right to the end. She was all agent, as brutal as any of the goons, and more dangerous than most. It had had to be done.

Melina sat up, battered and shaken. She had evidently not expected to be bested in combat by another woman. 'That was your wife?'

Quaid nodded. He had done it, and knew it was justified, but it still made him sick. Obviously Lori not only had not loved him, she hadn't even liked him. He had not loved her, but he *had* liked her. He had killed her with a far heavier heart than she would have had if she had killed him.

'What a bitch,' Melina said.

That pretty well summed it up. Eight years – or six weeks' worth of it – had been wrenched from his experience. It hurt.

Richter pounded impatiently on the service elevator call button. It finally arrived. He and Helm stepped inside. He remained sorry that Hauser hadn't made a break for it, so that there would be an excuse to kill him – in the line of duty.

Melina crawled painfully over to Lori and searched her pockets.

Quaid watched her. 'Drop by on your coffee break?' he asked sarcastically. 'Time off from work?'

144

'*This* is my work,' she replied.

'And The Last Resort, that's your hobby.' He knew he was being peevish, but he was sick of being left in the dark.

'That's my cover,' she said. She continued her search.

She was a professional, just as Lori had been. She did whatever she needed to do to protect her true mission. He could relate to that. 'I thought you didn't like me.'

'I didn't,' Melina said shortly. She found the key to the handcuffs and unlocked them.

'What changed your mind?' he asked, as if this were a conversation instead of a desperate escape.

'If Cohaagen wants you dead, you might be okay.'

Actually, Cohaagen seemed to have been trying to take him alive this time; the agents could have plugged him anytime, through that wall, but instead waited on the little scene with Edgemar and Lori. He refrained from clarifying that, however. Melina's reasoning was similar to his reasoning about her: if she refused to deal with him as long as she had any doubt about the nature of his loyalty, she was probably okay. Lori had been the opposite, and not just in the color of her hair. Sometimes it was necessary to see who a person's enemies were before deciding whether that person was a friend.

'So you dropped by to apologize?' he asked.

'Kuato wants to see you. Come on!' She pulled him to his feet and they tore down the corridor.

Richter and Helm ran out of the service elevator. Richter pulled up short at the sight of the bullet hole in Lori's forehead. The blood drained from his face as he was hit by a wave of disbelief and rage. The last time he had seen her, she had been so warm, so alive, and now . . .

No, he thought. *Not Lori. Not my Lori!* She had been the best thing that ever happened to him. Smart, beautiful and great in bed. He could not bear the thought of never holding her again, never seeing her smile, never hearing her sultry voice.

He was filled with a mind-numbing anguish that was quickly replaced by white-hot fury. Hauser had done this. That murdering, traitorous scum! Richter would avenge

Lori's death if it was the last thing he did. He'd rip the bastard's head off, he'd . . .

Helm touched his shoulder and pointed. Richter saw Quaid and Melina running down the hall. With an incoherent bellow, Richter opened fire, charging after them. Bullets whizzed past Quaid's ears.

Damn! He had feared there would be more goons erupting from the elevator, so that a gun battle would wipe him and Melina out even if they got Richter and Helm. But it seemed there were just the two men. Now any hesitation, any attempt to get into position to fire accurately, would put them at a fatal disadvantage. They had to keep running.

They came to an EXIT door. Melina pulled at it. It refused to open. 'Shit!' she exclaimed.

They kept running, having no alternative at the moment. They headed toward the big window at the end of the corridor. Outside the window there was only the red sky and geodesic framework, with no indication of any surface to stand on.

'Now what?' Quaid asked, seeing the dead end coming.

'Jump!' she replied succinctly.

Had he been in better command of his wits, he might have balked, but he remained a bit unbalanced from the knockout. Maybe it was the same with her. Well, if he was going to take a fall, she was the one he wanted to do it with! He remembered the dream –

They leaped together – and crashed through the window. They sailed through the air, and fell, and parts of Quaid's life passed before his eyes, and he gained a new understanding of what was buried in his mind. It *did* relate to the welfare of mankind!

Then he looked down and saw the rooftop just six feet below. Melina had known of it, obviously. The hotel was a series of terraces built right up next to the dome.

They landed, bounced, scrambled to their feet, and resumed their running. Richter and Helm appeared at the broken window and fired down at them. Then Quaid and Melina dashed out of range around a corner.

Quaid heard the crash as Richter and Helm jumped down to follow. This chase wasn't over yet!

146

They ran from roof to roof, dodging to stay out of the line of fire. Fortunately, their pursuers couldn't fire accurately while running, so were wasting shots.

But soon they found themselves boxed in, as they had been in the hotel, except that this time it was drop-offs that surrounded them, not walls. Where now?

Melina ran full speed toward the edge. Quaid followed with dismay. 'Again?'

Evidently so. He hoped she still knew where she was going. Then he saw the dome ahead. He tucked the gun into his waistband. He was sorry he hadn't been able to keep the plastic gun he had worked so hard to bring; it was a superior weapon.

They reached the edge of the rooftop, leaped, and grabbed onto the scaffolding of the geodesic dome. Again they had found an escape!

As he clung to a beam, Quaid glanced back. He saw Richter and Helm arrive at the edge of the roof. Richter raised his gun to shoot, but Helm smashed his arm down in time for the bullet to discharge into the floor.

'You trying to kill us?' Helm screamed.

Furious, Richter clouted Helm in the head and tried for another shot. Helm struggled fiercely with his much larger boss. 'You'll crack the fucking dome!' he shouted as he pummeled Richter.

True enough, thought Quaid, remembering the scene at the spaceport. A bullet could do it as readily as an explosive mask. The man was a shoot-first fool, as likely to kill an innocent party as the one he was after. But he must have come to his senses because the shot never came.

'By the way,' Quaid gasped as if they were doing this for fun. 'Ever hear of a company called Rekall?'

'I used to model for them. Why?'

'Just wondering.' Things were falling into place in his mind, even as they were coming apart in other ways.

Quaid followed Melina as she athletically edged along beams, slid down pipes, and swung from strut to strut. She might look like a woman of leisure, but now she was an acrobat!

But his contortions dislodged the gun at his waistband. Quaid couldn't catch it: with regret he watched it fall. Melina had either ditched hers on the roof or lost it similarly. Now they had no way to fire back.

Meanwhile Richter and Helm were climbing down the side of the hotel, a much easier and shorter task. They were gaining.

Quaid and Melina dropped to the ground next to a solid wall. Richter and Helm landed almost simultaneously. They ran forward, shooting.

Quaid looked around and saw nowhere to hide. He searched frantically for his dropped pistol, but it was lost amid the materials at the base of the dome, and there was no time to get it anyway. Things looked bad for the home team!

Richter slowed to a walk as he came within range. He leveled his gun, taking more careful aim. He was grinning. *He* intended to take no prisoners!

Then a car screeched around a corner, cutting off Richter and Helm. It stopped in front of Quaid and Melina.

It was Benny, the jivester cabbie! 'Need a ride?' he said.

They dived into the cab, tumbling over each other as Benny gunned it and fishtailed away.

'The Last Resort!' Melina gasped. 'Quick!'

Richter fired from the curb and the rear window shattered. Quaid pulled Melina down low to avoid the flying glass.

'Jesus!' Benny yelled. 'Ya'll in trouble?' He put the accelerator to the floor.

Behind them, Richter and Helm clambered into their car and peeled out into traffic, guns blazing.

Benny swerved into the main tunnel. 'Whatcha doin' to me, man! I got six kids to feed!'

Benny made a sharp left into a tubeway that led across the chasm. The motion flung Quaid and Melina together. He wished they could do it deliberately! As it was, he disengaged carefully, not wanting to set off any misunderstandings.

The pavement of this tubeway was not quite even. As the car passed from segment to segment at high speed, lights flashed and the tires made rhythmic sounds. *Calumph,*

calumph, calumph, transmitted through the chassis. The effect was oddly soothing.

The rear window shattered. Quaid and Melina ducked down, almost banging heads.

'You got a gun, Benny?' Quaid asked.

'Under the seat, man.'

Quaid fished under the front passenger seat and found a gun mounted in a concealed sheath. He pulled it out and checked it. It was a pro special, loaded. This cabbie knew how to protect himself when he had to!

He looked back. Richter was leaning out of his car. There was a muzzle flash. Benny's rearview mirror was blown off. Richter was getting better!

Quaid leaned out a window and fired back, carefully. The shot went true; Richter's windshield shattered.

The car swerved, but did not go out of control. That meant he hadn't hit the driver. Too bad. He saw a hand with a gun scraping the glass beads away. Then the fire resumed, from inside the car.

All he had accomplished was to make it easier for Richter to shoot at them! Indeed, it looked as if the man was bringing out heavier artillery. What did he have?

Richter fired. A fender was blasted off the cab. He fired again. Another window went. That was a heavy-duty piece, all right!

Quaid fired back, but his gun now seemed inadequate. Both men in the pursuing car were hunkered down, so he couldn't get a clear shot, and unless he scored on one of them, he wouldn't accomplish much. There seemed to be metallic shields guarding the front tires, so the car wasn't vulnerable to much more damage by his gun. That cannon of Richter's, however –

Richter fired again. This time the roof was blasted off the cab.

'Fuck!' Benny exclaimed. 'The cab ain't even paid for!'

There was worse coming. Benny's tire was blasted as they went through a curve. The cab went out of control and flipped over, sliding to a stop in the Venusville Plaza.

Quaid was hardly aware of what he did; probably his

Hauser-aspect had taken over again, as it did in utter crisis. He found himself holding Melina, wrapped around her as much as possible, protecting her from the crash.

Before the motion stopped, he acted. 'Out!' he snapped. They scrambled under the hanging seats and out through the broken windshield. 'Move! Move!' he urged, lurching to his feet and hauling Benny and Melina out.

'Aw, Christ,' Benny groaned. 'Now they're after *me*!'

The three of them started off at a run, barely in time. Richter's car zoomed out of the blind curve and screeched to a halt. He and Helm emerged, saturating the wreck with gunfire.

20
Kuato

The sound of gunfire must have alerted the bartender at The Last Resort. He held the door open as Melina, Quaid, and Benny dashed up and he slammed it shut behind them as they spilled inside. Quaid pulled up short, momentarily confused at the scene that greeted him.

Tony and the other miners had lifted their table and, with it, a piece of the floor. A hole gaped beneath. Was this an escape route of some kind?

Melina knew exactly what it was. She climbed into the hole and disappeared into the darkness. Benny followed, throwing terrified glances over his shoulder. Quaid snapped out of his stasis and quickly lowered himself into the hole.

The miners replaced the table and resumed their game of poker just as Richter, Helm, and six soldiers charged into the bar, loaded for bear.

The car players looked at the armed men with mild curiosity. The scene was as quiet and peaceful as a bridge club on a slow Thursday afternoon, but Richter was not to be fooled. He knew that these subhuman creatures were protecting the man who had killed Lori and, by that action, they had forfeited their right to live. He didn't care how many of them he had to kill in order to get the information he needed.

He grabbed Mary and held his gun to her head. It was the same gun that had taken the roof off Benny's cab. 'Where'd they go?' he demanded.

'Who? I don't know wha–' Mary's head was blown from her shoulders. Richter threw her body aside and grabbed Thumbelina.

'Maybe *you* know,' he suggested, his voice cold with menace.

Before she could respond, Tony leaped in a flying tackle and knocked Richter to the floor. As Helm ran forward to take aim at Tony, Thumbelina reached up, gutting him from crutch to sternum with a bowie knife.

It was like setting a match to a keg of powder. The rest of the miners exploded into action, attacking the soldiers with fists, knives, guns, bottles, and beer mugs. By the time Richter struggled free of Tony's grip, he saw that half of his men had been wiped out.

He dived through the window, guns firing after him. A large number of soldiers had assembled at the sound of gunfire and they covered his retreat with a hail of bullets.

Scuttling behind a barricade of car wrecks and overflowing dumpsters, Richter made it to where a military vehicle had pulled up to disgorge more soldiers. Bullets whizzed by his ears as he dodged, feinted, and rolled his way toward the truck. It had a rocket launcher. Richter's eyes gleamed. That would do the trick.

'You! Over here!' he commanded. He directed the launcher setup and was about to give the order to fire, when a soldier handed him a field videophone.

'Cohaagen,' the soldier said.

Richter gnashed his teeth as he took the call. 'Sir . . .' he began, but Cohaagen interrupted him.

'Stop fighting and pull out.'

No, no, no, this couldn't be happening. 'They're protecting Quaid!' Richter protested, his voice cracking with anger and astonishment.

'Perfect!' said Cohaagen. 'Get out of Sector G. Now.' Before Richter could respond, Cohaagen added: *'Don't think.* Do it.'

Richter saw the look in Cohaagen's eye and choked back a retort. Cohaagen had something up his sleeve. Richter didn't know what it was, but he knew it would be worse than anything the rocket launcher could propel. He followed orders.

Quaid dropped from the shaft into a tunnel and followed Melina and Benny. The tunnel appeared to be one artery of the vast mining complex that spread beneath the city in all directions. His suspicion was confirmed as he ran past miners chipping away at the rock walls with drill hammers. The miners ignored him. They seemed to be used to such sights.

The tunnel branched off into several others at an intersection on the far side of Venusville. Melina paused there for a brief moment to catch her breath, and almost stopped breathing altogether when a mechanical shudder shook the ground beneath their feet.

'My God,' she said, aghast. 'The emergency pressure doors! They're sealing us off from the rest of the city!'

No sooner had she spoken than – SQURRCHANG! A featureless metal door descended from the ceiling, closing the entrance to one of the tunnels in front of them. They rushed to the next one – too late!

Only one tunnel remained open. With the speed of desperation, they crouched, rolled, and dived under the last door just before it slammed into place. They'd made it!

The rebel survivors of the battle of The Last Resort peered cautiously through the jagged shards of glass that protruded from the bar's shattered window frames. The soldiers had ceased firing a short time ago and now they appeared to be packing up and beating an orderly retreat. The rebels didn't know what to make of it.

As the soldiers disappeared from view, the people of Venusville began emerging from whatever hole they'd hidden in during the battle. They spoke softly. Some looked dazed. Others looked suspicious. They were startled when the pressure doors clanged into place and no one knew what to expect next. A crowd gathered in the plaza, but it was strangely hushed. Then it got even quieter.

The giant fans which circulated air through the sector slowed and came to a stop. The silence was absolute. Every face filled with dread. Then . . .

The fans started turning again! Someone laughed with relief, but the laughter twisted into a strangled cry of despair as the papers that littered the square started flying upward, toward the great blades.

The fans were turning backwards! They were sucking the air out of Venusville!

Quaid stumbled as the tunnel opened out into a larger space. Melina took a flashlight from a shelf near the tunnel opening and shone it around an excavated chamber, illuminating the walls, which were honeycombed with niches.

'The first settlers are buried here,' she said.

Quaid noticed human corpses in the niches, naturally mummified without wrappings. He had heard of similar examples in some of the drier areas on Earth. Mummification depended on the climate, not the wrappings.

Melina led the way through a labyrinth of narrow corridors lined with open tombs. She remembered the first time she had come here, as a little girl clinging in fright to her mother's hand. Her mother had calmed her fears by telling her stories about each desiccated form, until they had become recognizable individuals, almost alive.

Her mother's stories had started Melina on the path which led to her joining the rebel forces. The first settlers had been a hardy breed, determined to create a colony that would be the envy of all the other planets. They had built a firm foundation, but the discovery of turbinium had undermined it. The Northern Bloc focused on the mines to the exclusion of almost everything else and living conditions deteriorated accordingly.

Vilos Cohaagen had made matters intolerable. The man was an insensitive monster. He made no effort whatsoever to listen to the people of his colony. He responded to petitions with arrests, and declared that any criticism directed at him would be punishable by death. Melina could not bear to see the dreams of the first settlers dissolve into dust, so she had joined the Mars Liberation Front. She intended to see the first settler's vision become reality. Benny's voice intruded on her thoughts.

'I heard about this place,' Benny whispered.

'They came to build a better life,' Melina said. 'But it didn't work out that way. Cohaagen skimped on the domes and turned us into freaks. He works us like slaves on our own planet, and he won't let us leave. He even makes us pay for the air we breathe.'

Something fell into place in Quaid's mind. *Air* . . .

'We're like his goddamn pet goldfish,' Benny grumbled bitterly.

'We could have had a livable planet by now,' Melina continued. 'But the Northern Bloc decided that creating an atmosphere wasn't "economically feasible". Not if it meant taking money and manpower away from the turbinium mines.' She was deeply disgusted.

Air. Quaid struggled to grasp the thought he had almost had, but it eluded him. He focused instead on the plight of the miners. He had known that mining turbinium was dangerous; in fact, there was more than a suspicion that the mutation rate on Mars was as much the fault of radiation in the mines as of the unshielded sunlight in the domes. Without the huge bonuses, no one would voluntarily emigrate to work in the mines.

And it wasn't until they got to Mars that they realized they'd have to spend most of those bonuses on air, Quaid thought grimly. Since the mines were the only game in town, the common folk had to work in them, just to keep on breathing. Even if they did suspect what it cost them – what choice did they have? Slow mutation was better than fast death.

He began to remember why Hauser had changed sides. If the folks of Mars had any alternative to mining turbinium, there would be a revolution. There was one already, but not enough of one, because Cohaagen controlled the air supply.

'And nobody down there on Earth gives a damn,' Melina continued. 'As long as the turbinium keeps flowing, as long as the Northern Bloc can maintain military superiority on Earth, nobody's going to upset Cohaagen's comfortable little apple cart.' She stopped and turned to Quaid with hope in her eyes. 'But maybe you can change all that.'

He looked away, embarrassed. If only he could unbury those memories, whatever it was that he was supposed to know that would change everything! But the chains on his mind remained firm. 'I'll do what I can,' he said gruffly.

They walked on through the catacombs, Quaid beside Melina, Benny lagging behind.

'It's something you *know*,' Melina said. 'Kuato's going to make you remember a few things.'

'Like what?'

'All sorts of things.' She hesitated and when she continued, her voice was husky with emotion. 'Maybe you'll even remember that you love me.' Quaid couldn't bear to hear the sorrow in her voice. He grabbed her arm and turned her to face him. He had to convince her that what was in his heart was real; that the false memories in his head didn't matter.

'Melina, listen to me!' he said. 'I don't need Kuato for that! I dreamed about you every night back on Earth. They blotted out everything else, but they couldn't destroy my feelings for you. When I slept, I saw you, and I wanted you, every night. The memory of our life together may be gone, but the feeling remains. It just wouldn't let go, till I couldn't go on with my life.'

Melina gazed into his eyes, and he saw belief forming. 'Then you really –'

'Forever!' He leaned closer, but before their lips could meet, Benny let out a yelp of alarm.

The corpses around them were moving! A whole section of the catacomb wall slid away like a door. Behind it stood seven armed men.

Quaid tensed, but Melina put a hand on his arm, calming him. 'It's okay,' she said, 'they're with us.'

One of the rebels stepped forward and gestured toward Benny with the barrel of his gun. 'Who's that?' he asked.

'He helped us escape,' replied Melina.

'Hey, don't worry about me, man,' said Benny. 'I'm on your side.' Benny put his left hand on his right hand and pulled. There was a click; then the right hand came off, as if it were the appendage of a marionette. It was artificial. Underneath was a deformed nub with a few vestigial fingers. Quaid felt slightly sickened by the sight, but the others looked on with mute sympathy.

Then the cabbie stretched out his arm and clenched his fist. There was something odd about the shape of the arm and Quaid's stomach lurched as he saw something squirm under the sleeve. The cabbie pushed the sleeve up and a second forearm unhinged from the first, a groteseque limb with long, bony, webbed fingers which slowly curled and uncurled. Even the rebels recoiled at the sight – but it served its purpose. They were convinced that Benny was one of them.

'Follow me,' the rebel said. They followed the armed men through a narrow tunnel to a large excavated chamber where other resistance fighters camped in small groups. Weapons and ammunition were stacked around the room, and a few men were poring over maps on a table at the far end. The rest were eating, playing cards, cleaning weapons, reading, and sleeping, but there was little talk and no laughter. The mood was very dark.

Quaid lost some respect for the rebels. They were an organized force, without a doubt, but he was learning entirely too much about them. A spy could make a fairly accurate report on their numbers and nature, if brought through here this way. The sensible procedure would have been to drug him unconscious, bring him here, then kill him if he turned out to be a spy.

The rebel in the lead turned to Benny. 'Wait here,' he ordered. And then, to Melina and Quaid: 'Come with me.' He escorted them to the table at the far end of the room. Now Quaid could see that there was a videophone among the maps and charts that littered the table. He could also see that the man seated at the table, the man who was obviously in command, was George, the affable miner from The Last Resort. He spoke urgently into the videophone and there was authority in his tone.

'Then ram down the pressure seals!' he said.

'We can't,' said a voice and Quaid stiffened when he heard it. It belonged to Tony, the hothead who had been with Melina at the bar. Peering over George's shoulder, Quaid saw that the miner was in no shape to fight anyone now. He appeared to be breathing with difficulty and Quaid could see others in the background, lying on the floor of the bar or draped over tables, gasping for air.

'Cohaagen depressurized the tunnels,' Tony continued. 'And they're rigged to blow up.'

George glanced over his shoulder at Melina and then looked back to the videoscreen. 'Okay, sit tight. Melina just got here with Quaid.'

'I hope it was worth it,' Tony said. George ended the transmission and paused for a moment, looking grim. He turned to face Melina and a faint smile passed over his lips.

'Glad you made it,' he said.

'You don't look so glad,' Melina replied.

George rose from his chair and the grim look returned. 'Cohaagen sealed off Venusville.'

'We know,' said Melina. 'We almost got caught ourselves.'

'What you don't know is that he's pumping out the air.'

Melina's hand flew to her mouth. She had known Cohaagen was ruthless, but she hadn't known *how* ruthless, until now. George looked at Quaid.

'You must know something pretty damned important, Quaid. He wants *you*.' Quaid was appalled. 'If we don't hand you over, everybody'll be dead by morning.' George led them to a fortified door. He punched in a series of numbers. The lock clicked.

'What are you going to do?' asked Melina.

'That's up to Kuato,' George said. He beckoned to Quaid. 'C'mon.'

Would Kuato be able to unblock his memory? Since Quaid himself didn't know what he was supposed to know, he doubted that anyone else could tell just by looking at him. Maybe they intended to drug him and question him. That was unlikely to work either. He still couldn't remember the Rekall experience clearly, but believed that they had encountered severe problems with his prior memory conditioning. It would be no different here.

Quaid glanced at Melina before following George. She held up her hand in a small gesture of farewell and for a moment looked precisely as she had in his dream. He wanted to go to her, to hold her to him and never let her go, but he wanted his memory, *needed* it, even more. Not only for their sake, but also for the sake of those who lay dying in Venusville. He had something trapped out of reach in his head and he had to free it and the people of Mars before he could be free to love Melina. He tore his eyes from her and followed George through the door.

He entered a dark, domed chamber which was as empty as the other had been full. There were no rebels in sight and no sign of Kuato. The man wasn't going to arrive after them, either, for the door had shut behind them and Quaid could hear the lock click back into place.

George led him to a table with two chairs. 'Sit down,' he said.

Quaid sat in one of the chairs and scanned the room for another entrance. Naturally Kuato would have his own entry, independent of the one used by the troops. Except that there was none. Unless they were better at masking the door than his trained eye was at unmasking it, which he doubted. He knew it was Hauser's eye doing the checking. Hauser –

Something clicked. Melina had known him as Hauser, not as Quaid. Yet in the dream-memory she had called him Doug. How could that be?

The answer was so obvious it made him smile. They hadn't changed his first name, just his last! Douglas Hauser had become Douglas Quaid. He remembered now, or thought he did. Unfortunately, it wasn't a signficiant memory. His thoughts returned to the present.

'Where's Kuato?' he asked.

'On his way,' George replied shortly. He seemed to mull something over before speaking again. 'You heard the rumors about alien artifacts?' Quaid nodded. 'They're true. Cohaagen found something in the Pyramid Mine, and it's got him scared shitless.'

Which explained why the Pyramid Mine had been closed down. Quaid felt the flutter of memory. There was something buried deeper in his mind than the turbinium was in the frozen Martian ground, but he could not dig it up. 'What was it?'

'You tell me,' George said. 'A year ago, you fell for Melina and said you wanted to help us. So we said. "Great. You're on our side now? Then tell us what's in the mine." You went away to find out. And that was the last we heard of you.'

'My dream!' Quaid exclaimed. 'My memory! I went there with Melina, and fell into the pit –'

George unbuttoned his jacket and threw it on the back of the other chair. 'We didn't know whether you died in the fall or got captured,' he continued. 'Or maybe you were just jerking us around. But if that was the case, why is Cohaagen so desperate to get you back now?' George shook his head. 'No. Cohaagen's big secret is locked away in that black hole you call a brain. And we need to know what it is.'

There was no question about that, Quaid agreed. Obviously he hadn't died in the fall, and had been captured. But how long had he been free in that alien complex before they caught him? What had he learned? Because he knew he *had* learned something amazing, something bigger than any of them had imagined. A whole chapter of his life was missing, and he wanted it back.

George sat down across from Quaid, close. 'Now, my brother, Kuato, is a mutant. Please don't show revulsion.'

'Of course not,' Quaid agreed, bracing himself. So the man had three arms, or teeth in his ears. What counted was what he could do.

George unbuttoned his shirt. There was something odd about his chest, Quaid realized. It had looked pretty solid, as if the man were perpetually thrusting it out, a braggadocio. Now this was revealed as a front, a plastic form. A man's version of falsies? It must be rough when someone punched him there: rough on the man's fist.

Then George removed the shaped plastic, revealing –

Quaid stopped his jaw from dropping only with an effort. *A small second head was growing from the man's chest!*

Wrinkled and hairy, the head was a cross between a fetus and an old man. Its eyes were closed in sleep. Evidently it was only partially formed, like Benny's claw-hand. Mutations were seldom beneficial; most of them were negative, being not only grotesque but useless. Yet some were otherwise . . .

George turned to Quaid and held out his hands. 'Take my hands,' he said. Then, noting Quaid's hesitation: 'Go on.'

160

Quaid reluctantly held George's hands. He was trying not to be finicky, but the notion of being close to the mutant repelled him. So did the notion of holding hands with a man.

'I'll leave you with Kuato,' George said. He closed his eyes and seemed to fall asleep.

Simultaneously, the Kuato head twitched, yawned, and woke. One of his eyes was abnormally large.

Kuato stared intently at Quaid, opened his toothless little mouth, and spoke. 'What do you want, Mr Quaid?'

'Same as you,' Quaid said as evenly as he could manage. 'To remember.'

'But why?'

Quaid was puzzled. If Kuato knew his name, why didn't he know his mission too? 'To know who I am.'

'You are what you do,' Kuato said. He paused, letting that sink in. Unfortunately, most of what Quaid had been doing recently was searching for his memory, and trying to survive.

'A man is defined by his actions, Mr Quaid,' Kuato continued. 'Not by his memories.' He stared at Quaid, who had difficulty returning that uneven geaze. One eye was so big, the other so small!

'Now open your thoughts to my presence . . .'

Quaid couldn't help staring at Kuato's large eye. It was hypnotic. He found himself falling into a trance.

'Open . . .' Kuato said.

Quaid seemed to fall toward that huge eye. He saw himself reflected in the pupil. It was as if he were zooming in on his own image, on his own reflected head, his eye, his pupil, in which he saw the reflection of . . .

21

Revelation

Quaid saw the Pyramid Mountain rising like the Matterhorn from one side of a canyon. He floated, seeming disembodied, contemplating it.

'Go inside,' Kuato said, from somewhere in another reality.

Quaid discovered that he could move simply by willing it. He jumped to the side of the mountain, then traveled into the tunnel in its side, as in his dream. The tunnel went deep inside, then dead-ended at a hole in a stone wall. He glided through that hole and into an abyss.

A gigantic metal structure seemed to fill the central core of a dark pit. His dream-pit – but somehow different. The structure – it was in its fashion alive, not dead, and dynamic rather than passive. He had seen it before and thought it defunct; now he knew it was not.

He floated to it. There were huge metal trusses, like the arched understructure of a bridge.

He moved on toward the centre of the structure and saw a forest of gigantic corroded metal columns.

Kuato's voice came again. 'What is it?'

Quaid didn't answer. He didn't need to; Kuato was reading his mind. The questions were merely to focus his attention.

He dropped down, down, down, as if on a tether, as he had in the dream. But as he passed the point where the dream had ended –

His hands, of their own accord, found the line at his waist and closed about it. They clamped automatically, and suddenly were jerked up as they tried to break his fall. His arms were wrenched almost out of their sockets as they took the full falling weight of his body. Even in the lesser gravity of Mars, it was a shock. He swung, hurting – and smashed into the wall of the pit. The shock was transmitted through his suit, stunning him. His gloves slipped on the line, starting him down again. He knew he couldn't afford that; he was still a long way from the bottom.

He willed his hands to hang on, whatever the cost. But the cost was his consciousness. He felt himself swinging again, into . . .

The galaxy was crisscrossed by lines of communication and trade. Lightspeed limited both, on the interstellar level, but species that took the long view prospered. They sent out missionary ships, knowing that they would not see any results in the lifetimes of those aboard, or in the lifetimes of any of the creatures extant. But they continued, for that was the nature of the long view.

The galaxy was actually the debris being drawn into the monstrous black hole that was its center. It had started as a cloud, formed into a quasar, and swept the gas and dust of its vicinity into itself, its appetite insatiable. In the course of billions of years it had dimmed somewhat, for the substance around it was thinning, but it remained a well-organized system.

Hauser recovered consciousness. He was at the bottom of the pit. He had suffered a brief vision of a black hole, but while his mind was out, his hands had evidently eased him on down safely.

He detached himself from the cord. He needed freedom to explore. Then he would climb back up and –

And what? Melina had heard him fall. She would know that something had gone wrong, and would head back for help. He should have told her he was all right, only he had gotten knocked part way senseless. He wasn't sure how long he had been out. So his mission –

What *was* his mission? He couldn't quite remember. That disorientation –

But it was coming back. He was trying to find out about

this alien artifact. What it was, what it did, who had left it, anything. So that Melina –

Whatever thought had started was preempted by another. *He loved Melina*. He closed his eyes and pressed a hand to his forehead. How could he have allowed this to happen? He was an experienced professional, not some lovesick trainee. His love for her had been a pose, a means to an end, the oldest trick in the book. He had used her to infiltrate Kuato's rebel forces and he had succeeded in that, though he had not succeeded in locating Kuato himself. Now it was time for the rest of the plan to go into action. It was time for him to return to Cohaagen, to the world of intrigue and double-cross and cold calculation.

But it looked as though *he* had been double-crossed, by his heart. He had sensed the loss of control, of detachment, a while ago, but he had ignored it, suppressed it, tried to forget it. He could do so no longer. Melina's courage and determination had pierced his amoral armor – and awakened feelings in him that he had never experienced before.

He loved Melina. He could deny it no longer. And if betraying the rebels meant losing her, then he could not betray them. He didn't care what Cohaagen thought his mission was. He was doing this for her.

He set out to explore the alien device whose struts towered above him in the near-darkness. He had for a moment seemed to understand the aliens, their missionary ships, their long view – or was that something he was about to learn? His memories were jumbled, with chronology seeming to be something other than a straight line. The memory implants, laid over each other, one, two, three of them, synaptic turbulence where they interfered with each other at the fringes – how could he be sure what was real? Focus on the lowest level, exclude what hadn't yet happened . . .

He found what might be a footpath, but for other feet than human. The surface was rough, almost like sandpaper, with crisscrossing corrugations. It was like a tape, curving around on the contour, without guard-rails, and he had to duck to pass under other tapes that crossed above it. It dead-ended in a drop-off into a hole, and picked up again a few feet below. It was as if the tape had been folded at right angles, then straightened out again at the lower level. Whoever had walked this hadn't been much concerned about continuity.

He jumped down and resumed his walk, determined to find out where this path went. It stood to reason that it went somewhere, and that it might offer some hint about the alien structure. He had no better notion how to proceed than this.

The path seemed determined to thwart him. It made a right-angle turn up, proceeded along a low ceiling, then turned the corner to the top of a substructure within the giant complex. If this really was a path, the creatures who used it must have feet like those of flies, so that they could walk up walls or upside down on ceilings. Did that make sense?

He persevered, managing to climb back to the level surface so that he could walk normally again. There was always a clear way forward; sometimes he had to proceed on hands and feet, but it never blocked up completely. From this he judged that the aliens had been about half the height of a man. They were also unafraid of heights, for some paths he passed extended straight up the sides of towering columns. The image of a fly was growing stronger, distressing as he found it. Could flies be builders? What would they build *for*? Some titanic framework for the airing of carrion?

At last he came to a kind of central plaza where a number of paths converged. There was a squat column in the center, covered with what looked like carvings in relief. They were of all types, from straight geometrical designs to weird blobs.

He walked around it, looking at the figures. Many of them were reminiscent of ants.

Ants! Ants could walk on walls and ceilings, and were longer than they were tall. They built mounds, and tunneled through wood. They had quite an organized society, and even made war, in the fashion of man. Could the aliens be ants?

Then he spied a picture of a man. Immediately he concentrated on it, suspecting he had misinterpreted it, too eager to spy something familiar. But it was definitely a man – and beside it, definitely a woman. The figure was naked, and the female reminded him of Melina in her perfection of form.

Melina . . .

There was no doubt now: he was getting warm! He knew these figures had not been carved by men; they were part of the alien structure. The aliens had put them there. Why?

Could this be a message intended for men?

He studied it. Both the man and the woman were looking out from the column, interest in their faces. Hauser looked in the direction they were looking. There, at the edge of the circular platform, was a chamber. It was about the size and shape of a man.

It seemed an obvious enough invitation. He could step into that chamber – and what? Be pickled for future reference, a specimen of Homo sapiens? The term meant 'rational man', but he wasn't sure it would be rational to take the suggested action!

Yet if the aliens had known of man, they must also have known how to capture a specimen if they wanted it. They didn't need to set a roach trap for the adventurous soul who found this hidden place.

He looked again at the figures on the column. Could these be examples of many creatures the aliens had known, the males and females of the systems of the galaxy? One set of each, like in Noah's ark? So was this some kind of memorial, and any creature who visited it would find himself represented?

But why?

He looked more closely at some of the other figures. Many were indecipherable, but others were vaguely recognizable. For example, there was a perfectly good set of BEMs – Bug-Eyed Monsters – of the type usually drafted for Evil Menace duty in comic videos. Their bugging eyes

166

were gazing out at – a chamber evidently designed to contain a BEM.

One figure looked like a cross between a giant spider and a small snake. Sure enough, there was a chamber made for it too.

Since there were no such creatures on Earth, and never had been, as far as he knew, any such beings who appeared here had to be galactic travelers. They would not fall for any roach trap!

Then it came to him: communication! These must be communications chambers, each for its own species. A central phone system, maybe, so that travelers could call home, or at least find out where the local facilities were.

Did he trust the ancient aliens?

What did he have to lose?

Hauser went to the man-chamber and stepped inside.

There was a faint flash of green light, and a measured clicking, as of something starting up. Then –

The galaxy was crisscrossed by lines of communication and trade. . . .

So *this* was where he had remembered this from! The alien indoctrination tape. Now he had it in its proper order. He listened and looked, not with his senses but with his mind.

At the edge of the galaxy, still far from the maw of its central black hole, dust was spiraling in, and new stars were forming. Some of them acquired planetary systems, some of which were suitable for the development of life. Some of these 'living' planets were prospects for new trade, to replace those being lost at the interior as their systems entered the event horizon and were lost. Experience had shown that the process could be facilitated by seeding: by presenting advanced technology to nascent traders, and facilitating their development to full trader status. Thus the network of the galaxy was maintained at a constant level despite the continuing loss of advanced planets. The appearance and chemistry of the new species did not matter; the only requirements were that they be capable of mastering advanced technology and using it in a positive way.

167

The normal course was for a trading species to develop after several billion years of life on a planet, if some natural cataclysm didn't wipe it out. Such a species could proceed from the first realization of mind as a commercial force to interstellar travel in just a few million years. It could then achieve galactic contact and trade in a few hundred years – if appropriately seeded. The chance of an unseeded species reaching full trading status was only one in ten: about half destroyed their planets and therefore themselves in the course of making the breakout to space. Many of the rest lost interest and turned away from space, preferring the security of isolation. But seeded species had a 50 percent chance because they were caught at the first surge of their ambition and were able to follow through before destroying their habitat by war, depletion of resources, or accident.

But there was risk in seeding. Sometimes a species that would have been eliminated by natural selection (destroying itself) was enabled to survive. Such a rogue species could then embark on the destruction of legitimate species, using the technology in a negative instead of positive manner. The rogue species tended to like conquest for its own sake, failing to appreciate the advantage of normal trade. If allowed to continue, such a species would wreak the same havoc on the galaxy as it did on its home planet, culminating in destruction on a far broader scale.

Yes, Hauser thought, and the presentation paused the moment his private thought took over, allowing him time to assimilate the material in his own way. Give a child a gun, and he may start shooting other children. That wasn't smart.

So precautions were taken, and these were effective. One such precaution was in requiring the prospect species to achieve limited space travel on its own, before being seeded; that ensured that only a species capable of a sustained and well-executed effort of the proper nature would profit by it. Another was in concealing the full nature of the seeding so that an incurious species might not take advantage of it. The third precaution was unspecified.

However, the time between the establishment of the seeding and the implementation of it ranged from thousands to millions of years. It was possible that not only the individuals who did the seeding but their entire species would be defunct before the seeded species manifested as a trader. Once the seeding was done, it would not be reversed. There would be no second-guessing. That made the decision critical.

Hauser reacted again. Before a man gave a child a loaded gun, he should think very carefully about it! Especially if he knew that he would have no way to take it back. So he might set it on a high shelf so that the child wouldn't be able to reach it until he grew up, and then he might conceal its nature so that the child who didn't inspect it carefully might throw it away unused. But the child who grew up and had the wit to understand the gun might find it very useful in protecting his home from molestation.

It wasn't a perfect analogy, but it would do. Mankind was in certain respects childish, and this was evidently a most sophisticated alien construction, on a grand scale. What was it for? It didn't seem to be a spaceship, though he couldn't rule that out.

Well, man had achieved limited space travel, so the first requirement had been met. If he could figure out what this thing was, and how to use it, that would be the second. That would leave only the third. Unspecified? What did that mean? That it varied with the species? Well, maybe he would find out, after he figured out the rest.

He relaxed and let the show continue. He was on his way to learning what he had come for, and it promised to be far more than he had imagined!

The normal course for a trading species was to rise within its planet, achieve travel between planets, receive the seeding, progress to galactic trading, seed new prospects, and retire as its stellar system was carried into the central maw of the galaxy. There were many variants of this process, and the duration of the trading species varied widely. Of course, a species could survive beyond the demise of its home system, by colonizing systems farther out, and many did. But generally the heart of a species died when its home system was lost, and the species preferred to expire with it, leaving the ongoing process of civilization to those who followed.

One such trader was the No'ui. The No'ui were specialists in seeding, and had done it for a wide variety of prospective species. They were good at large construction and especially strong on chemistry. None of their seedings had failed for inherent reasons; their analysis and technology were sound. Thus they were the ones to seed some of the more difficult prospects.

The present prospect was difficult. The initial survey showed a species of warm-bodied, four-limbed, nontelepathic, two-sexed creatures who were unusually aggressive. This local species (there was the slightest pause as the program allowed Hauser to fill in the blank with 'the humans' because the No'ui name would have made no sense to him) was advancing rapidly across its native planet of 'Earth' and was developing increasingly sophisticated tools. It was judged that this species of humans would achieve interplanetary travel within fifty thousand years. However, the prospect for them to become successful traders on the galactic scale was only one in three, even with seeding.

Hauser whistled in his helmet. One in three! That meant that the No'ui believed that mankind was twice as likely to fail as to succeed, by No'ui standards. Double or nothing!

But the human species *had* made it here, and now Hauser was finding out what the nature of this alien construction was. That was two steps out of three, as he understood it. So maybe the odds were evening, or even turning positive.

This is the No'ui, the presentation continued. A picture of a giant ant appeared, confirming Hauser's guess. The No'ui were six-limbed, warm-bodied, semi-telepathic, two-sexed creatures, which made them virtual clones of the human species, by galactic standards. Anticipating a question here, the mental narrator paused to flash a picture of a more distant type of species.

It was like a fire-breathing jellyfish with lobster pincers. But it was its mental nature that really set it apart. It seemed to orient on Hauser – and his stomach roiled, his breathing became gasping, his heart skipped several beats and

170

pondered before resuming something approaching a regular schedule, and his mind felt as if it were being stretched sideways and folded in on itself. He hastily agreed: the No'ui were near-clones!

Now the presentation oriented on the actual work being done on the monstrous structure. No'ui were walking on the walks, and sure enough, their feet clung firmly to the rough surfaces, so that they moved upright, vertically and upside down with similar facility. Actually, they needed only three or four limbs for walking; two or three were used for other purposes. Some guided floating objects to their assigned places, while others used complex tools to do indecipherable things. The place was like an anthill, unsurprisingly, with constant traffic along the paths, yet no collisions. Were they all one-way paths? No; when two individuals met, one would slide around and walk on the underside of the strip until the top was clear again. Because they were semi-telepathic, they were in constant communication with each other, and were never surprised by encounters.

The view closed on one particular No'ui. This was – a pause to apply a suitable designation from the mind of the recipient – Q'ad, a specialist in the demolition of temporary structures that were no longer required, so that their elements could be used in new structures. Q'ad used a device that powdered metal or stone, and the powder was then sucked up and stored. Q'ad was male, and strongly proportioned. He was expert at his specialty, though he had not had it long.

Hauser paused here to reflect. It was evident that this presentation was being heavily edited to relate to concepts he understood. The No'ui had studied the human species two million – no, it must have been more like fifty thousand years ago, because it was modern man, not an apelike man, who had spread across the globe and used increasingly sophisticated tools. It had been just a guess about the age of this complex: evidently no one had used any sophisticated dating methods, or announced the results if they had. At any rate, the No'ui had studied man, and known his nature, and set this up to relate to that. But much of the detail was sheer spot adaptation. For example, the name provided was Q'ad, not alien, so that he could relate comfortably to it: it was an alienized variant of his name. How could the ancient aliens have known that a man named Douglas Quaid Hauser would come to receive this presentation? The answer was that they couldn't have known, but had left a telepathic (or semi-telepathic – he wasn't clear on the difference, but after seeing the non-clone alien he didn't care to explore that further) computer program to indoctrinate the subject in the most expedient manner. That spoke volumes for the sophistation of the No'ui!

And they were only the local seeders, in a galaxy full of traders! Just a typical species doing a minor job before moving on to the next system requiring seeding. How could the human species even compete? Yet the No'ui thought it could, if it managed to qualify. Were the No'ui still around? Quite possibly they were, elsewhere in the galaxy, for they took the long view.

Hauser felt excitement and awe. He wanted to meet the No'ui! He knew he never would, for they might be fifty thousand light-years away now. But this message was almost as good. He suppressed his thoughts and tuned in again.

Q'ad was not on duty as a duster at the moment. He was with M'la his ad hoc mate, as they carried their egg to the hive nursery for hatching. They had seen in each other the possibility for superior breeding, so had done it. Now they were about to discover the proof of their effort.

The egg was about a quarter M'la's mass; she had lost working time generating it, but this was acceptable. Good new workers were always needed. They took turns carrying it. If their hatchling passed muster, it would be a vindication for both.

The hive nursery was deep under the construction site, in the most projected region. It was a job carrying the heavy egg down the vertical path; their foot-grippers tried to pull loose, and they had to use all six limbs to hold on, gluing the egg to one of their backs. Finally they had to march in tandem, each supporting an end of the egg casing. Q'ad went first, carrying the front end glued to his hind section, while M'la followed, the rear of the casing glued to her head between her antennae.

By the time they reached the bottom, both were exhausted, but the egg was safe. It was now close to hatching; the movement affected it, and the increased atmospheric pressure of the depths.

They brought the egg to the queen of the nursery. She touched it with her antennae, and read the stirring mind within. *It is time*, she agreed. Because their kind was not fully telepathic, they were required to formulate specific thoughts for projection; fully telepathic species had complete understanding without having to do that.

We wish to witness, Q'ad thought.

She paused, about to lift the egg. *You are aware that the chance of a hatchling in this region qualifying is only one in three?*

Yes, they agreed together. The radiation here caused a severe incidence of uncontrolled mutation, and until they established an atmospheric shield they were confined to the depths, and even so their eggs were likely to be damaged. Q'ad had bred once before, with L'ri, and the egg had failed and been destroyed, its elements salvaged for food. But the auspices seemed better with M'la.

Hauser paused again, interrupting the presentation with his active thinking. L'ri? That hadn't happened yet! Which meant that even this memory of the experience was being modified, to attune to those names and events that related best to his present awareness. For the original Hauser the name should have been different. The alien program remained in his mind, still operating in its special way. The memory implantation technique of the No'ui compared to the Rekall method as a three-dimensional hologram compared to a little flat TV screen. He was awed.

Then you may witness, the queen thought. *But you will only receive; your sendings will be barred.*

We understand. They went to a receiving booth. They knew why their sendings were barred; they might otherwise try to influence the responses of their hatchling.

173

They watched the wall of their booth, which reproduced the sight and thought of the hatching chamber. The egg was there, and already it was stirring, as the conductive thoughts of the chamber affected it. The egg rocked, then cracked, and finally opened, and the hatchling climbed out and dried in the bright ambience of reconstituted No'ui homestar light. That homestar was a hundred thousand light-years distant, and none of the staffers of this mission had even seen it, but it remained their home. When this seeding mission was done, perhaps in another hundred thousand years, their distant descendants would return. That was their dream!

The hatchling was male, and looked fit, and holographic scanning verified it; there were no physical mutations. Q'ad felt M'la's relief; the first hurdle was over.

But now came the interrogation, and that was more critical. A trace physical defect might be tolerated, such as an extra set of limbs, but not a significant mental defect.

Hatchling: what is your nature? The queen's thought came.

The hatchling had been experimentally walking around the chamber, coordinating his six legs. Immediately he answered, for the No'ui were made with genetic memory. *I am a male No'ui.*

What is your purpose?

To serve the will of my species.

What is planetary transformation?

The hatchling hesitated, and both Q'ad and M'la stiffened. Had the technical transfer taken?

It is the adaptation of a hostile planet to a compatible phase, the hatchling responded. Again Q'ad and M'la relaxed.

Given sufficient quantity of hydrazoic acid and water, how would you generate an atmosphere three-quarters nitrogen and one-quarter oxygen, approximately?

The hatchling paused again. This was not just technical information, it was an exercise in application. If the hatchling got this right, he would qualify mentally.

Question permitted?

Permitted.

Are there facilities for nuclear fusion?

He was getting it!

There are.

I would initiate a controlled fusion reaction for power, the hatchling thought carefully. *I would use that power to separate the hydrazoic acid into its component elements of one part hydrogen and three parts nitrogen. I would also separate the water into its components of two parts hydrogen and one part oxygen. This would yield three parts hydrogen, three parts nitrogen, and one part oxygen. I would then merge the hydrogen to helium by continued nuclear fusion, leaving the nitrogen and oxygen in the required ratio. I would store the surplus helium in compact state awaiting some future use.*

Q'ad and M'la did a little dance of joy! He had gotten it! Of course it was a considerable oversimplification, but what could be expected of a hatchling with no experience of the universe? He would learn all that was required. Two parts of the test were done.

But the third was apt to be the killer. They tensed again.

Explicate this concept: (FIGURATIVE)

The hatchling paused, and again, Q'ad and M'la stiffened.

The hatchling's antennae quivered. Then the little body relaxed. *I am unable.*

Why are you unable?

It is a concept alien to my nature.

Q'ad's antennae met M'la's antennae in an expression of rapture. Their hatchling had qualified!

They left the chamber. They would have no further contact with their hatchling, unless later he was assigned to the same project as one of them. Their part had been done: they had produced a true No'ui individual.

But the episode reminded Q'ad of the alien concept. What *did* it mean? He had struggled with this before, but it had always remained beyond his antennae. It seemed to suggest that something was not precisely as represented, yet indicated the essence. That was incomprehensible. A thing either was or was not: it could not be approximate in other than the purely physical sense, as in the case of an estimate instead of a direct count. Yet it appeared that the verbal language of the human species utilized this concept, and that humans understood it. They were of course primitive; perhaps they would eliminate such meaningless terms from their vocabulary as they matured. Still, it bothered him that a primitive species should be able to grasp a concept that no No'ui could.

Q'ad and M'la were now free to return to their assignments. But in time they would breed again, because their combination had proved to be successful. They had each justified their effort, by producing a viable hatchling in this hostile environment.

Q'ad found that he was now assigned to work on the surface. They were nearing the time of the test transformation and certain modifications had to be made in the landscape. M'la would be working with the genetically modified plants that would be able to root in the sands of this harsh planet. They both had to wear space suits, because until the project was completed there was insufficient atmosphere to sustain them. Actually, they would have to use suits once the atmosphere was established, because of course they could not breathe the alien mixture.

Then the presentation left Q'ad and M'la and zoomed above the planet, showing the time of its temporary transformation. An atmosphere was generated in the general manner described by the hatchling, oxygen-rich but suitable for human sustenance. Water flowed, and the special plants sprouted. The nuclear reactor had elements extending far across the planet, which were used to dissipate its enormous heat, at the same time bringing the temperature of the ground up to the level required by the plants, which was between the freezing and vaporizing points of the water that now collected in the declivities.

The test was a success; it was evident that the human species would be able to live on the surface of the planet if it activated the prepared mechanisms. The No'ui shut them down and restored the planet to its prior condition, except that the flow of water had changed some features in irrelevant ways. The plants were eliminated; their seeds were stored where they would be dispersed when the system was activated at a later date by the arriving human creatures. The activation itself would be simple; the complex was primed to come to life when a particular action was taken. That action was made clear to Hauser. He could readily do it.

But how did they know that the humans would be suitable traders? Hauser wondered. Suppose they abused the equipment?

In answer, he saw a representation of the planet Mars, with the Pyramid Mountain highlighted: the site of the nuclear reactor he had seen them building, and where he now (in memory) stood, receiving this presentation. There were three courses: it could be used as intended, and not only would it transform the planet so as to be livable by the human kind, it would yield its secrets of technology to human scientists, and enable them to catapult their species into galactic space, becoming full-fledged traders. Or it might be ignored, in which case the human species would make its own way as far as it was going to, perhaps achieving trader status in some later millennium. Or it might be abused, in which case it would be destroyed. A little nova symbol appeared, evidently indicating the destruction.

Now the program addressed him directly: *Go tell your species, D'gls Q'ad H'sr. Make it understand that the choice is upon it. We No'ui put the matter on your appendages.*

The presentation ended. Hauser found himself standing in the booth, and it was only a booth again. The alien presence was gone.

For some time he remained, awed. He knew that there were levels of this message that would take him hours, weeks, or years to understand completely. Right now, he knew what this complex was for, and how to activate it. That was enough.

He also knew that whatever loyalties he might have had in the past had been preempted by the No'ui. He was now their emissary.

22

Betrayal

Now, as Quaid, he understood so much, yet still not enough. He knew there was danger, immense danger, but wasn't sure of its nature. Had Cohaagen's men captured him, there in the alien complex? If so, what had he told them? His mind had been opened to the No'ui, but not to his own life, which had been blotted out by the memory implant that had lopped off his past identity and made him Douglas Quaid.

Somehow he knew that he wouldn't have told Cohaagen about the true nature of the alien complex. Cohaagen was the wrong person; he would be an abuser rather than a user. Maybe Cohaagen had subjected him to the memory implant in an effort to make him tell. Somehow the alien knowledge must have been proof against Cohaagen's interrogation. But who was the right person to tell?

He saw an expanse of ice, now, at the bottom of the complex; he must have moved to another region. The ice was punctured by hundreds of round wells, like a giant pegboard. He looked up and saw that a column was suspended directly above the hole, like a peg.

A peg. A peg that could be lowered into the hole, where it would start a reaction, activating the system, starting a complex chain of events that would in due course . . .

Kuato had not been able to read much of the No'ui message: that had been for Quaid alone. Evidently the No'ui knew how to shield against telepaths too, even in a memory of a message received fifty thousand years after being recorded! So they must have been able to keep it from Cohaagen. But now Kuato caught on.

'A nuclear reactor!' he exclaimed. 'To make an atmosphere!'

But Kuato's attention remained on Quaid. 'Think, Quaid! How does it work?'

Quaid returned to the memory. He soared up through space, needing no support because he was exploring a design that was now stored in his head, and could be explored by mere thoughts. It was the eidetic implant of the No'ui: the alien presence in his mind. He passed temporary scaffolding on the side of the abyss. He approached a ledge at the very top of the pit. There was a walkway leading to what he knew was a control room. He floated into it.

There were electronic consoles surrounded by enormously complex mechanical systems – the tops of the corroded columns. But the corrosion was nothing; the No'ui would have guarded against it had it mattered. The key elements of the machinery were protected. He passed a textured wall.

He knew how to start this device. The question was whether Kuato was the one to tell. There was something that made him doubt, not because Kuato was a bad person – that wasn't the case – but because of a wrongness in the situation. Something didn't jibe, and until he knew exactly what was wrong, he was stalling.

'There!' Kuato cried. 'Go back . . . More . . . There.'

An abstract mandala, a concentric configuration of geometric shapes that might represent the cosmos, had been sculpted into the stone. It was covered with weird hieroglyphics that did not derive from Sumer or Egypt or any Earthly culture. It was a No'ui representation, and Quaid understood it now, but did not care to interpret it for anyone else. The wrongness was still there – not Kuato himself, but –

'Closer,' Kuato said eagerly. Evidently he could read the mandala, see the figures, but did not know their meaning.

In the center of the mandala was an image of startling familiarity: a human hand.

Kuato saw the hand, but didn't get it. 'How do you start the reactor?' he demanded. 'Concentrate!'

Quaid focused on the hand, tracking toward it, as if drawn into it. Oh yes, he knew –

Suddenly the hand began to vibrate. A low-pitched rumbling filled the chamber. Quaid's eyes snapped open and the rumbling continued. It wasn't part of his vision!

Sand and gravel rained down from the ceiling. Hairline cracks spread through the walls and then expanded into wide fissures. A mining mole bored through the chamber wall and burst into the room. Quaid leaped from his chair and George followed suit, buttoning his shirt as he ran for the door. A rebel threw it open and then entered the chaos of the outer chamber.

Another mole had bored into the catacombs, churning through the mummified bodies. Fifty soldiers mowed down the outnumbered, outgunned rebels. The mole ground its way out through another niche-lined wall, heedless of the sacrilege. Soldiers followed the juggernaut farther into the chamber. Some rebels tried to fight, but they had been caught unprepared. This was no more than a mop-up operation for Cohaagen's forces.

'Where's Kuato?' said the rebel at the door. An explosion ripped through the room, throwing everyone to the floor. Quaid helped George to his feet and bent to lend a hand to the rebel fighter, but the man was dead.

Melina and Benny found their way to Quaid's side. George's bloody shirt had been torn open in his fall and they stared at Kuato's wizened head in amazement. But there was no time for explanations.

'This way!' George shouted. He led them through a concealed door into a passageway. Soldiers tried to block their path, but Melina mowed them down. Benny and Quaid grabbed guns from the fallen soldiers and ran on through a series of chambers until they reached an airlock. Quaid guarded the rear as George, Melina, and Benny squeezed through the door. As he closed the door and flipped the lever to bolt it in place, he heard more gunfire – from *within* the airlock!

Quaid spun just in time to see Benny riddling George's body with bullets. There had been a traitor in their midst. Kuato himself would have known it had he looked into Benny's mind. But he had been watching Quaid and so had overlooked the obvious. Benny had used Quaid as a shield to get near Kuato.

Before Quaid could move, Benny seized Melina and pointed the gun at her head. 'Freeze!' he shouted. Quaid froze and Benny sneered. 'Congratulations, folks. You led us right to him.'

Quaid ignored the jibe and knelt to examine George's still form, trying to find a last flicker of life. If Kuato could strike at Benny's mind, set him back just long enough for Quaid to –

'Forget it, bro,' Benny said. 'His fortune-telling days are over.'

Kuato's head was dead weight. George's head hung limp. The body seemed dead.

Melina glared at Benny, as astounded as she was outraged. 'Benny, you're a mutant!'

The man's lips quirked. He displayed a flashing beacon hidden in his artificial hand. 'It pays to keep in touch. Your boys never checked me. Hell, *Kuato* never caught on. He may have had weird powers, like the rumors say, but he wasn't smart, and this organization wasn't smart. You can bet nobody would've sneaked into Cohaagen's den like this!'

Quaid had to agree. He had noted the laxity of the rebels himself. They had depended too much on Kuato's mutant power, and let something obvious and stupid happen. They weren't professionals.

But Benny was. His eyes glittered cruelly as he added: 'Sorry, Mel. I got five kids to feed.'

Five? 'What happened to number six?' Quaid asked.

Benny grinned. 'Shit, man. I ain't even married.' Then he was suddenly authoritarian. 'Now put your fucking hands on your head!'

From alien majesty to human ignominy, so quickly! It seemed that the No'ui had been right to doubt the likelihood of man's success. With men like Cohaagen in control, the alien gifts weren't worth it.

As Quaid complied with his order, Benny pulled Melina with him while he edged over and kicked open the bolt on the airlock door. Quaid remained alert for any mistake on Benny's part, but the man was alert, too. Only by sacrificing Melina could he have gotten the man – and Benny knew he wouldn't do that. Benny had been standing right there when Quaid had acknowledged his love for her.

Then Quaid heard a muffled choking sound from Kuato's head. He bent close to hear the barely audible whisper.

'Quaid . . .'

'Back off, Quaid!' Benny snapped.

Kuato struggled to speak again. 'Start the reactor . . . Free Mars.' Quaid jumped back as a burst of gunfire obliterated the head. He heard a muffled exclamation from Melina. He looked up – and there was Richter standing above him, holding an automatic rifle.

'Make a move,' said Richter. '*Please*.'

Quaid's eyes burned into the man with hatred. But he was helpless. Benny's betrayal had wiped out both the Resistance and Quaid's hope.

Quaid and Melina were roughly shackled and thrown into a mole for transport. 'I'm sorry,' he told her, over the roar of the engine. 'If it hadn't been for me, Benny wouldn't have gotten to Kuato.'

'I brought you in!' she said. 'I thought – feared –'

'That I was the traitor,' he finished for her. 'I know. I don't remember much of what we were to each other before, but I think for me it was supposed to be business. When I fell into the pit, I realized that I loved you. That's why that memory kept coming back to me. It was the last I had seen of you. I guess Cohaagen didn't know about that, or thought the memory implant would wipe it out. It did wipe out all the other memories, but not the love.'

'I couldn't forget you,' she said. 'I didn't know whether I could trust you, but somehow . . .'

'I guess we were destined for each other, corny as that sounds. But you know, there was more I found down there, before they – I guess they captured me. I don't remember that, but I remember the alien message.'

'The what?'

'The No'ui. An alien trading species. They set this up for us, when we came of age. If we qualified. Which I guess we don't. But –' He paused, remembering something else. 'Do you know anything about hydrazoic acid?'

She concentrated, as they bumped along in the mole. 'It's a colorless, poisonous, highly explosive liquid. I sniffed some once. It was vile!'

'What would it be like on a planetary scale? I mean, thousands of tons of it?'

'Like hell, I think! Why?'

'The aliens – they were going to use it to make air. I mean, with water. They were going to melt the ice, and combine – I don't know, I'm no chemist. Does it make sense?'

'I'm no chemist either, but I think it could make sense only to an alien!'

'But with advanced alien technology, would it be possible? I mean, to break apart hydrazoic acid and water, and recombine them into air, and use the extra for a nuclear reactor to power the whole thing?'

She shook her head. 'I'd have to ask someone who knew more about it than I do! But it sounds crazy to me.'

He sighed. Maybe it *was* crazy. But it was also in his mind. He hoped the aliens did know what they were doing.

The mole ground on, carrying them to Cohaagen. Quaid did not expect to enjoy the encounter.

23

Worse

The next morning, still shackled, uncomfortable, but not actually mistreated (to Quaid's surprise), they were hauled into Cohaagen's fancy office. He had assumed that Richter would beat on him even if forbidden to kill him, and that Melina would be fair game for the goons, as a beautiful and helpless (because bound) woman. But they had been given food and a chance to use sanitary facilities, and left alone (but monitored) to sleep. Naturally they had not talked, knowing that their every word could be examined for evidence against the Rebels. So it had been uncomfortable but not bad.

Now he knew it was going to get bad. They had been saved for Cohaagen's direct interrogation, and Quaid knew that the man would do whatever he thought was required to achieve his ends. Richter was a thug, brutal but without the imagination to generate real mischief. Cohaagen, in contrast, was a white-collar criminal, less violent in manner but ten times as dangerous overall.

Go tell your species . . .

Tell Cohaagen? Not likely! The man did not have the interest of the species in mind, let alone the interest of the galaxy. He wanted only what was good for the Mars Colony, as defined by himself: in short, power for Vilos Cohaagen. The No'ui science represented power beyond that known by man; it must not fall into the hands of this petty dictator.

In fact, Quaid expected to suffer horrible torture, rather than yield that information. Cohaagen did not know about the alien message center; it had been hidden amidst the tangle of twisting paths, so that only a person with a special curiosity and persistence would find it. Hauser had been assigned by the Resistance to discover the meaning of the riddle of the alien artifact, so he had been motivated; otherwise he would not have been so persistent. Also, fresh in the realization of his love for Melina, he had done it for her, to make her trust him, and love him back. No, he would not give the No'ui message here!

Make it understand that the choice is upon it. For mankind had either to ignore the artifact, as it had done so far, or to invoke it and use it positively, as the No'ui intended. If a man tried to use it negatively, it would be destroyed. That was what the nova symbol meant: a nova was a flaring star, in effect an explosion, destroying what was around it. The alien complex would explode, perhaps by setting off that hydrazoic acid buried beneath the subterranean glacier, taking itself and the local human colony with it. That was the choice: to use it or lose it. But Cohaagen would only pretend to use it properly; he would instead make a scientific monopoly of it, using that power to make himself the dictator not only of Mars but of the entire human species. That was what the aliens hadn't counted on, being unfamiliar with duplicity. To them a thing either was or was not; they could not grasp even the relatively innocuous concept of 'figurative'. They were literal-minded creatures, hatched with their knowledge genetically encoded, their values set.

We put the matter in your hands. That was the essence of their conclusion. They had given their message to one person – the one who happened to come to their message center – and trusted him to do what was right. They had made him their emissary, and he intended to honor the trust they had extended. He wanted mankind to become a trader, one of the significant species of the galaxy. So he was going to keep the secret from Cohaagen, letting the alien complex be destroyed rather than perverted. He was prepared to give his life and Melina's to that end. He knew she would want it that way. He had told her nothing so that she could not give away the secret herself.

Melina! Suppose Cohaagen had *her* tortured in Quaid's presence? Surely Cohaagen *would*, if he thought that would be effective. Could Quaid hold out against that?

There was only one answer: he had to.

Maybe they would be lucky, and Cohaagen wouldn't know what Quaid had discovered. After all, it seemed he hadn't known before, when he set up the memory implant and sent Quaid to Earth. The traitor Benny hadn't caught on, otherwise he wouldn't have killed Kuato. He had thought the only secret was that the alien artifact made atmosphere, and knew how to turn it on. That was the least of it!

Quaid's thoughts were interrupted by men tramping into the office, carrying a body. They dumped it onto the conference table. It was Kuato, the shriveled head growing from George's chest.

Cohaagen stared down at it. 'So this is the great man!'

Richter and Benny, standing guard over Quaid and Melina, chuckled. They were pleased with their accomplishment. They had unriddled the mystery of the leader of the Mars Liberation Front, and destroyed him and his organization.

Quaid saw Melina wince. She still blamed herself for the colossal mistake of bringing Benny into the inner sanctum. Yet how could she have known? Benny had been on her side, helping her cause, helping them escape pursuit. Benny had been a pro; that said it all. It would be better to blame Quaid, or his Hauser-aspect, for not recognizing another pro when he saw him.

Cohaagen gingerly examined Kuato's head. He grimaced with disgust. 'No wonder he kept out of sight.' He turned away, nodding to the goons, who picked up the body and hauled it away. Another goon wiped off the table. Cohaagen was fastidious about appearances; he didn't want any ugly smears remaining.

Then Cohaagen walked over to where Quaid sat, and clapped him on the shoulder. 'Well, congratulations, Quaid,' he said jovially. 'You're a hero.'

Quaid's reply was to the point. 'Fuck you.'

Cohaagen, oddly, was not annoyed. He smiled. 'Don't be modest,' he said. 'Kuato's dead; the Resistance has been completely wiped out; and you were the key to the whole thing.'

Quaid saw that Melina was regarding him ambivalently.

She had never been quite certain of his loyalty to the Resistance, and wasn't certain now, despite her love for him.

'He's lying,' Quaid said. They might both be about to die, but he wanted her to believe in him.

Cohaagen spoke to Melina. 'Don't blame him, sweetheart. He didn't know anything about it.' He smiled. 'That was the whole point.'

Now Melina was confused – and so was Quaid. What was the man talking about?

'You see, Quaid, the late Mr Kuato had an uncanny ability to detect our spies,' Cohaagen continued. 'We didn't know he was a telepath, or whatever. None of our people could get near him. So Hauser and I sat down and invented *you* – the perfect mole.'

'You're lying,' Quaid said. 'Hauser turned against you.'

'That's what we wanted you to think. Actually, Hauser volunteered to be erased and reprogrammed. That was after he failed to get to Kuato the first time. This canny bitch –' Cohaagen nodded toward Melina, who responded by making a gesture of spitting in his face. 'She never took him into the catacombs. She took him directly to the Pyramid, never saying a word about the entrance there. Just that empty cave they never used. When he dropped in the pit, she didn't flee to Kuato, she went back to the dome and her cover. It was all for nothing; they just didn't trust Hauser. Nor far enough. We needed some way to nudge them into complete trust.'

'Get your story straight,' Quaid said, disgusted. He pointed to Richter as well as the shackles permitted. 'He's been trying to kill me since I went to Rekall. Harry too, and Lori, back on Earth. You don't kill somebody you're trying to plant.'

'Richter wasn't in on it,' Cohaagen said. 'The others were under his orders.'

'Then why am I still alive?'

Cohaagen smiled with a certain pride. 'He's not in your class. And we gave you help. Benny here . . .'

Benny made a little mock bow to Quaid. 'My pleasure, man.'

'The fellow who gave you the satchel,' Cohaagen continued. 'That little bag of tricks that came in so handy.'

Quaid didn't accept this for a minute. 'I don't buy it. Too perfect.'

'Perfect, my ass! You pop your memory cap before we have a chance to activate you. Stevens gets killed tracking you down at that hotel. Meanwhile, Richter here is fucking up everything I spent months planning.' He glared at Richter, who looked down. 'I'm amazed it worked.'

Quaid nodded his head, reluctantly impressed. It did make sense. Suppose Hauser *had* been an agent for Cohaagen. Then when Melina didn't lead him to Kuato, despite their more-than-friendly relationship, he would have had to find a way to write himself out of the part. So he could have faked a fall and waited for Cohaagen's men to 'capture' him, setting up the fancier ploy. His dream had been of the last episode before the memory implant took over his life.

But two things had happened they hadn't counted on. He had realized that he really did love Melina – that what might have been pretense had become real – and he had discovered the No'ui message. That would have changed everything!

But then why would he have volunteered to undertake the sophisticated mission that was highly risky for himself (even without Richter's interference), only to betray the woman he loved and the No'ui who had converted him to a higher cause? That made no sense! So Cohaagen must still be lying.

Was this just another little ploy to try to get him to tell something useful to Cohaagen's program? Or did Cohaagen suspect that Quaid knew more about the alien artifact than he let on, so this was building up to some way to get that information? That wasn't going to work!

'Well, I have to hand it to you, Cohaagen,' he said, as if giving up. 'This is the best mindfuck yet.'

'Don't take my word for it, Quaid. There's a friend of yours here who wants to talk to you.'

'Don't tell me,' Quaid said. 'Let me guess.'

Cohaagen turned on a television screen. Sure enough, Hauser appeared, in the same clothes and setting as in the previous disc message.

'Hello, Quaid,' Hauser said. 'If you're listening to this, that means Kuato's dead and you led us to him. I knew you wouldn't let me down.' He laughed, and there was a hint of cruelty in it that was foreign to Quaid's present nature. 'Sorry for all the shit I put you through, buddy, but hey, you're just a program.'

Quaid's last wall of resistance crumbled. It was true: Hauser *had* volunteered! But why? Why betray Melina, and . . . ?

'I'd like to wish you happiness and long life, old pal, but unfortunately that's not gonna happen,' Hauser continued on the screen. 'You see, that's my body you've got there, and, well –' The figure shrugged, almost apologetically. 'I want it back.'

Quaid was chilled. If his present identity had been made up, then it could be unmade. The villainous Hauser would take over again!

'Sorry to be an Indian giver,' Hauser said. 'But what's fair is fair, and I was here first. So adios, amigo, and thanks for not getting yourself killed.' He smiled, in the manner of a victor who is being generous to his fallen foe. 'Who knows? Maybe we'll meet in our dreams.'

The videodisc message ended.

Quaid, in shock, looked at Melina. She was as appalled as he, realizing how they both had been betrayed.

But still the nagging question: what, then, of Hauser's love for Melina? Why would he have done this to her? And the No'ui message –

Then he made the connection. Hauser had known better than to tell Cohaagen about the No'ui – but how could he avoid it, since he worked for Cohaagen? Knowing that Cohaagen would probably pick up Melina and torture her to make her tell where Kuato was? He had needed a way to save Melina, and to conceal the alien secret. Until he found the right people to tell it to.

So he had conceived a way to do both. He had

volunteered for a mission that not only required that Melina be left alone, so that she would be there for Quaid to find, but that would suppress the alien message in his mind! He had fed Cohaagen a bill of goods that caused Cohaagen himself to hide the thing he would have wanted most! He had hoped that Quaid would remember the No'ui before he led Cohaagen to Kuato. And he almost had.

Almost.

Now, in restoring Hauser's fuller memories, they would surely discover his secrets too. It was possible to do a memory implant without reading the prior memories; they were simply suppressed. It was a bit like recording a new message on an old videodisc; nobody cared what was being written over. But to restore the old – they would have to check it at every point, to be sure it was accurate. No secrets there!

Cohaagen, having wiped out the Rebels, would gain much more than he had dreamed of. Because Hauser's desperate ploy had not quite worked.

Damn!

The worst of it was that Melina would never know what Hauser had tried to do. That somehow hurt worse than the very tangible mischief Hauser's failure had done.

24

Break

In due course Quaid and Melina were strapped into examination chairs in an industrial-scale version of the Rekall implant clinic. Quaid had watched for a chance to break free, but the goons had been very careful to keep them both shackled throughout. Even if he had been able to get loose himself, Melina would still have been hostage.

Suppose he just accepted the implant. Was there a chance the technicians wouldn't realize the significance of what they were handling, so that Hauser could be restored with his secret intact? He doubted it; for one thing, the implant equipment sounded an alarm if anything out of the ordinary occurred, and the alien message would set off a six-alarm clamor. Yet what could he do, bound as he was?

Cohaagen watched as a doctor and six assistants prepared the reprogramming procedure. Melina already had an IV drip in the back of her hand. Quaid bucked and struggled as a technician inserted the needle in his hand. It wasn't the momentary sting of the puncture that bothered him, but the finality of the coming injection of a drug that would pacify him for what was to be the loss of his personality – and worse.

'Relax, Quaid,' Cohaagen said. 'You'll like being Hauser.'

'The guy's a fucking asshole.' Actually, he had been, up to a point: the point at which he had realized his love for Melina, and received the No'ui message. Then he had done his best to make up for a misdirected life – and in the process destroyed the Mars Liberation Front. So the description stood.

'True,' Cohaagen said. 'But he's got a big house and a Mercedes. And you like Melina, right?' He glanced at the woman, who grimaced, not appreciating even his look. 'Well, you'll get to fuck her every night. She's gonna be Hauser's wife. Not only that, we're reprogramming her to be respectful and compliant and appreciative – the way a woman ought to be.'

Quaid and Melina looked at each other in horror. If he had wanted such a woman, he would have been satisfied with Lori, who had played the part perfectly. But even before his memory cap blew, he had been dissatisfied with her, and longing for Melina. His taste was for a real woman, with independence and courage. Then if she loved him, it meant something. If he went wrong, she would set him straight in a hurry! The idea of making such a woman into a docile puppet appalled him. And she – he knew she had no more desire to be that kind of whore for real than she had to turn traitor to her cause. She had played the part of a whore, but it had been only a part. What would it do to her, inside, to be locked into that part of life? She might as well be lobotomized – which was what this resembled.

A call came through on the videophone. An assistant answered, then said to Cohaagen: 'Sir, it's for you.'

Cohaagen turned impatiently to the screen, where a nervous technician stood in front of a wall of dials and gauges.

'What is it?' Cohaagen snapped.

'Sir,' the technician answered. 'The oxygen level is bottoming out in Sector G. What do you want me to do?'

'Don't do anything,' Cohaagen said.

'They won't last an hour, sir,' the technician said.

Cohaagen pressed a button on the videophone and it displayed three quick views of Venusville. Everywhere, people were sprawled on the ground or slumped in doorways, their mouths open, gasping for breath. Melina turned her head, unable to look, while Quaid struggled angrily against his shackles. He had to get free! He had to stop this madness!

Cohaagen switched back to the technician. 'Then it will all be over soon,' he said. He ended the transmission.

'Don't be a shithead, Cohaagen!' Quaid shouted. 'Give the people air!'

'My friend, in five minutes, you won't give a fuck about the people.' Cohaagen turned to the doctor. 'Fire it up.'

The doctor lowered the helmet over Melina's head. She tried to move her head out of the way, but could not: she was captive.

Then the doctor got ready to lower Quaid's helmet, when Richter interrupted him. 'Uh, excuse me, Doc – but when he's Hauser, will he remember any of this?'

'Not a thing,' the doctor assured him.

'Thanks.' Then Richter slugged Quaid in the face with all his might.

Lights flared. He would have a black eye, and maybe a concussion, but the headrest had braced him against the worst of it. He glared at Richter, who just grinned.

'You have a lot of courage, big man,' Quaid remarked ironically.

Cohaagen pulled Richter away. 'Sorry, Quaid. This'll be over soon, and we'll all be friends again.'

He'd be as well off making friends with a nest of scorpions! But that was the least of it. How could he protect the message of the No'ui from discovery?

The doctor turned on the implant machine. It made a horrible whining noise reminiscent of an old-style dentist's drill, the kind still used in horror videos. Cohaagen grimaced and led Richter out of the lab. He paused at the door and turned back to Quaid.

'By the way, I'm having a little get-together at the house tonight. Why don't you and Melina drop by, say around nine-ish?'

Quaid gritted his teeth, refusing to answer.

Cohaagen turned to the doctor. 'Doc, you'll remind him?'

'Mm-hmm,' the doctor replied, nodding absently.

Richter waved good-bye. 'See you at the party.'

And he would express surprise at Hauser's swelling eye. So the man was a hypocrite; that was the least of his faults.

Cohaagen and Richter left the lab. Now the sounds of the equipment became really terrifying, not for their mechanics, which were physically painless, but for their significance. It was as if the living brains were being sawed apart so that portions of brains from a morgue could be grafted on.

Both Quaid and Melina struggled against it. They concentrated to fight the effects of the reprogramming, but their resources were small, facing overwhelming force. Quaid pulled against the metal brackets holding his wrists and forearms and ankles. They didn't budge.

'Please keep still,' the doctor said.

Now there was pain, both physical and mental, as his skin was abraded by the bonds, and his mind tried to oppose the brainwashing. Both types of pain became more acute. Quaid grimaced, as if that could drive away the hostile program.

'Don't fight it,' the doctor said. 'That's what makes it hurt.'

Quaid saw Melina struggling vainly. Tears were flowing down her cheeks, and spittle drooled from her mouth. He thrashed in his chair, trying to break free. The whining of the equipment was excruciating, but that was nothing compared with the pain of struggle and loss. He seemed helpless, yet he could not just let it happen. Was this what a woman felt when she was being raped? For surely it was a kind of rape.

'This is a delicate procedure, Mr Quaid,' the doctor cautioned him. 'If you don't keep still, you'll end up schizophrenic.'

Would that prevent them from discovering the No'ui message? If so, it might be a way out. But he didn't trust it. He summoned all his strength to hold his identity intact and break free from the chair.

The shackles did not give at all; Cohaagen had made sure they were sufficient. But the screws holding the chair together started to creak.

'Turn up the sedative,' the doctor told an assistant.

That would do it! Quaid knew that this was his last chance. Yet his strength was at its limit; what more could he do?

No'ui! he thought. *I need help!*

And from some untapped resource came a flow of strength. The noise, the pain, and his thrashing all reached a crescendo, and it seemed that he could endure no more, but he felt that strength increasing. Maybe it was the strength of madness, that the No'ui implant knew how to tap. It didn't matter. He tensed his arms even harder, and opened his mouth to cry out.

Then, with a roar both vocal and structural, he ripped the right armrest from the chair! It hung on his forearm like an unwieldy splint. He was breaking free!

Immediately he smashed the IV out of his other hand, stopping the sedative. With one hand partly free he could –

The doctor rushed over to restrain him. Quaid swung the armrest like a clumsy weapon and drove a long, exposed bolt through the doctor's throat.

The assistants converged. One grabbed Quaid's forearm. Quaid curled him into a one-armed hug and snapped his neck.

Now he had a moment to help himself. He lifted the helmet from his head. That took care of the implanting process! He felt an awful headache as it went, as if wires were being ripped from his brain; then it was over.

Another assistant, behind Quaid, grabbed his wrist. Quaid grabbed the man's hair and pulled him brutally forward over his shoulder. The head landed between his knees. He snapped his knees together, putting pressure on the skull as if it were a walnut in a nutcracker. The man screamed and collapsed.

Quaid reached over and released the bracket over his left wrist. Now both arms were free. He saw Melina still fighting her brainwashing. 'Hold on!' he cried.

Three more assistants converged on Quaid, grabbing his arms. Yet another assistant attacked with a long metal pole. Quaid pulled one man in front of him, like a shield. The pole plunged through his eye. That was all for him. The others, appalled, froze for a moment. In that moment, Quaid reached down and unshackled one ankle.

Immediately he kicked the assistant closing in before him in the crotch; he remembered exactly what that felt like, from Lori's kick. The man fell aside.

Quaid pushed himself up and stood. One leg was still immobilized, but he couldn't take time to get it loose. Two more assistants were after him, baiting him like a bear, using the pole and a fireaxe. Quaid dodged the swing of the axe, grabbed the pole, then bent quickly to unfasten the last ankle bracket. The fireaxe came swinging down on him, and he spun away just in time.

Now fully free, Quaid impaled the assistant who had wielded the pole with his own weapon. Then he went to pull the helmet off Melina.

The remaining assistant did what he should have done at the outset; he activated the alarm and ran for the door. Quaid leaped after him, caught him, and accelerated him face first into the door. The man's nose left a bloody streak on the door as he slid down, unconscious. Too bad it wasn't Richter, who deserved a return tap on the snoot. Not that it could make the man any uglier than he was.

Quaid returned to Melina and started releasing the shackles on her arms and legs. 'Are you all right?'

She nodded.

That wasn't suficient. She had been under the treatment longer than he. 'Are you still you?'

She considered. 'I'm not sure, dear,' she said in a perfectly docile manner. 'What do you think?'

Quaid was aghast. Then she smiled. 'Let's get the hell out of here,' she snapped.

That irritation was music to his ears! He flipped the last buckle. She stepped out of the chair, grabbed the axe embedded in the remains of Quaid's chair, and ran for the door.

They charged out of the lab. Alarms were screaming. Two soldiers rounded a corner. Melina swung her axe into one soldier's sternum. Quaid swung his pole against the side of the other's head. Two down.

They grabbed the soldiers' guns, ran to the elevator landing, and pressed the call button. Quaid doubted that it could be as easy as just catching the elevator down, but neither could they afford to ignore it.

Ding! The elevator was going up. It stopped, the doors opened – and there were a dozen soldiers inside.

Quaid blasted away with his gun, hosing them down. Ding! The elevator doors closed on the mess.

The other elevator arrived. Ding! Going down. The doors opened. This one was empty. It seemed that even elevators learned from experience! They hopped in.

Quaid turned to Melina as the elevator descended. 'In case we don't get another chance to talk, I want you to know that I – no matter what I may have been before –'

She stepped into him and kissed him. 'I know,' she murmured after a bit.

'But that Hauser disc –'

'You could have had me on a platter if you'd just relaxed,' she said. 'Instead, you fought like hell and freed me. So I knew it wasn't that.'

'I do want you! Love you! But –'

'But not at the price of the betrayal of Mars,' she said.

'Yes. But also –'

The elevator came to a stop at the ground floor. 'Later,' she said tersely.

The doors slid open. They emerged into frantic activity. Alarms were blaring. Miners were moving around like swarming ants. Mining vehicles and security vehicles were speeding in all directions. Soldiers were on alert. Apparently the alarm had galvanized the establishment into frenzied but pointless stirring.

They exchanged glances. *Could* it be this easy?

They stepped out, trying to look busy in the same way as the others. No such luck. They were seen. Soldiers started firing at them.

They ran. Quaid jumped into a moving mole, pulled the driver out of the cab, took his place, and took the wheel. He looked out the window for Melina. Soldiers were firing at him: the bullets were bouncing off the metal hide of the mole.

He couldn't find her. 'Melina!' he cried, alarmed.

'Over here,' she replied.

His head whipped around. There she was in the

passenger seat, slamming the door. She hadn't waited for his call.

Quaid gunned the motor. The mole leaped forward, suddenly becoming a monster. Soldiers and miners scattered.

Cohaagen stood before the floor-to-ceiling window in his office and stared moodily out at the domes. The horizon was pink, signaling the approach of dawn. Alarms wailed in the background, muffled but insistent.

Richter fidgeted on the other side of the room. What more proof did Cohaagen need? Surely it was clear by now that there was only one way to deal with the traitor that Hauser had become. 'Well, sir?' he said finally.

Cohaagen remained in silent thought a moment longer. Hauser was a top agent. There would be hell to pay before he could be gotten under control again. Friendship went only so far. The man had outlived his welcome. Without turning around, he answered flatly: 'Kill him.'

'It's about fucking time,' Richter muttered, turning on his heel and dashing from the room.

If he had thought Cohaagen couldn't hear him, he was wrong. Cohaagen stiffened at the words. If it hadn't been for Richter's messing in, the Quaid programming might have gone smoothly. Certainly, the man would not have developed such a strong attachment to his temporary identity. A man could get to believe in himself if he had to fight for his life. After this ugly job was done, Richter himself would be expendable. It was about fucking time, indeed.

Cohaagen's pent-up anger at the man exploded. He glared at the fish swimming harmlessly in the bowl on his desk, and swept it to the floor, where it smashed to bits. The fish floundered desperately, unable to breathe. Cohaagen smiled.

But there were more important things to do. Cohaagen had suspected that Hauser knew more about the alien artifact than he had let on. Now he was sure of it. He could afford to wait no longer.

He picked up a phone. 'Get the demolitions team,' he said. Then he stared intensely into space. He didn't like doing this, destroying Hauser and the alien artifact. Both could have been far more useful to him, in other circumstances. But security came first. He had built a kind of empire here, and he couldn't afford to let either friendship or greed threaten it.

25

Reactor

'Do you know the way to the Pyramid from here?' Quaid asked as the mole charged along.

'Yes,' she said, looking. She pointed. 'Turn right, there.'

He swung right, into a wide tunnel, and careened down it at top speed, almost trampling miners who ran for their lives.

'Watch out!' she cried. She didn't want to hurt the common folk, only Cohaagen's minions.

'We have to get there first,' he explained tersely. 'He's going to destroy the reactor.'

She was mortified. 'No . . .'

'If Mars has air, Cohaagen's finished.' But that was the least of it!

Quaid swerved to avoid a fallen miner. He zoomed on down the tunnel, seeing the way now clear.

'If Mars has air,' she said, realizing, 'we'll be free.'

'We'll be free,' he echoed. 'But there's more. The No'ui –'

'What?'

'I never had time to tell you – and it wasn't safe anyway, as long as Cohaagen could interrogate you,' he said. 'I – that is, Hauser – did more down in that alien pit than just desert you. He –'

'Desert me?' she asked, frowning.

'Hauser was a spy. I remember now. He was only playing you along. He faked the fall so he could get "captured" by Cohaagen or seemingly killed. His mission for Cohaagen was through, because you were too smart for him. But that wasn't the only reason.'

'I understand. You don't have to explain.'

'Yes, I do! You *don't* understand. Hauser was

Cohaagen's man. He was an emotionless machine, ready to use anyone in order to carry out Cohaagen's orders. And then you came into his life. You showed him what it meant to believe in something, what it meant to be good. He grew to admire and respect you and then . . .

'His feelings for you were so alien that he didn't know what they were. He suppressed them, he fought to control them, and it wasn't until he found himself in the Pyramid Mine that he realized he couldn't betray you because . . . he loved you. So he wandered around down there, really trying to do the mission *you* had sent him on. And he found the aliens.'

Her face turned to him, amazed. 'He –?'

'They had left a – a message. That the artifact was built by the No'ui, an intelligent galactic antlike species, for us, when we came of age. To make air for Mars, and to share technology, so that we could become a species like them, a galactic trader, spreading civilization.'

'Missionaries!' she breathed.

'Right. And Hauser – well, he was impressed. The No'ui trusted him to do the right thing, to tell his species what the artifact was for and how to use it. Because if we use it well, we'll be traders, but if we use it the wrong way, or try to destroy it –'

'There's a self-destruct mechanism!' she exclaimed, catching on.

'Right. The thing is primed like a bomb. Do the right thing and it's okay, great for man in fact, and it will usher in a new age for us, greater than any we have known in the past. But do the wrong thing, and it blows. That hydrazoic acid – there must be hundreds of thousands of tons of the stuff, down below the glacier. Maybe that's what does it.'

'I can imagine!' she said. 'If that's released, it could wipe out the whole human colony here!'

'Yes. No'ui don't pussyfoot around. I saw one of their hatchlings. Just out of the egg. And he had to answer questions I couldn't answer and show he was one of them, or they would have killed him on the spot. We either use it right or we lose it; we don't dare use it wrong. So if

Cohaagen tries to destroy it, it won't be just the atmosphere we lose, it'll be all our lives.'

She was awed. 'And that converted Hauser?'

'That finished the job you started,' Quaid agreed. 'He couldn't stand to see you tortured, which he knew Cohaagen would do next, to make you tell where Kuato was. But he also knew he couldn't let Cohaagen know the full nature of the artifact. Cohaagen must already have figured it would make air, so he tried to hide it away so it wouldn't ruin his monopoly. But if he had learned how much more it meant, that he could learn the alien technology and magnify his power a thousandfold, he'd –'

'He'd take over Earth too,' she said. 'He'd pretend to be a good guy, using the reactor to make air and seeking to learn more about it, but once he had the information, he wouldn't need his air monopoly. He'd be able to take over everything.'

'Exactly, Hauser – I'm not making any apologies for him, he was an asshole, but you – you were a good influence on him, and the No'ui – it was really a kind of mind implant, and it converted him, and he wanted to do what was right. But Cohaagen routinely mind-checked his agents to make sure no spies had infiltrated, and he would've learned about the No'ui. So Hauser –'

'Volunteered for a new mission,' she concluded.

'Right. That saved you, and the artifact. But now –'

'I'm right with you,' she said. 'Do what you have to do, Doug. We have to get there and activate that thing before he destroys it.'

'And then we have to see that he's dead,' he said. 'So he can't pretend *he* started it, and that he's a hero who should remain in charge. That man could talk the warts off a mutant toad! We may die doing it, but –'

'Kuato and the Resistance Fighters have given their lives,' she said quietly. 'I can do no less.' Then she leaned over and kissed him on the cheek.

'Does this thing have a radio?' he asked. 'Better check on the pursuit.'

Immediately she turned on the radio. It was a standard

unit, able to receive commercial bands as well as private transmissions. She sampled stations. 'They must be maintaining radio silence,' she said. 'So others won't catch on to what's going on.'

'Then they can't coordinate to cut us off,' he said with satisfaction. 'It's a straight horse race.'

She stopped at a news station. '. . . results of the special election will be announced as they occur,' the announcer said. 'Meanwhile on the science front: astronomers report another "inexplicable nova" discovered. That makes seven so far. According to scientists, these novas shouldn't be happening, because they aren't the right type of stars. They –'

Something connected in Quaid's mind. 'Oh, my God!' he breathed.

Melina looked at him again. 'Something wrong?'

'That news item – those novas – I just realized –' He choked off, not wanting to believe it.

'What's the matter, Doug?' she asked, alarmed.

'Those novas – they're artificial,' he said. 'That's why they don't seem to make sense. They're seeded, same way as the No'ui seed species.'

'I suppose, if the aliens are as powerful as you say,' she said doubtfully. 'But I can't believe that –'

'Believe it!' he said. 'You haven't seen the sheer scale of that reactor! If they can build something like that, and use alien science to make air in a way we couldn't, they can seed a star to go nova!'

'Well, maybe so, if you say so. But what has that to do with this?'

'I told you, they don't pussyfoot! It's all or nothing with them. No second chance.'

'Yes, but –'

'The destruct symbol,' he said, feeling the horror rise as he spoke. 'It was a nova.'

Melina shrugged. 'Why not? We put a skull and crossbones to indicate poison. We don't mean it literally. It's figurative.'

'They don't know figurative. They're a literal species,

maybe because of the way they come genetically preprogrammed, like ants. To them, something either is or it isn't, or it is ignored. It can't be part way, unless it's something under construction. So when they use a nova symbol –'

Now the horror came to her face too. 'You mean – ?'

'I mean that when they say nova, they mean *nova*! If we abuse the reactor –'

'Our sun will go nova,' she said.

'It must be keyed in. The moment the reactor starts to go wrong, it sends the destruct signal to the sun. The sun flares up and takes everything out, maybe through the orbit of Jupiter. Just a little flare, on the galactic scale, but our species will be gone. Just as those other species went, thousands of years ago when they didn't pass the test, and now we're seeing their novas. There are three requirements, one being that we achieve limited space travel on our own, another that we are able to recognize the nature of the artifact, and the third is undefined – but now we know that it means to do it right, or else.'

'No second chance,' she agreed, staring straight ahead.

'We're shooting for all the marbles!' His face felt frozen. He remembered the dream he had had, of mankind ending. No dream, but an alien warning!

'All the marbles,' she echoed hollowly. 'God, Doug –'

'Yeah.' He arrowed on down the passage, feeling numb.

The mole passed an intersecting tunnel. A second mole pulled out of the tunnel and took off in pursuit.

Melina looked back. 'That's Benny!' she exclaimed. 'Watch out – he knows how to drive!'

Indeed he did. The moles were supposed to be uniform in speed, but the one behind was gaining. Its drill started spinning.

'Look out!' Melina cried.

But there wasn't much Quaid could do. He watched in the rearview as Benny's mole caught up and bored into the back of his own mole. The giant screw was made to handle rock; how would it react to metal?

There was a horrendous screech of metal chewing metal.

Shrapnel flew through the cabin. The whole vehicle vibrated violently.

Ask a silly question! Quaid had already been traveling at top velocity, but somehow he managed to coax more from the engine and pull ahead. It was no good; Benny caught up and drilled again.

The spinning drill bit appeared in the cabin, chewing hungrily. They leaned forward to avoid it, but had too little room. The sound was deafening. The thing could grind them into sausage!

Then it stopped, inches from their backs. Melina stared at it. 'I guess that's its limit,' she said. 'It's meant for rock, and rock will crack open and fragment away. It's stuck in the metal.'

'Stuck, eh?' Quaid smiled grimly. 'Then maybe we have him by the balls.'

'Balls?' she inquired, glancing sidelong at him.

'Whatever. Let's see how this pecker likes our action.'

Quaid swerved left, then right, making his mole rock back and forth in the passage. Benny's mole, held captive by its proboscis, was whipped into the stone walls. He hastily braked and disengaged from Quaid's mole. It wasn't enough; he ended up with two wheels propped against a wall.

'I'll keep that ploy in mind if I ever don't like your action,' Melina murmured.

Quaid kept a straight face. Behind, he saw Benny's mole maneuvering clumsily, its gears grinding. Then it flopped back on the level and resumed its forward motion.

They entered a dark chamber. Quaid turned his headlight to the side and saw that there was room here to make a loop. He shut off the light and began to turn in darkness.

'What are you doing?' Melina asked, alarmed.

'Maybe I can get him in the ass this time,' Quaid said. 'See how he likes his own medicine.'

He completed most of his loop and slowed, lights out. He saw Benny's headlights, then the nose of the mole, coming slowly in. The lights cast about, scanning the chamber.

Quaid gunned his engine and turned on his lights. They illuminated the side of Benny's mole, glaringly bright.

With his drill extended straight forward, churning ferociously, Quaid headed directly for Benny's cabin. 'Screw you,' he said succinctly.

He saw Benny's eyes and mouth open wide, in the glare of the lights, as the man saw the drill coming straight at him. He tried to gun his own mole out of the way, but was too late. Quaid's mole bored through the cabin, having no trouble at all with glass and plastic, and chewed it up as if it were being fed into a giant food processor. Benny was shredded into chopped meat, in a manner literal enough for even the No'ui.

Benny's mole had been near the far cavern wall. Quaid's mole couldn't stop; it drilled right on into the wall. Sand and gravel poured in through holes. The whole machine rattled.

There was nothing to do but keep going. The stone wall started to crumble. Quaid ground forward, hoping he wouldn't get stuck. But he was in luck; the other side of the wall was hollow space.

'Doug!' Melina screamed, staring ahead.

Now he realized that the luck he was in was bad. There was nothing ahead. They were drilling into the abyss of the alien reactor!

He slammed on the brakes. The mole tilted through the aperture, starting its fall. But the torn rear of the mole lodged against the top of the tunnel, making it pause a moment.

'Jump!' Quaid shouted, tearing away his seat belt.

The two of them barely had time to jump out of the doors and grab onto scaffolding before the huge machine dislodged itself and fell into the depths.

But why weren't they suffocating? The abyss of his dream-memory had been a near-vacuum; they had used space suits to enter it. How could he forget the frustration of trying to kiss Melina through the helmet! But there was air here; this was pressurized.

Then he remembered a bit more of his Hauser knowledge: the main part of the reactor was pressurized, because Cohaagen had been trying to find out more about it.

Cohaagen had been cautious, which was just as well: if he had done anything ignorant to it, the nova would have been set off. The pressurization hadn't affected it; the reactor was constructed to handle atmospheric pressure, because it was part of the process that made the atmosphere. Hauser and Melina had entered the unpressurized, unexplored section that Cohaagen thought didn't matter – and had discovered that it mattered very much. It wasn't just one unit, it was an interlocking complex of units, with the nuclear reactor just the tip of the iceberg in an almost literal manner.

They hung from the scaffolding on opposite sides of the hole, then got their footing and scanned the vast reaches of the abyss.

'You're right,' Melina whispered, awed. 'I never saw this. It's ten times as big as I ever imagined, and –'

'And a hundred times as complex,' he said, awed himself, though he had explored much of it in his prior visit and in his buried memory of that visit, and had experienced the No'ui explanation of it. 'This is our future – man's future – if we can get it started before Cohaagen destroys it.'

They continued gazing at it. An enormous metal truss stretched from the wall into space, reminiscent of the ancient Eiffel Tower laid on its side. Four such arches supported an immense round platform in the middle of the abyss.

The platform was a metal pegboard which braced a bundle of huge columns running through pegholes. The columns reached from the top of the abyss down toward its bottom, lost in darkness. Other arches and platforms braced the columns at various other levels, above and below.

Quaid climbed down and dropped onto the truss. 'Come on,' he called to Melina, gesturing.

She climbed down next to him and contemplated the long treacherous bridge they had to cross, which stretched into inky darkness. This might have endured for millennia, but it seemed insecure now.

Suddenly a frightening crash thundered through the abyss, making them both jump.

'The mole,' Quaid said, catching on. It had reached the bottom. It had seemed like several minutes since they escaped it, but it had probably been several seconds; the splendor of the reactor had made their perception of time distort. He thought.

'They'll be here soon,' Melina reminded him. 'You have to do it first.'

'Let's go!' he agreed. 'How's your nerve for skywalking?'

'Not great,' she admitted. 'But considering what's at stake, I'll manage.'

'Good girl.' But she was no girl: she was a woman.

They started across the truss at as fast a clip as they dared, not looking down.

26
Decision

The streets of Venusville were deserted. The people there had somehow managed to pull themselves back to their wretched hovels to die. In The Last Resort, a small canister of air was passed from hand to hand. Tony sat on the floor, back-to-back with the bartender, cradling Thumbelina's head in his lap. There was nothing they could do but wait for the end.

In the Pyramid Mine, Richter and sixteen soldiers stood on a platform and looked down. Richter shone a powerful light around the edges of the hole bored by Quaid's mole. He shone the line around the area and saw the truss leading from the stone wall to the next lower platform.

He concentrated, spying something. Like two ants, Quaid and Melina could be seen walking along the truss.

Richter smiled. This time the quarry wouldn't get away. As for the woman – he knew what he would do with her. Quaid was responsible for Lori's death, so Richter would repay him in kind. An eye for an eye. But the rebel slut wouldn't die as cleanly, as quickly, as Lori had. Oh, no. And Richter would make sure that Quaid watched every minute of what happened *before* he killed her. Before he was done, Richter would make Quaid beg for her death.

He piled into the elevator with the soldiers.

Quaid and Melina climbed with difficulty from the truss onto the platform. There was an elevator built into the centre, with its cables stretching up into the gloom. This struck him as odd, because the No'ui normally didn't use such devices. But of course they had made this for human beings. The two of them wandered through the forest of columns, still awed. These were virtual metal sequoias with corroding bark.

'The whole thing is a gigantic nuclear reactor,' Quaid repeated. 'Turbinium rods slide out of these sheaths and drop into holes in the glacier below. That starts a chain reaction. Radiation splits the ice into oxygen and hydrogen. The gas goes up, gets trapped by gravity . . .'

'And Mars has an atmosphere,' Melina finished.

'Not yet. That's just water vapor: hydrogen and oxygen. We couldn't breathe that. The hydrogen is used for nuclear fusion, merging to form helium, like the old-time hydrogen bomb. That provides the energy for the larger process. The hydrazoic acid stashed below the glacier is broken into its components, and its nitrogen joined with the oxygen from the water to make the air we can breathe. The mixture will be a bit oxygen-rich, but that's to compensate for the reduced pressure at the outset. It will be adjusted when the atmosphere is complete. The whole thing will happen fast – much faster than any process we understand could do it.' He was amazed at how much he knew, as the rest of the No'ui information in his mind surfaced. 'But that's still only one stage. Mars is cold, so it needs to be heated so that plants can grow and people can live on the surface without space suits, just as they do on Earth. There are heat conductors spreading out all through the –'

He broke off, hearing something. The elevator was stopping. There were sounds of doors opening and boots walking on metal grating. They saw flashlight beams in the distance.

Quaid pulled Melina behind a column, but as they brushed against it a scab of corroded metal crashed to the platform floor. Suddenly all the flashlight beams were pointed in their direction. 'Time for Plan B,' Quaid murmured.

'Plan what?'

'You'll see.'

As the soldiers advanced, they saw Quaid running and hiding behind a column. Richter and the guards rushed over, surrounded the column, and opened fire as they moved around it.

Amazingly, Quaid was not there. But four soldiers were shot and killed!

Richter scowled, uncertain how this fluke had occurred. 'Spread out.'

They searched the area. A soldier closed in on Quaid, not yet seeing him.

Quaid fiddled with his watch, and a hologram became visible nearby. Melina's eyes widened appreciatively. So that was how he had done it! She hadn't caught it the first time. He had a holo projector, oriented on the user. Clever ruse!

The soldier spied the hologram. The soldier shot at it, charging in to be sure of his man.

The real Quaid stepped behind the soldier and broke his neck. Hauser might not have been a great person, most of his life, but he had certainly known how to fight; his reflexes made easy what Quaid might have balked at.

Richter's search continued. Quaid popped out from behind another column.

Several soldiers spied the figure, this time. They surrounded it. They shot through it. Their bullets scored on each other. Four more bit the dust.

'Cease fire!' Richter cried. 'It's a hologram! Don't be fooled!'

But he was too late for the nine soldiers already dead.

Quaid threw the holo-watch to Melina.

Two soldiers in different places saw Melina wander near them. They both opened fire on her hologram – and shot each other.

Three soldiers sneaked up on Quaid. They had him dead to rights. He smiled. 'You think you found me, don't you?'

But he wasn't looking at them, but to the side. That was weird. They realized that it must be a hologram. They glanced around for the *real* Quaid.

But this *was* the real Quaid. He turned straight at them and gunned them down. 'You did,' he said.

Two soldiers advanced, game to the end. Melina stepped in front of them. They shot through her. Jagged craters appeared in their chests from bullets the real Melina put in their backs.

The real Quaid met the real Melina, touching hands just to make sure. They ran cautiously from column to column toward the elevator. It was open and empty. They dashed inside.

Quaid swung the doors closed. The elevator rose at an amazing speed. They held each other, relieved.

'I didn't know they'd gotten any of this alien system working,' he remarked. 'Must be some residual power, or maybe they ran a line in. Cohaagen must have been really curious about this artifact.'

'Shut up and kiss me,' she said, lifting her face.

Suddenly her eyes widened, and she went stiff. What was the matter?

Then he heard a faint noise above them, and looked up himself. One of the ceiling panels was sliding open a few inches. Richter was on the roof! The barrel of his gun was poking through the slot. It fired. The bullet spanged around the interior, missing them.

Quaid shoved Melina out of the way somewhat less romantically than he might have wished and whipped up his gun. He and Melina returned fire, but their bullets ricocheted back at them. They would take themselves out if they continued!

Richter had not depended on his soldiers. He had let them be a diversionary force while he set up his clever little ambush, knowing that Quaid would survive and come here. Richter was protected, while the two of them were not. Richter was getting smarter.

Quaid and Melina moved erratically around the cabin, trying not to be sitting ducks. But it wasn't enough. They remained fish in a barrel. Richter kept shooting, and winged Quaid in the shoulder.

This was no good! Quaid swung the door open. He and Melina climbed out and scaled opposite sides of the elevator. Richter shot down at them, and they shot back. Now they were outside, and Richter was no longer protected by the invulnerable metal of the elevator. He had to keep his body out of the line of fire.

Melina dodged a bullet, lost her balance, dropped her

gun, and saved herself only by holding on with both hands, her feet swinging over the void.

Richter aimed at Quaid. Quaid grabbed his arm.

In that moment, Quaid looked up. Behind Richter he saw the next platform. The elevator was speeding toward it. Anything extending outside the elevator car would be guillotined! Quaid was like dough watching the cookie-cutter come at his extremities. Richter saw it too. He grinned crookedly.

Quaid tried to climb up on top with Richter, but Richter pushed him away. Quaid grabbed Richter's other arm – and hung there. All four arms would be severed any second.

Now Richter heaved back, pulling his arms out of danger and effectively giving Quaid a helping pull onto the top of the elevator. The last thing he wanted to do was save Quaid, but he valued his own flesh. Quaid curled his feet out of danger barely ahead of the seemingly falling edge.

Melina trapezed herself into the elevator an inch ahead of the blade that sliced down on her side of the car.

Cohaagen stood near the alien control room as the demolition experts unloaded their equipment. He had hoped to get something useful from this alien contraption, but he couldn't afford to have it start to produce air for Mars. He didn't know who Quaid might have told his suspicion about that air, and couldn't be sure that every last Rebel agent had been exterminated. Obviously the Rebel woman had corrupted Quaid, and she could have blabbed the secret far and wide. So he had to destroy it now, before any more pseudo-patriots got smart ideas. Monopoly was a funny thing: once it was lost, it could almost never be put back together. The specter of free air would generate an endless number of would-be revolutionaries. So it was time to put a stop to the whole thing, by eliminating the possibility. He had been foolish to delay it this long, but there had been a nuisance about preserving alien artifacts, and Earth-government officials had been pestering him. Well, after this he would give them free access to the Pyramid Mine, and they could admire the alien wreckage to their hearts' content. One thing was certain: there would be no free air, and his power would be secure.

He peered down the elevator shaft. He saw two tiny figures fighting on top of the rising elevator. That meant that Quaid had survived Richter's cleanup mission and was still making trouble. He had to admire Quaid's persistence; he was drawing on the skills of Hauser, who had been matchless as an agent. Too bad the man had gone wrong. He had been much better than Richter would ever be.

But it was time for a real pro to take a hand. Cohaagen brought out a grenade and carefully placed it in the gears of the elevator. Then he jogged off to the control room.

Boom! The grenade, crushed by the gears, exploded, destroying the elevator mechanism and blasting the elevator gantry from its moorings.

Cohaagen gazed at it with satisfaction. That should take care of Quaid *and* Richter, who had about outlived his usefulness.

Quaid and Richter, fighting viciously, heard the explosion and felt the elevator shake. The cables whipped around dangerously. The elevator ground to a stop.

The elevator gantry swung out from its moorings, slowly, its measured pace like that of the second hand of a watch.

Richter looked up, fathoming what had happened. 'Shit! He cut me off too!' he exclaimed.

'It's so hard to find good friends in the snake pit,' Quaid said with mock sympathy.

Then the two of them hung on for dear life as the gantry levered out over the abyss like falling timber.

Quaid, despite his mockery of his enemy, was not at all sure of continued life. It looked like a long way down!

Then the gantry caught on one of the enormous trusses, forming a bridge across a small arc of the pit. They wouldn't fall – yet.

But as the gantry caught, the shock traveled back, and the two of them were jolted off the elevator car. Both reached out desperately, grabbing hold of anything.

Quaid caught a loose elevator cable. Richter did the

same. But it was no good: the cables were unattached. They were faaaaaaaalllllllling . . .

Quaid's whole life did not flash before his eyes, not even all of his recent life. His only thought was of Melina, who would look out of the elevator car to see him gone, and he suffered brief regret that their relationship had to end here. Theirs – and humanity's, when the No'ui's nova was triggered.

Hwang! Their plunge unexpectedly snapped to a halt. The cable had snagged on something.

No – Quaid and Richter were hanging on to opposite ends of a long piece of cable, which was draped over the gantry. They were swinging wildly back and forth, serving as counterweights to each other, about twenty-five feet down. They had saved each other: another irony.

Quaid looked around for some way off. There was none; they were dangling below the gantry, and there was nothing else within reach. Quaid caught a glimpse of the open elevator door and saw part of a form, unmoving. That would be Melina, lying semiconscious in the elevator car, jolted by the same shock that had thrown them off. What could she do, even if alert and active? Quaid and Richter had to survive or fall together, on their own.

As they swung, Richter took advantage of Quaid's distraction to maneuver himself close. He kicked Quaid in the crotch. Quaid managed to twist just enough at the last moment to take the brunt on his thigh, and his unanchored body swung away, diminishing the impact, but still it hurt.

The motion caused the cable to slip a little. Quaid was a little heavier, and he slid down, while Richter was pulled the same amount up.

'Don't!' Quaid cried.

On the next swing, Richter was higher. He kicked Quaid in the ribs. Again Quaid tried to turn, making it a glancing blow, but again it was too solid a blow for comfort.

'Stupid – !' Quaid cried. 'Listen to me!' They were swinging out of range of each other at the moment, but that was temporary. 'If you kick me off, you'll fall too!'

'Bullshit!' Richter replied. Then, swinging close, he kicked at Quaid's head.

Once more Quaid was able only to decrease the force of the blow, not to stop it from scoring. His ears were ringing. 'Think about it!' he exclaimed. 'If I let go, my end of the cable will slip right over the top!'

Richter looked up, and finally realized that Quaid was right. He held back the knockout kick. He hadn't been bright enough to see the danger, and wasn't bright enough to see the solution either. Just as well.

Quaid grabbed Richter's foot and quickly tied the dangling end of the man's cable around his ankle. Richter furiously tried to kick him away. 'What are you doing?'

Quaid pulled himself up his own cable and unleashed a furious barrage of punches and kicks at Richter, who was surprised to be attacked so foolishly.

'Stop it!' he cried. 'Stupid!' Just as Quaid had, moments before.

Quaid pummeled Richter, who fought back defensively, afraid to attack. He saw the void open below and was fazed by it. 'If I fall, you fall!'

'Wrong,' Quaid said. With a mighty punch to the face, he dislodged Richter from his handhold. Tied at the feet, Richter fell headfirst. His momentum caused the cable to slide over the gantry, dropping him another twenty feet and simultaneously raising Quaid all the way to the gantry.

Quaid wrapped himself around the gantry and called to Richter, who was hanging upside down, like a swinging sandbag. 'See you at the party, Richter.'

Richter tried to say something, but fear contorted his face as he realized he had been outmaneuvered.

Then Quaid let go of the cable. 'Bottoms up!'

Eight more feet of line whipped through his hands, over the gantry, and Richter plummeted headfirst. His terrified scream followed him down.

Quaid hoped there was another quick way up. He still had to stop Cohaagen from destroying the reactor – and the whole human species.

Cohaagen and his crew were busy in the reactor control room. It was a stone chamber filled with complex mechanical systems and electronic consoles, just as in Quaid's memory triggered by Kuato's mindscan. All of the huge columns had tapered to smaller columns here. Sunlight poured in through the quartz ceiling. On one side was a stone wall with the hieroglyphic mandala.

Soldiers worked in different parts of the large room, planting explosives, running cable, and drilling holes for charges with jackhammers. The noise was excruciating.

A soldier drilled attentively. Someone tapped him on the shoulder. He looked up. It was Melina. Amazed, he froze.

Behind him, Quaid grabbed his jackhammer and drove it through his chest.

A nearby demo-man saw Quaid and came after him with his jackhammer. But this was Quaid's weapon of choice. 'Am I boring you?' he inquired as he bored through his opponent, plus two more who converged on him as he made his way to the mandala.

Cohaagen grabbed the detonator and hid.

Melina picked up a fallen soldier's gun. She looked around.

A demo-man was sneaking up on Quaid and was about to bore through his back. Melina shot the man in the nick of time.

Cohaagen connected wires to the detonator.

Quaid dueled with the demo-man at the mandala, churning him to a pulp. Then he threw down his jackhammer, yanked the explosives charge from a hole drilled in the mandala, and threw it far away.

He reached out to place his palm against the hieroglyphic stone palm, when Cohaagen called out.

'Sorry, Doug. I can't let you do that.' Quaid turned to see Cohaagen holding the detonator. He signaled Quaid away from the altar. Quaid backed off.

'Once the reaction starts, it's spread to all the turbinium in the planet,' Cohaagen said. 'Mars would go into global meltdown. That's why the builders never turned it on.'

'You don't know what you're talking about,' Quaid said.

'And you do?' Cohaagen's voice dripped with sarcasm. 'The great Doug Quaid, here to save the planet. Sorry to

217

disappoint you, but in thirty seconds the great Doug Quaid will be dead. Then I'll blow this place up and be home in time for cornflakes.'

Cohaagen sighed and shook his head sadly. He had spent so much time training Hauser, honing him into the perfect Agency machine. Together they had discussed the uses of power, of terror. Hauser had been a natural. He had also been as close to a friend as Cohaagen had ever had. He missed the man. 'I didn't want it to end this way. I wanted Hauser back. But no. You had to be Quaid.'

'I *am* Quaid.'

'You're nothing!' Cohaagen shouted, suddenly furious at the man who had taken the place of his friend. 'You're a stupid program walking around on two legs. Everything about you, I invented: your dreams, your memories, your pathetic ambitions. "You coulda *been* somebody,"' he mocked. 'You could have been real. But instead, you chose to be a dream.' Cohaagen held the detonator with one hand, while he pulled a gun out of his jacket with the other. He raised it. 'And all dreams come to an end.'

The sound of a gunshot rang through the reactor. Cohaagen fell backwards, hit in the shoulder and arm. Melina stood by the elevator, blasting away. Quaid ran to kick the gun out of Cohaagen's reach and saw that the man had somehow managed to keep hold of the detonator. No, Quaid thought, the man was bluffing. Cohaagen wanted to live as much as anyone. He wouldn't be eager to set off the blast that killed him.

Cohaagen saw the doubt in his eyes. He grinned evilly. And activated the detonator.

A huge explosion shook the room, destroying almost everything except the mandala, whose charge Quaid had removed. Cohaagen had not been bluffing!

A hole had been torn in the quartz roof. A powerful suction drew everything toward the aperture. Objects and bodies twirled up in a spiral, an inverted tornado.

Cohaagen clung to a piece of the reactor. Melina lodged herself in a corner. Quaid, sucked halfway toward the hole, made a Herculean effort to crawl down against the wind to reach the mandala. It had not been destroyed, and it was the key; if it remained operative, there was still a chance! How much destruction did the reactor tolerate before it triggered its own destruct mechanism? Had the No'ui allowed for the possibility of unrelated damage, such as a meteorite striking it? Maybe it wasn't hair- triggered. He could only hope so!

He grabbed hold of a rope made taut by the wind and pulled himself down. The dome had been holed, but as long as there was a rush of wind out the hole, there was air to breathe. When that air ran out . . .

Cohaagen pulled himself over and stationed himself between Quaid and the mandala. He knew that it wasn't necessarily over.

Quaid held on with his left hand and reached for the hiereoglyphic palm print with his right.

'Don't do it!' Cohaagen screamed above the rushing roar. 'You'll kill everybody!'

Quaid hesitated. Cohaagen's voice rang with passionate intensity. Quaid was assailed by sudden doubts. How did he know that the memories Kuato had allowed to surface were real? What if they had been implanted, too? If Cohaagen were right, the alien machine would kill everyone on Mars. And Quaid would be responsible.

Cohaagen kicked at him, still arguing. 'Every man! Every woman! Every child!' He furiously bashed Quaid's left hand with his heel. 'They'll die, Quaid! They'll die!'

Quaid's mind was suddenly filled with the faces of every man, woman, and child he had seen in Venusville, the listless faces of people who had been drained of every vestige of pride and self-esteem. People who had been used and discarded like so much human refuse, mercilessly, remorselessly, by the very man who was now pleading for their lives.

One face in particular stood out: the deformed face of the child Quaid had glimpsed briefly from Benny's cab. That memory had not been implanted. It was as real as the pain in his left hand. What kind of future would that child have under the rule of a man like Cohaagen?

Quaid knew the answer. He'd seen it all around him in Venusville. Cohaagen was lying – again. Cohaagen was playing games with his mind – again. Cohaagen was trying to manipulate him just as he manipulated everyone else. Cohaagen would say anything, do anything, to hold on to his power. *He* was the one who would destroy every man, every woman, every child on Mars, if he was allowed to continue.

But this time Quaid would stop him.

'Bullshit!' he shouted at Cohaagen. He stretched and placed his right palm against the hieroglyphic hand.

He felt a tingle. A voice seemed to speak in his mind. *Done.*

An awesome low-pitched rumble shook the control room. It was starting up! The other controls must have been mere window dressing, or intended for spot adjustments. Cohaagen had destroyed them, but it might have been like breaking the knobs off a radio: it might make it hard to adjust, but the guts of it remained operative.

All the mechanical systems started to move. The ancient machinery creaked and groaned. Hundreds of rods simultaneously descended.

Cohaagen's armhold receded into the floor. He had to let go. He was sucked up to the ceiling and out the hole.

The rods dropped out of their sheaths into the pegholes in the ice. The whole glacier, far below, started to glow. The process was starting, and operating on its own now; Quaid's action had been enough. The chemical processes would begin, and the nuclear fusion, and would continue until all Mars had air and heat and liquid water.

Melina was sucked closer to the hole. Quaid let himself be blown over toward her and tried to hold her in place. If they could just hang on until the pressure equalized – but that seemed impossible. First it would drop, here, finishing them.

All the junk in the abyss was regurgitated. There were more bodies, rifles, pieces of moles, rocks, sand. When it was all gone, and the air pressure dropped, the two of them would die too – but Mars and mankind would be saved. At least he would die in Melina's arms; if he had to go, that was the way he wanted to do it.

The chamber filled with a hurricane of mist. It had a strange smell, and was warm and damp.

It was the air and water vapor from the reactor! Already the process was operating to make the new atmosphere!

More refuse was disgorged. Benny. Richter, still trailing his length of cable.

Melina was pulled toward the hole. Quaid clung to her but was drawn along with her by the unremitting wind. In fact, it was stronger now, as the No'ui's factory gained momentum. Quaid knew that most of the air was going out through other vents, all around the planet, but as long as this hole remained, it would leak out here too.

They sailed up toward the dome, still linked. Quaid stretched out and tried to block the hole, but the pressure was too strong. It doubled him over, shoving him and Melina out.

Outside the wind quickly dissipated. Quaid and Melina dropped to the side of the volcano, a few yards from Cohaagen's body. That was a grotesque thing, its eyeballs ruptured, tongue swollen and protruding, and blood at the ears. Cohaagen had had countless people executed by depressurization for such minor things as resisting false arrest; now he had been served similarly. That was justice.

The air was drawn out of Quaid's lungs. He and Melina gasped for breath.

Quaid squinted, trying to protect his eyeballs as long as possible. Even in this hopeless state, he was fighting for life, for just a few more seconds!

A mammoth geyser of water vapor and gas was spraying out of the dome, forming a huge white cloud. The warmth of it blasted out at them.

Quaid grasped Melina's hands and felt her fingers squeezing his. They were dying together, knowing that Mars and mankind would live.

The mountain vibrated as the No'ui equipment intensified its operation, and wind tore out of it. The dirt was shaken from the side of Pyramid Mountain, revealing traces

221

of an actual alien pyramid underneath. Its nature had been concealed, but now it needed to be hidden no longer.

Quaid's and Melina's mucous membranes started to bleed. They clung tightly to each other's hands, knowing that this was the end.

Then the expanding cloud engulfed them. Drops of warm water splattered against their bodies, and bits of fluff sailed by. Those were the winged seeds of the special plants the No'ui had engineered, he knew, being flung out on the wind, to take root and start converting the hostile Mars soil to organic matter so that regular terrestrial plants could grow there later. It was the start of the terraforming of Mars, making of it an Earthly paradise. He was very glad he had seen this before he died.

Then he realized that he was breathing! Melina was panting beside him. They drew in more air, hungrily. They looked at each other. Was this the other side of death, and their spirits were breathing free?

The cloud moved on, but they still could breathe. They looked up.

The red Martian sky was turning blue in the region above the mountain.

The new air was spreading out, and they were close enough to receive its benefit! That was why they had suffered but not died, and now the air was thickening, and they were breathing almost normally! They were not dying after all!

They recovered some of their strength and sat up. They became aware of the chill of the air. It had burst from the mountain warm, but as it expanded it cooled. Snowflakes were falling on them. But the ground itself was warming now, as the heat of the nuclear reactor spread out, so they were merely cold, not freezing.

They noticed the snowflakes on each other's hair. They touched them and licked them off each other's faces.

They looked around again, awed. The sky was blue, but it was snowing more heavily now.

They clung to each other, for warmth, but they also kissed. Life was wonderful!

That thought was echoed in the shouts and cheers that rang through Venusville.

All of the domes on Mars had collapsed when the reactor kicked in. Deprived of their protection, people fell where they stood, in an agony of depressurization. The wealthy tourists writhed in the lobby of the Hilton Hotel, and the miners still at work in the great mining hub had dropped their tools and stumbled to their knees.

For the rebels, the shattered dome was almost a welcome sight. Depressurization was a horrible way to die, but it would at least put a quick end to their slow death by suffocation. In The Last Resort, Tony had just enough strength left to shake a weak fist at the sky and then –

A miracle occurred. Thumbelina stirred on the floor and then sat up. The bartender raised his head from his chest and inhaled. Tony stared at them, stunned. He took a deep breath, and then another. There was air! There shouldn't be – the great fans hadn't started up again – but there was! He gulped in great lungfuls and laughed out loud. There was air!

In a moment, they were all laughing. Soon they were up and dancing a jig of joy. They danced out into the street and were joined by others – men, women, and children – who joined in their crazy conga line as it wound its way around the Venusville Plaza and through the streets. There was air! The tyranny of the Cohaagen monopoly on air was broken!

It did seem like a miracle.

Quaid and Melina looked down at their feet. The snow was melting as it landed, and the ground was wet and spongy. Water was trickling over the parched soil. There would be some erosion – but already the No'ui plants were landing. They would be rooting quickly, taking hold of the dirt, anchoring it, turning it into humus. Red Mars would become green!

Melina nestled up to him. 'Well, Mr Quaid, I hope you've enjoyed your trip to our lovely planet.'

' "Enjoy" is not the word,' he replied somewhat gruffly. They had won the right to move on, as people and as a species, but the horrible cost remained too fresh in his mind.

'Come on. Didn't you see the sights, kill the bad guys, and save the planet?' She smiled seductively at him. 'You even got the girl of your dreams.'

She was teasing him, but her familiar words chilled him. 'I had a terrible thought,' he said. 'What if this really *is* just a dream?'

'Then kiss me quick,' she said seriously. 'Before you wake up.'

Quaid cast the specter away. He took Melina in his arms and kissed her robustly. He was through with dreaming; reality was much better.